# THE WORLD

# OF

# HOLLY PRICKLE

## Mary Allen Redd

Shenandoah Books

Cover concept by Brenda Nowlan
Cover design and illustration by Bill Harrah


Library of Congress Catalog Card Number: 93-92632

ISBN: 0-9636548-0-2

Manufactured in the United States of America


Shenandoah Books
3151 Lindenwood Lane
Fairfax, Virginia 22031

First Printing

10 9 8 7 6 5 4 3 2 1

*To my wonderful parents*

Also by Mary Allen

LITERARY CRITICISM

*The Necessary Blankness: Women in Major
American Fiction of the Sixties*

*Animals in American Literature*

# CONTENTS

# THE WORLD

## OF

# HOLLY PRICKLE

# 1

# *Beltway  Bandits*

"Holly, you do too much for men," Fiona said in the office one day, seeing Holly straightening her boss's desk. "This is the nineties, honey. Learn to get what you want."

"I try to be modern," Holly said. She smiled at Fiona. "I joined a health club. I permed my hair. I have joint custody." But the part about hating men wasn't so easy, not when you're thirty-four years old and you hyperventilate when you go on a date.

And she liked working for Bill. He was a good man. He called his wife every day from the office just to say hello. His voice got soft. "How are you pal?"

Fiona held out her long, red fingernails, squared off at the end. "Has he done anything about your promotion?"

"Not this week. You know Bill is hurting."

"Well, demand what you deserve, Holly. It was the same in your marriage, wasn't it, where you gave and gave and got nothing in return." Fiona centered her pearls on her black silk blouse and looked down at the cactus on Holly's desk.

1

"I got Walter," Holly said, turning to the picture of her nine-year-old son.

"You must be somewhat hostile to your ex-husband," Fiona went on.

"Of course I am." Just hearing Eddie's name gave her nervous indigestion, and they'd been divorced three years. "You know I'm thrilled I never have to see him." Not even when he delivered Walter. Eddie was a policeman, and her greatest fear was having a patrol car pull up and be him.

"Why you let that man have joint custody I'll never know," Fiona said.

"I've told you why," Holly answered in a low voice. "Now let's go get some candy."

Fiona got a Kit Kat bar from the machine, claiming it was less fattening because of the cookie inside. Holly had a Butterfinger. And when those sweet flakes land on your tongue, it's hard to despise this life. "All right, I do kowtow to men. But I can change," she said, feeling a lump of the buttery candy come unglued from her teeth.

"Good," Fiona said. "Remember that."

The phone was ringing down the hall. "I better run get that," Holly said. "See you later."

She hurried to her desk and grabbed the phone. "Beltway Consulting. No, I'm sorry Mr. Moss isn't in. Could I take a message?" It was Mr. Wall from HUD, sounding mad. "What? A million-dollar mistake in our deliverable report? That's not possible. Here at BelCon we specialize in quality control."

She gave herself a spray of the perfume she kept handy on her desk for these emergencies. "Don't worry, we'll locate the disk it's on and make any changes you want. *OK*." Mr. Wall was steamed. Meanwhile, Bill had already gone downtown to "massage" some other irate Project Officer in the government.

2

She would have to take this HUD problem to Ned Bird. He was their Sub-Deputy Director, and he liked things perfect. A typo made his face go red. Not that she didn't agree, a typo is a zit on the page.

Holly went down to Ned's office. Grrr. Who said she wasn't hostile? There was his secretary, Rita Staples, who bragged about all the overtime she did. She also idiotically went out with a married man.

Rita was wearing her rat-colored dress, which maybe she thought would hide the pet hairs on her lap, but it did not. Rita put down the romance novel she was reading, *The Volcano of Love*. Who could bear those ridiculous stories. Holly had stopped reading them herself three years ago.

"Where's Ned?" she asked. "I need to discuss a problem at HUD with him."

"Out," Rita said, blowing smoke towards the ceiling with her bottom lip stuck out, not that it made any difference, smoke is smoke. After being around her, you took the smell home with you in your underwear. "And since when do higher-ups 'discuss' things with secretaries?"

"Well, maybe they should," Holly answered.

"Here, give this to Bill," Rita said and handed her Ned's updated version of their corporate capabilities.

"Thank you, Rita."

On the way back to her desk, Holly went by the elevator where she might see a friendly face. Here came the car. Ping.

The doors opened, and standing there was BelCon's CEO, Mr. John E. Johnson. He was a tall man with blond blow-dried hair, his face tanned by a sun machine, and bunny teeth. He carried one of those slick little attaché cases executives have, only his had a lump in it. The secretaries discussed what it might be. A treat Mr. Johnson's wife put in? Extra jogging socks, since he was a known health nut?

Standing behind Mr. Johnson in the elevator was a computer person known to be one of the few eligible men at BelCon, cringing against the wall. He did not make eye contact. That's the trouble with the men in Washington, D.C. They're workaholics. The male situation was so bad that even in the singles bars you couldn't come up with scum. The men hunch over the counter watching football, football, football, worshiping the town's team, the Washington Redskins. It's a brutal sport, football. And Holly didn't say that just because of what happened to Eddie.

She got a drink at the fountain to calm herself. Then she went back to her desk to proofread Rita's work, getting excited at the thought of finding mistakes in it. The trouble was Rita was good.

"Beltway Consulting (BelCon)," Holly read, "located in convenient northern Virginia, is a consulting firm made up of a cadre of trained professionals. The company, promulgated by a hard core of Navy individuals, has expanded its growth curve capacity to encompass the non-military sector and harness real-life solutions to a vast spectrum of human-related problems."

Beltway bandits is what they were—the consultants outside the road running around the nation's capital who compete for government contracts.

Rats, she couldn't find any mistakes. Then she gave a happy shout. Yes, there was one. Rita had forgotten to capitalize the word *company*. Holly circled it and put the correction in the margin the way their editor did it.

Now she had to take this HUD problem to somebody. Maybe Mr. Johnson. He did have an open-door policy.

4

"Drag your boss's dirty linen up to him?" Fiona said when Holly went around and asked her. "No, I wouldn't do that. Get one of the analysts to deal with it."

"Everybody's out except Leonard Pudding, and he has that sleeping problem," Holly reminded her. "It's getting so he drifts off in the middle of his own sentences." Not that Leonard was a stupid person. He had a Ph.D. degree in something. But he was a thirty-nine-year-old strange guy who'd probably never been out on a date. And he brought meatloaf sandwiches to work.

"I'll get the gun," Fiona said. It was a water pistol they used to keep Leonard on his toes.

They went down to his office and looked in. His chair was rolled over to the window with his pinstriped body tilted in it. He must have been watching for snow. In Washington they close the government down when it snows. And it is scary wondering if you'll make it home, with cars crisscrossed in the road and driven into ditches as you edge along in the white, lost.

"Holly, come shoot Leonard. Show that you can stand up to men."

Right. Squirting some poor guy asleep in your office definitely proved that you were liberated. Still, she aimed and she fired—getting drops that barely spurted up to land on Leonard's white collar.

His hand woke up and slapped his neck. Then his head flopped to the other side, and he went back to snoring, a ragged snore, the sound of paper caught in a machine.

"You do it, Fiona," Holly said and handed the gun to her southern friend who was no wimp. Fiona stepped up and squirted Leonard in the temple. He lurched out of his chair, sending papers flying off his lap like flapping birds. Water dripped down through his short haircut. "Did I miss a meeting?" he croaked. "Where am I?" he moaned.

5

"It's not a meeting, Leonard, sugar," Fiona said, and they gave him the message from HUD.

But before he read it, he rolled his chair over and stuffed the newspaper on his desk in the drawer. This wasn't like Leonard to hide anything. He was a person who said things straight out. When Bill asked him if he had a minute, Leonard stated, "Nope."

"I don't deal well with people," he said.

They knew that. Leonard liked charts and graphs. And if he wasn't doing a matrix for a proposal, he made up his own. He did a Punctuality Profile of Employees in Special Projects that he distributed to everyone in the office. Then he wondered why nobody would talk to him.

Leonard was glaring at them now.

"Bill's going to be proud of you," Fiona said, tapping Leonard's gray sleeve with her bright fingernail, "if you iron out this HUD wrinkle."

"Who cares?" he answered gruffly. And you almost had to believe it, coming from a guy who posted a No Smoking sign on his door when he worked for a chain smoker.

They left Leonard grumbling about how he hated to make calls as he dialed Burt Wall's number. "He better watch his attitude," Fiona said.

"And why did he hide the newspaper?" Holly wondered.

"Maybe he's looking for another job. And for good reason," Fiona added quietly. "They fire you in these places if you don't fit in. And I'll bet somebody here will be terminated before this proposal season is over. You watch and see."

Holly hurried back to her desk, afraid of the recession.

She got the *Commerce Business Daily* out of the mail, the *CBD*, which announces all the government contracts. And Bill wasn't picky. He would bid on anything. "Go for

6

the jugular" was his motto. Not that he understood the projects they won. When she was hired at BelCon she asked him what consultants did. Bill got a laugh over that one. At least when she worked for Star Kist out in Long Beach, where she came from, she knew what tuna fish was.

She put the *CBD* on Bill's desk. It was his favorite publication.

Then she stood at his window, looking down on the beltway. The traffic was getting thicker, heading into rush hour. He was down there somewhere, hurrying around to fix the mistakes he'd made. Losing a contract may be nothing in the world of homeless people, but Bill was still a human being, trying for things that don't work out.

Holly hoped he didn't get fired here at BelCon. A manager can lose his job as quick as anybody else these days.

She could see a wreck on the beltway now, cars collecting like suds in a stream. Here came the flashing blue lights of a police car. One day the officer approaching her on these roads would be Eddie.

She went back to her desk, got a scented tissue, and inhaled it.

All right. Tomorrow she would approach Bill about her promotion. He would bounce back from losing that last big bid. He always did.

And she wouldn't procrastinate. She would confront him the first thing tomorrow morning.

# 2

# *Bill Moss*

Bill got to the office early, pulled off his jacket, and sat down. He dug a *Request for Proposal* out of the mail. He had to win the next bid. But how? What do you have to do, put females on a project to win one anymore?

The women of today scared him silly. They want jobs in management. And girls not wanting to be secretaries any more. Hell, it couldn't be that bad of a job. Nice surroundings. Even Holly was getting ideas lately.

The *RFP* was from USDA. He'd never gone that far off the military track, bidding for a job at Agriculture. But with Defense cutting back, what are you supposed to do?

Then when he saw what the job was, he almost peed his pants. The National School Lunch Program. And if BelCon did a project about food, maybe he could understand what they were doing. He might even get booted up to Division Head if he could win this one.

*Hail Mary Moss faded back to throw the football, sailing it forty, fifty yards down the field . . . landing on the money! The guy had it, he was dancing into the end zone, the way those black guys do. Moss had led his Prairie Dogs to the state championship!*

But that wasn't the way the big game of his life had turned out. Everything was hanging on that last touchdown pass he threw—overthrew, you might say. Yup, it smacked the goal post.

He needed to win a big one bad, with his life going down the toilet here.

*OK, don't rush it this time. He set up in the pocket, said his prayers . . . and let loose a bomb—*

Damn, the chair was sliding out from under him, and he landed on the floor.

He looked up. Holly was standing there. "Bill, are you all right?" He fumbled for the loose football, clutching the busted leg of the chair.

"Oh, hi." He got up on his pulled hamstring. "You want to give me a hand here, Holly."

"Bill, I need to talk to you." Thwonk. A woman wanting to talk. He limped over to the sidelines and benched himself, putting his head down in his hands. "It's about my promotion," she said.

"Hold that thought for one second." He reached for the phone and dialed his home number. "How's it going, chief?" he greeted his wife, winking at Holly. "Got to check in with the boss," he whispered. "Don't go away." Back to the missis, "Nah, never too busy to give you a buzz. What, Ronnie failed his skills test again? Dang it."

As he hung up, the cold nausea of defeat rose in his gut. "It's my boy Ronnie. He failed his skills test to get promoted into the second grade."

9

"Bill, I'm sorry."

"Ouch." He leaned down and rubbed his Achilles' tendon. "The trouble with these Virginia schools is all the brainy Asian kids. All they do is study. Their whole family studies for them. How's your basic American kid supposed to keep up?"

"You could get a tutor," Holly suggested. "Get an Asian tutor."

Jap eyes stared at him through vines, planning how to take over more American companies. "I'll give Ronnie's principal a call. See if they can't beef up that test in line with my boy's capabilities. Hell, any kid who knows the number of every Redskin on the team must have some kind of brain."

"I'm sure he does." Holly turned her chair to face him. "Now, can we please talk."

Hike. Punt. "You betcha. But first, check this job at USDA."

"You're bidding for a contract at Agriculture?" Holly stared at him. She laughed. "We don't have any experience in that field. Nothing. And how will you relate BelCon's military expertise to the school lunch?"

"What about that Army study we did, Morale in the Barracks? Institutionalized meals type of thing. You interface the chow hall setting with the school cafeteria scenario," he said excitedly. "Those same kids grow up and join the military." Holly eyed him suspiciously. "Sorry, I forget your husband went to Nam."

"And Eddie suffered from that war." Holly cleared her throat. "Not that he was disabled. But he got spit on afterward. I'm sure it's a reason our marriage broke up."

"Those guys had it tough." Bill turned through the *CBD*. They even had the menus in here. "*Pizza, chocolate milk, cling peaches . . .*"

10

"That's in a government document?" Holly grabbed the page. "Not that I'm a big fruit eater. You know my mother died from bottling peaches. She had a stroke."

"Sorry about that. Everybody needs their mom." Bill paused. "OK, now, we'll need a gimmick to win this one."

"And you *will* run the proposal through editing this time," Holly said. "Claire would never have let a million-dollar mistake get by her." A cloud came over Bill's playing field. Claire Whittle flaunting her brain made him feel like a pea. "What was the mistake in our HUD report, anyway?" Holly asked.

"Ah, probably just a paper error." It wasn't easy explaining this consulting business to the gals, trying to put it in words. Actually, words *is* what it was. "Heh, time for lunch. You want to go for Italian? Looking at these menus has made me starved."

The lasagna Bill had was still settling when his wife called. She asked if he was ready for the big occasion that night. "You want me to stop for a pizza? Uh, not when you're making me a special birthday dinner. Right."

He'd forgotten that today was his birthday. Forty big ones. A guy is supposed to be a success by this time. And he'd done OK here at BelCon, making Head of Special Projects. But if you want to see hustle, John E. Johnson made CEO at age thirty-seven.

Bill reached back and touched his hair where it was getting thin. Did the skin show through yet? He didn't want to be one of those old guys who comb their last hairs over the bald spot.

He got out a pack of cigarettes his wife had missed in her frisking routine. One helluva wife. Actually, smoking sharpened his brain, not that anybody will believe you telling them that.

11

Cancer, sure. But you can't sit on your colon day-dreaming about that, can you. Cancer research. There's the ticket.

"You're needed in the conference room," Holly came in and told him.

He sat up. "Dang, did I forget a meeting?"

"Just go."

He traipsed down the hall, getting the feeling somebody was ganging up on him.

Yup. Everybody was crammed around the conference table. And they had a birthday cake for him. "Chocolate, my favorite. How'd you know?"

"I am your secretary." Holly waved across the room to him. "And it's homemade."

"You gals will do anything to get out of work," he said, chuckling. The secretaries groaned.

They didn't ask him to cut the cake, either. At his house, the person with the birthday always did it, even if they messed up. Guess these gals wanted to keep the place tidy. They handed him a slice on a paper plate that sank in his hand as he took it. The cake had nuts on it. Good girl, Holly.

"Bill," she said, taking him off to the side, "don't forget, I have to leave early today to pick up Walter."

# 3

# *Walter*

There he was, her Walter, skipping down the handicapped ramp of his school with a ratty notebook in one
hand and eating something out of the other. His dark hair
fell in his face, and for a second he was . . . his father. But
those sturdy legs didn't come from his dad's side.

He saw her, he was waving.

Holly leaned on the horn. She probably shouldn't,
parked here behind the bushes without a release slip to
pick him up on her noncustodial day. However, an officer
of the law had asked her to do this, Walter's father, the
cop. He'd left a message at BelCon saying an emergency
social engagement had come up. This she found hard to
believe, as nobody invites a policeman to a cocktail party.

Having an Officer Prickle call you at work did not look
good. It was bad enough having all vehicles with something on the top remind you of police cars—taxis, student
drivers, even pizza deliveries.

But at least today she got to see Walter. He bounced
onto the seat beside her. "Hi, Mom."

13

"Honey." She hugged him. His cheeks were cold. "How was school? I'll take you to McDonald's."

"Bor-ing." As they drove, he turned to watch a motor-cycle go by, making farting noises. His dad was a bike freak, too. "Did you ask for your promotion?" he said.

"I did talk to Bill, but he's so involved. Listen, though, Walter, I *am* going to stop being subservient to men. You watch." Oops, she swerved to miss a young man filling a pothole in the road ahead of her. His torso was god-like.

"Get real, mom. You enjoy doing stuff for people."

"Whoever said that?" she asked as they turned in to her apartment. She had to feed Warren, their rabbit, and water the plants.

She had a lot of plants, and branches greeted them as they went in. It was a jungle in here. A new crop of leaves had littered the floor since that morning. "Why are these plants dying, Walter? It's not as if I don't water them. I give them plenty." Holly got down and crawled around picking up the brown fern fronds. Fern. That was her mother's name. And she should learn from the way her mother had died, knocking herself out for others —although she had enjoyed bottling her husband's favorite fruit. "Just give me Fern's peaches for dessert," her dad would say. That was back in the days before husbands divorced their wives for no reason.

All this foliage in her apartment was in honor of her father who ran a nursery in Long Beach, The Green Hand. Her older brother Woody also lived in southern California. At least his answering machine was there, with that dorky message, "I'm all tied up." Woody wasn't a mean brother. He just ignored you.

"Mom, you need a rake in here," Walter said, swatting the dieffenbachia, which dropped a big spotted leaf on the rug. "You water these too much. You're drowning them."

14

"Really?" When you come from southern California this does not seem possible. "All right. I'll try to restrain myself. Now let's feed Warren, then we can go."

The pellets pinging in his dish brought Warren galloping out of his hutch in the bedroom, sliding across the kitchen floor to get his supper. He had been just a handful of white fur when they got him. Now he wouldn't stop growing. They bought the biggest hutch they could find, but his fur squeezed through the slats as he grew to the size of a puppy. Soon he would be a sheep. Holly only hoped that nobody from the rental office caught sight of him, as you were only allowed to have lap pets here.

Warren finished and scrambled into the living room to gobble the last green leaves there. "Get him," she called to Walter, who chased the big bunny and caught him around the waist, getting ears in his face. Then her son kissed that rabbit on his pink twitchy mouth.

A mother should get upset about such things, but Holly was glad her son was affectionate. And speaking of making out with your pets, rabbits are better kissers than drooling dogs.

Walter took Warren in to his hutch then came back looking for his shoes. "Did you make cookies, mom?"

A pain went through Holly's heart. "Honey, no. I'm sorry. I didn't know I'd get to see you tonight."

She thought of her plan to stop kowtowing to males and wondered if it counts when you'll cook anything your son wants. "Have some chocolate chips to tide you over," she told Walter. "Then put on your shoes, and we'll go."

He came out of the kitchen with his hand in the bag of toll house morsels but no satisfaction on his face. "There aren't any left in here. You ate them all."

Groan. She was such a bad mother. "Those packages are getting stingier. Come on. We'll get you a Big Mac."

15

It wasn't until they roared up to the golden arches that Walter dropped his bomb. "I'm having the McNuggets."

You drive kids through traffic to get their favorite meal, and then they order snacks. "You're having chunks of chicken at the home of the world-famous hamburger?" If she'd trucked Walter over to Colonel Sanders, he would probably want a hot dog there.

"Get real, mom. McDonald's is junk food."

She knew that. Every mother is fully aware of that fact. You just want your child to be happy (and to have a delicious French fry in your mouth yourself). "Well, the government has stated that ketchup is a vegetable."

"Dad eats McNuggets," her rude child informed her.

"Because his taste buds are ruined by the meals he gets. You did say the cooking at your father's was terrible. Walter, just tell the truth. Describe it to me, son."

"Wendy goes in for salads."

"Honey," Holly inhaled, "you don't know how it hurts when you refer to that creature as a person."

"She is *married* to dad," Walter reminded her, loading their tray and heading to a booth with it, leaving Holly talking to his back.

"What a name, Wendy," she said, sitting down on the hard plastic seat. "To me that's a hamburger." She took a gulp of diet Coke. "And Walter," Holly said, lowering her voice, "she's barely out of her teens, and a husband snatcher."

Walter dangled a French fry over his python throat. "Dad didn't even meet her until after you were div—"

"I've told you, Walter," she muttered, ripping at the tiny little packet of extra ketchup they give you if you beg. "I've asked you not to mention that awful word in my presence, please. Now, just describe the disgusting meals you get at your dad's place."

16

"No good desserts," he said.

"No desserts?" The pickle squished out of Holly's bun, squirting onto her lap. "Son, I hope this doesn't make you cranky. Or you could feel deprived later in life if you don't get any sweets. We'll make chocolate chunk cookies tonight, Walter. We'll get Hersheys on the way home, and you can put in any size chunks you want."

"Yum." He slurped a French fry. She really should discipline him. But after a day at work, who has the energy to be a nag?

"Did I tell you BelCon is bidding on a project to revise the school lunch?" she said.

"Yuck." Walter pointed his finger down his throat and made a gagging sound.

"Son, that gesture is unbecoming. Now be a gentleman and just describe the menus you get at school."

"They stink."

"Sh," Holly warned him, looking over at a nice family of daughters in the next booth who were using napkins. "You just don't blurt out a word like *stink* in a public place."

"That's what all the kids say. Yesterday they gave us lima beans."

Holly's throat contracted. "They fed you those icky things?" she squawked. "Now I know we have to win the school lunch contract, so you kids can have a decent meal."

"You must have an important job if you can fix that slop," Walter said, the dear boy.

"A proposal is a team effort," she explained, "although I will have more to say when I'm an admin assistant."

"How big of a raise will you get?"

"Honey, don't discuss money with your mouth full. It isn't polite."

17

"How much do you make now?" Walter asked.

"You're too young to ask these things. Now clean up your plate."

It was late when she took Walter back to his father's place that night. She'd been a bad mother again, letting him watch all his favorite TV shows.

The neighborhood was quiet, made up of cul-de-sacs, known in the real world as dead ends. These were the so-called single-family dwellings, although nearly every home anymore is made up of families combined. All those stepparents. And the many, many stepchildren.

Holly eased down the block in her Ford Escort, keeping on the lookout for Eddie's old black Corvette, or a patrol car he might have borrowed for the night. Nobody was coming.

She pulled up to the hydrant at the end of the block where she always stopped. It was far enough away so she wouldn't see the person at the door, but she could still watch Walter make it inside. "Wake up, honey," she whispered, shaking him.

He flopped out of the car, staggering onto the sidewalk doing his Frankenstein act. Her son, who no doubt wished that he'd been born a monster.

"Don't make a ruckus," she called into the frosty air. He yawned, and his breath came out like smoke.

Holly slid down below the dashboard, where she could sneak a look at Walter but not be seen. He walked along the curb then stepped in their flower bed. Good. He went up to the door. It opened. She hid her eyes.

When she looked again, Walter was gone.

Now she had to get out of here. Cold crept into her heart. What if her car wouldn't start, and she got stranded here for the night? A leftover wife, stuck like an ice cube to the seat of her car outside her ex-husband's house, waiting for what?

But her car did start. She thankfully patted the dashboard as she drove out of Eddie's neighborhood and made it to a friendly 7–Eleven. She stopped and went inside, getting that jolly late night feeling of being with other junk food lovers buying their favorite treats. And she didn't have any smart aleck son on the premises to call out the cholesterol count to her across the store.

She bought a Tastycake and ate it in the car, thinking about her nice evening with Walter. Joint custody isn't so bad. It gives you time off to relax.

On her way home she went by the church in her neighborhood where there was a lighted message out front, a sort of memo for people who hadn't made it to the services lately. Singles do have hectic schedules on the weekends.

She stopped and turned the car lights off, sitting there to read the words on the bright billboard. They said: "Your cookie may be crumbled, but your soul can still be whole." It did seem sacrilegious to use cookies that way, but as she thought about the message, her eyes grew warm.

"Thank You for letting me make it out of Eddie's neighborhood," she said into the night. "I'm sorry my son comes from a broken home. Not that I'm asking to meet another man, although somebody for companionship might be nice. No one I'd really care about, though, Lord. With a job and a son to raise, I can't afford to be wiped out by love.

Also, nobody with a disease. I've always believed Your teaching that our body is a temple. Amen."

Holly opened her eyes. Then as she reached to start the car, her fingers froze on the key. A police car was pulling up in front of her. This was it. She was getting punished for being a bad mother, a no-good wife, and now for wanting to be liberated.

The officer got out. Her lungs stopped working as she watched. Thank heavens. He was too big to be Eddie. The badge gleaming in her headlights sat up on a huge chest.

He came over to her window and looked down at her with chins. "You OK, miss?"

"Fine. So fine."

"Just thought I better check. Your car's been sitting here a while," he said.

"Sorry, I meant to get home earlier. Tomorrow's a big day at work. We're launching a proposal. Thank you, officer."

# 4

# *Kickoff Meeting*

As the proposal kickoff meeting was about to start, Rita, who had been out sick, arrived with her face puffed up like a biscuit baking. "Maybe you should be home in bed," Holly told her.

"It's nothing you'll catch," Rita answered, blowing out cigarette smoke. "I'm not missing this meeting." Then she coughed to prove that she had something—or else it was smoker's hack, which she could use at any time to pave the way for calling in sick.

Holly got up and moved to the other end of the table. She noticed that Leonard was absent, so she left and went down to his office to wake him.

"Kickoff meeting," she whispered in his ear as he dozed on his desk.

Leonard lifted his face off the blotter. Burp. "I'm coming."

When everybody was seated in the conference room, Bill made his entrance, ramming his hand through his hair, making it stand up in black spikes. Bill liked to give the

21

impression of being a lovable klutz. And he was. "How's it going, troops?" He grinned around the room, making eye contact to the point that he forgot which meeting he was in. He looked over at Holly. She pointed to her mouth to signify school lunch.

"Uh, right. You ready to leap into a new market area? Ever hear of the National School Lunch Program? That's right. We're going after Agriculture. And everybody in town'll have their fingers in the potty on this one."

Leonard, who'd been holding up his hand the whole time, waved it. "So, what's on your mind?"

"Bidding on this is stupid," Leonard said. "We aren't qualified."

"Now, don't get steamed, Pudding," Bill said, taking out a ballpoint pen and chewing on it. "You finesse it. Hell, that's what we've always done. Just plug in a data base from some other prop, cut and paste, type of thing. It's what I call user friendly."

"What is this school lunch project, anyway?" Leonard asked. "What are we supposed to do?"

"Uh," Bill said, "I don't think it's necessary to actually understand what it is we're talking about here. You tell them, Ned."

Ned read from the *RFP* that the contract called for "'recommended alternate selections of nutritional deliverable components for recipients of the school lunch program nation-wide.'"

Leonard was snoring by now, and Holly put her head down to rest.

Suddenly she heard, "You mean we fix the menus?" spoken by bossy Rita. Holly opened one eye and looked over her arm at Bill, who was gnawing deeply on his pen with Rita pestering him. "I don't see as anybody here knows diddly about food," Rita said.

22

Holly reared up. "We are, too, qualified. Everyone here has . . . eaten the school lunch."

"I never did," Leonard growled. "I went to private school. And what is this supposed to mean?" he asked, holding up the Statement of Work, the SOW. "It says here Plate Waste Analysis."

"Sounds like garbage to me," Rita said. Who else?

"Tell you what, Leonard," Bill said. "We'll make you our Plate Waste Analyst. Give you some hands-on experience in the high school cafeteria scenario. And you can eyeball the cute girls."

"Will I get a raise?" Leonard asked.

"What a character." Bill laughed and took a gulp of coffee. "Uh, sure. If we land this deal, I guess there ought to be something in the pie for everyone."

Good, Holly thought. Bill was practically announcing that he would be promoting people.

"Except we can't bid on this," Leonard stated. "The *RFP* says it's a set-aside for a female-owned business."

"Cripes, let me see that." Bill snatched Leonard's copy. "You call females minorities? No pun intended, gals," he apologized. "Women these days with their own damn businesses," he muttered. "Well, OK. We'll smoke out some female operation and put their names up front. Work them in on the production side."

"Who else but women will teach you gentlemen about the lunches?" Fiona asked in her southern voice.

"We're not talking about the peanut butter and jelly sandwiches you gals put together for your kids," Bill said.

"Kids do eat the lunches," Holly reminded him. "And they like treats, which doesn't mean apples. What is worse on Halloween than getting an apple dropped on your cookies? Chocolate chip cookies, that's what people like."

"So?" Rita butted in. "They already have those."

23

Holly could hardly sit in her chair. "So—we could spruce up a basic food and also be responsive to the *RFP*—where it says 'recipes should be in line with the preferences of today's students.' We could put chocolate chips in the bread. Or better—chocolate chunks. Think of it: BelCon's Chocolate Chunk Bread."

Leonard's eyes stayed open. Ned Bird stopped biting his fingernails. And Bill chewed hungrily on his pen. Then a dark blob of ink oozed out on his lip. Holly pointed to Bill's mouth, but he just grinned, probably thinking she was still referring to the school lunch.

"Holly, good idea," Fiona said (politely covering her smile as she looked at Bill). Meanwhile, Ned Bird patted his lips conspicuously with his handkerchief to point out Bill's problem to him. But he still didn't catch on. "And if you gentlemen will install an oven in here," Fiona suggested, "I'll be happy to test the bread."

Bill's eyes got as big as loaves, and he said with his navy blue mouth, "I smell a winner here. OK, now. This prop isn't due until April 1. Pass them the schedule, Holly. How many pages can you gals type in a day, anyhow, minus trips to the powder room? To save dough, what we ought to do is install bedpans in the typing pool."

The room became silent. "Bill, there is no such typing pool here," Holly informed him. And she handed her boss a mirror.

Leonard complained that editing had been left out of the production schedule, as usual. "After that screw-up with HUD for a million bucks, you'd think we'd shape up."

Holly looked around, realizing that their editor, Claire Whittle, wasn't present at this meeting. That was because Bill hadn't invited her.

"OK. We'll try to jimmy in the wordsmithing," Bill said, rubbing his dark mouth with his handkerchief.

24

Then he rambled on about his management plan so that it was after six o'clock before the meeting ended. Too late for Holly to make it to her racquetball class tonight. She would definitely go next week.

Bill was feeling good as he came in the office after the meeting, trying to chin himself on the door frame, although he barely got his feet off the rug. The exercise did turn his face the color of a watermelon. "Everybody seemed hyped up about this prop, don't you think, Holly?" he asked with a big smile.

"They did," she agreed. "But don't forget you promised to add editing to the production schedule. Bill, you've got to put Claire Whittle in the loop. She is our full-time editor. That is what she gets paid to do."

# 5

# *Claire Whittle*

Claire looked at her watch. It was only three o'clock. She held it to her ear. Yup, still ticking. Move, you piker.

How do these people do it, drag themselves in to work every day, for the whole week—for their whole lives? Not that she hadn't worked her tail off in graduate school. But you didn't have to start in the morning and go all day.

The constant optimism in this place also wore on her nerves, "the sky's the limit" ad nauseam. She missed the angst of academia, the soothing discussions of nihilism that get you off the hook of life.

Hmm. It was mighty quiet around here this afternoon. They must be having another meeting. Good.

Claire got up and strolled to the window, checking a white speck floating by, begging for it to be snow. She'd rather be stranded in a Washington storm than ensconced in this room for another interminable afternoon.

She didn't mind the editing. If only they would give her some to do. Bring on the hyphenations. Let her plug in the bullets going down the page, those dark dots that take the place of logic. However, the terminology of consulting was taking its toll on her sensitive soul, once nurtured by the nuances of Shakespeare, driven by the demons of Dostoevsky . . . now whittled down to the bottom line.

And to Claire's horror, consulting jargon came out of her own mouth. Phrases such as *hands-on experience* and *market thrust* issued from her pristine lips that once massaged nothing but poetry. Last night in bed she even told her husband Jack that she was "too tired to interface."

Maybe she should quit this job and become a writer. Family and friends had always insisted that she had talent. And her master's thesis on alliterative patterns in post-modernist poetry was so well received by her committee that they cried for its publication. She could analyze the stuffing out of a poem, no question about that.

Ah, but the cash flow problem.

What she should do is write those romance novels that are the big sellers. You just follow a formula. It's two hundred pages of foreplay with a happy ending.

Here's how it goes. A virginal-type heroine, always with long hair, meets a thirty-fivish, cynical hero sporting blue-black locks. His kiss melts her bones (which for some reason infuriates her), and she stays mad at him for the whole book. But she's smitten for life, and her hormones cease to function in the presence of any other male.

Each episode gets hotter than the last, interrupted by barriers that the author throws in to keep the tension building up to the last steamy scene. Finally, the hero's tough hide cracks, and he grudgingly admits that he cares. Bingo, they're off into the sunset.

Claire took a legal pad out of her drawer and placed it on her barren desk. Her fingers quivered with anticipation as she wrote the title for the romance that had been

27

festering in her: *Forbidden Fruit.* Magnificent. She could see it on the best-seller list. It would be her ticket to freedom from the corporation—perhaps her passport to immortality.

She sat with her pen poised, waiting for her block-buster opening to surge through her fingers onto the page.

It did not.

All right. Maybe you have to make an outline first. And a novel has to have a pattern of imagery. She hadn't majored in English for nothing. Ah, images of fruit, of course. She rapidly wrote down all the fruit she could think of.

Her heart was contracting like an orange in a juicer now as her story surged up in her. OK. The first sentence has to set the scene, introduce the characters, and suck the reader in. She had studied the novel and knew these things.

*Reeling under Rodney's riveting lips, Ramona furiously slid across the satin sheets (decorated with a papaya pattern) to escape the scorching caress of the only man she could ever love.*

Claire stopped to breathe. Magnificent. It was realistic, too. The satin sheets her mother-in-law gave her and Jack sent them flying out of their king-size bed. Dear Jack, whose electrical engineering language (which once bored her silly, although his body never did) would now be the vocabulary to capture the magnetic essence of her romance.

That opening sentence was good. But maybe too good. If she didn't slow her characters down they'd be sexed out by the bottom of the page. You're probably supposed to start the story before the hero and heroine meet.

OK. She would need an exotic setting, someplace where fruits grow. Hawaii with its honeydew . . . the pomegranates of Polynesia . . . breadfruit baking in Borneo. A person could get carried away doing this. Or, her characters might meet on neutral grounds, the equator, say, in a love boat type of scenario. Yes.

*The hot air hugged the humid hull of the* Mango Maiden *as she glided on her virgin voyage through the Gulf Stream, head-on to the equator, where east and west would meet.*

*Rodney Rhodes, the world-famous climatologist (with blue-black hair), stared cynically with slitted eyes out at the still sea. He passionately wished the breasts of the waves would rise up with white tips, but they did not.*

*At the opposing end of the deck, unbeknownst to him, red-haired, reclining Ramona put her glasses on (with no prescription in them), and opened her book,* Principles of Hotel Management. *This would prove that she was no airhead sex symbol, even though she had won numerous beauty contests and was the reigning Tangerine Queen of Florida. For her talent number she had flow-charted her rise from mail person to receptionist at the Muskmelon Manor, her father's hotel.*

*Suddenly, the sky grew dark, and a hot drop splatted on her cheek. She better go get ready for the party tonight celebrating her parents' twenty-fifth wedding anniversary —and proof that not everybody gets divorced in this storm-tossed world. Vaguely, only vaguely, did Ramona miss her boyfriend, Ed Ward. He was a nice young man who was totally attentive and thus did not excite her.*

"Claire?"

She looked up. It was Leonard Pudding, the office nerd. "What is it, Leonard?"

"Do we have to capitalize the word *company*?"

29

"Yes," she snapped.

Leonard disappeared.

*Ramona hurried towards her stateroom. But not so fast. The passageway was blocked—by the carved magnificence of sinewy male shoulders.*

*Furiously, she tried to breeze past, but the man grasped her wrist. "Care to watch the storm arrive?"*

*His touch sent an electric shock through her, triggering her spinal cord and shorting out her brain. "Excuse me!" she said, summoning all the voltage she could into her nineteen-year-old voice, although not enough to withstand the magnetic grasp of this god.*

*"Climactic agitation turns me on. I'm Rodney Rhodes." His tongue caressed his manly lips, foreshadowing a deeper hunger to come.*

"Do you want anything from the candy machine?" a voice said.

Claire put down her pen. "Hi, Holly. What?"

"Sorry," Holly answered. "I won't disturb you," and she quietly closed the door.

*Ramona tried to wrench her way past Rodney, but his charged fingertips grazed her bare arm, sending a current of desire through her beauty queen's body more potent than the pina coladas on this ship. He crushed her to his rock-hard body. And as thunder stomped across the grape-colored sky, his lips pressed hers, transforming every fiber of her being to purée.*

*When Ramona opened her eyes, Rodney was looking up at a blond woman on the deck above them, who darted out of sight.*

*"Damn," he muttered.*

30

*"You rat! I knew I couldn't trust you," Ramona cried, wrenching away and stumbling back to her claustrophobic cabin (forgoing the fresh fruits presented by the steward), where she threw herself on the narrow bunk and was inundated in a tidal wave of tears. This brought on a migraine, puffy eyes, and the intolerable ringing of a bell.*

Claire jumped. The phone on her desk was ringing. Good grief, it was almost five o'clock. And she never worked late.

*Ramona's mascara-stained fingers reached for the throbbing receiver and picked it up.*

"Uh, Claire, you got a minute to come in my office?" Let's see, whose voice was that? Oh, the guy she worked for. Bill Moss.

"Sure," she answered. And secreting *Forbidden Fruit* in her drawer, Claire swept out of her quarters and down the gangway to her boss's office.

Bill leaned back in his fat cat leather chair and said, "Uh, Claire, you want to get to work on the résumés for this school lunch deal."

"School lunch?" Her nostrils dilated at the memory of that awful cafeteria smell. Visions of unwanted fruit floating in tubs of juice rose up before her eyes. Meanwhile, she had no idea what this man in a military consulting firm was talking about.

"It's this big new prop we're going for," Bill continued, munching on a pencil. "You know."

"Solicited or unsolicited?" Claire asked, stalling, fully aware that no organization acquainted with BelCon would invite them to submit a bid. However, she nodded attentively and wrote something down.

*Ordinarily, any male who solicited Ramona would be dead meat. But Rodney Rhodes, inviting her to dinner on the* Mango Maiden—*and begging for a chance to apologize—undid her body and her brain. Would her answer be "Yes!"? Would it be "No!"? She wagged her head from side to side until her neck was weak.*

"What's that, Claire?" Bill asked, moving his head in unison with hers and holding out his ear. He would make a wonderful deaf mute, she thought. "So, go ahead and beef up the résumés," he said, "in line with the school lunch, kind of thing."

*"Beef? Yes indeed," Rodney assured Ramona. Prime rib, filet, and savory sirloin tips were all in abundance on the menu in the ship's dining room. The choice was hers.*

"That's it?" Claire looked up from her note pad. And noticing that it was after five o'clock, she said she had to go. "I'll do the résumés tomorrow."

She heard Bill grunt as she walked out. No matter.

Claire sailed down the stairs, swept through the lobby, and floated out BelCon's front door, where she stepped across the pigeon droppings there. Another time she might have stopped to note their symbolic significance in relation to this company.

But not tonight. She rushed out into the frosty February night. The air smelled of snow, but none was falling yet. Hurrying to her car she almost stumbled, trembling with desire to get home to Jack.

# 6

# *Spa Baby You*

Holly jogged up to the desk at her health club, gulping, whoa, would you look at that attendant handing out the towels. A dream in a tee shirt, with the name of the club—Spa Baby You—spread-eagled on his chest.

"Your membership card, miss?" Her body sang a song.

"Certainly." She fumbled in her tote bag, leaning forward to catch his name tag. Mitch, oh God. He took her ID, and his fingertips touched hers, causing her legs to become water. "Could I have a towel, thanks."

He passed it to her, warm and fluffy. "Here you go, Holly," he said, already knowing her name. That was so nice.

OK, somebody behind her was getting shovy. She stepped out of the way of a person who had obviously worked out with weights to build her pecs, which were not a pretty sight.

Holly moved to the other end of the counter and looked behind it to see if Mitch was wearing shorts. Too bad, no. But those contours in his warm-up suit were definitely

33

buns. She pumped on upstairs to the racquetball courts with the warm towel Mitch had given her around her neck. Whew, these steps were steep.

Mr. Pound, the racquetball instructor, was waiting with his roster. He was probably considered handsome by the young girls in the class. They hounded him with questions such as, "How do you hold the racquet?"—obviously wanting him to demonstrate personally with his hands. Well, to Holly he was just plain scrawny and cocky. He was also a prejudiced person, putting her on the bottom of the almighty club ladder when he'd barely seen her play one time. Big deal, a ladder, if you're the type of person who has to be on top of others to feel secure.

Mr. Pound also consistently hassled you. "Aim for the corner," he would holler, when you had the whole wall to hit. He nagged you to "move your feet," as if it's possible to concentrate on forty-five things at once. And he spied on you through the glass wall of the racquetball court, rather, a wooden cell. Holly did like the ball used in this game. It was soft and blue and spongy and didn't hurt when it hit you as much as other balls do.

"Prickle, court four," Mr. Pound commanded.

Holly tugged on her headband and got down to crawl through the opening made for midgets going into the court. Either that or Spa Baby You was getting cheaper by the day.

Her opponent was already warming up. Yikes. She was an Amazon, galloping across the whole room and swatting the ball as if she hated it. But being that tall she probably didn't have a personal life, which was sad. One size does not fit all. She said her name was Jocelyn.

"You ready?" Jocelyn asked, looking down at Holly, with sweat rolling off her giant limbs.

"You bet." Go for the jugular.

34

Jocelyn smacked her serve against the wall then hogged the middle of the floor, leaping with her oversized feet. Well, Holly was glad she didn't have to buy shoes of that size. She preferred shoes that were for girls. She jumped as high as she could for the next ball (though not to the point of giving herself a hernia) and missed, feeling as short as a toenail. Then Stilts slammed one straight at the glass, which was something you didn't do in Holly's upbringing. Those who break windows pay.

Before she knew it, that game was over. Fine. Maybe they could take a break and get a soda.

But her opponent couldn't bear to have a pit stop with her one-track mind, play, play, play.

All right. This time Holly was determined to get a point. The ball flew at her head, and she gave it her jugular swing. Crack! She'd smacked her own skull.

And did Jocelyn say she was sorry? Not in the least.

Holly touched her scalp and felt a lump, and her fingers came out sticky. OK, it wasn't blood. But sweat is not nothing.

Naturally Mr. Pound was gawking into the court at that moment, always on the lookout for when you messed up.

Holly raised her dizzy head. "Play ball." She would hit a winner this time or else.

The ball came whizzing at her, and Holly smacked it towards the corner. It landed exactly in the crack, although not in the corner she had aimed at. However, this tactic did cause her opponent to practically fall over herself trying to get another greedy point. Jocelyn lurched for it but missed this time. Holly's point, hurrah, in this beautiful game of racquetball.

She looked to see if Mr. Pound appreciated her now. But the little worm had gone. That's what's wrong with the men of today, no attention span.

35

Finally, the buzzer sounded. And Jocelyn had no trouble getting her tall body out of that low door pronto, gloating over to Mr. Pound to record her fabulous score.

Holly squeezed out the stubby hole and went over to slump down at a table and rest her pounding head.

When she looked up, a man was sitting at her table, facing the other way, watching a game. He had blond hair that was getting thin in back, but at least he didn't swoop it across the balding spot. And his tan legs were stretched out with gold hair curling on them, as opposed to the legs of the gentleman at the next table, which were as smooth as muskmelons, although not as appetizing.

The blond man turned and looked at her with eyes as blue as the skies out west. "Have a good game? You were giving it a go."

"You bet." Holly fluffed her perm over the lump on her head. "But some people take games so seriously. I think sports should be fun."

"Yup." He smiled and didn't show a single cavity. "But it is more fun when you win."

"I'm sure you did," Holly answered, admiring his shoulders. Some women might consider them heavyset, but to her they were laid-back muscle. The dark sweat on his navy tee shirt looked as if a hand had touched him on the chest. It was so masculine it was making her crazy. "I do enjoy most sports."

"What else do you play?" he asked, shifting his magnificent legs.

"Why, most anything," she answered, daintily removing her headband and wringing it out. "What's that game where you bat the ball with feathers on it?"

"Badminton."

"Right. I've played that at parties."

36

"I like athletic women," he said, stretching his arms up behind his head, showing more of his sexy sweat. Her headache was completely gone.

"My wife Maxine never got into sports." Holly's nostrils flared. Men love to rub your nose in it, don't they, always bringing up their other women. "But my kids are athletic. Swimming, soccer, you name it. My two boys live with me."

"With you?" Holly swallowed. "Just you?"

"Yup. Their mom, she passed away. Last year."

A dead wife, oh, God, You are too good. "You poor man, left with that responsibility. I have a son myself and know. How did your wife die?"

"She—" He stopped as a player crashed into the glass wall in front of them. Whang. "It was a type of stroke."

"I'm sorry. My mother died of a stroke."

"Is that right. Say, the boys want to crack crabs this weekend. Would you care to join us?"

The racquetball pinged off the window in front of them, it sang off all the walls. "Very much so. And I won't have my son Walter with me, although it would be nice if he could meet your boys sometime."

"You have cracked crabs and know what you're getting into."

"I'm sure I have," Holly said. She liked the sweet meat of crabs, not that it could compare with her favorite seafood, tuna fish.

"I'm Les Moore."

Les Moore? At least his parents got half of it right.

Holly introduced herself and explained that she had been named after one of the best-selling shrubs in her father's nursery.

Les laughed and said that he would call her.

# 7

# *A New Man*

Holly whispered Les's little name into her pillow until it got big. He was a nurturing man, a new man, who took care of his children. And he'd complimented her racquetball game. She smiled into the floral pattern of her pillowcase, dreaming of their date that night.

And Les called that morning as he'd said he would, a man who didn't lie. He wasn't sure what time they'd be going for crabs because he had to take his boys to the pet store first. What a father. Lassie.

"Aren't pets great," Holly said, holding Warren's ear up to the phone. He leaped off her lap. And Les was so nice to take his boys along on his date. He was a generous man, too. Crabs are not cheap meat.

That afternoon when Holly went out to get rabbit food, she passed a place called Leroy's Crab House. Outside was a picture of a crab hanging down, looking like a big red spider. When she saw this, she decided maybe she hadn't cracked crabs after all. The Neptune salads and crab cakes she'd eaten were impeccably prepared.

38

She decided to check out Leroy's and see what you wore to such a place. It was a warm day in winter, with everybody out in the thaw, and she pulled into the last muddy parking spot, next to a disgusting van. Those drivers with dirty beards and drugs stashed in the back did not appeal to her. She walked way around the van.

As she went up on the porch of the frame house converted into a restaurant, the smell was enough to knock you over. She wiped a place off the grimy window and looked inside. Ugh. Garbage was piled on the tables, and the customers were pounding on their food with mallets.

She went inside Leroy's to get a better look and make sure she wasn't dreaming this up. A waiter in a filthy apron brought in a bushel basket and dumped it on the table, leaving a pile of muddy shells with pink sticks poking out. If those were the crabs, they didn't resemble the white pieces of meat they dunk in butter on television at all. A man in a Redskins tee shirt picked open his crab's stomach, lifting it up as if it were a flip-top lid. Holly stepped over to get a closer look at the entrails, which did not increase her appetite. Then she saw the worst. Sitting on the edge of the crab's shell were two dark little knobs with long hairs coming out of them. *Eyes.* Yes, crabs have eyes and watch you eat them.

She hightailed it back out to her car and fastened her seatbelt. Who was this Les Moore, anyway, inviting a person to such a place? Maybe she should call and break the date, although you have to be cruel to do that, and she wasn't that liberated yet.

When she walked in her apartment, the phone was ringing. It was Les. "Holly, you want to take a rain check on those crabs?" Her bodily functions stopped. "My kids asked me to fix burgers instead," he explained. "You're welcome to join us."

Her breath came back. And you can't get mad at a man for cooking his kids' dinner. "OK."

"You do like hamburgers? The boys think mine are pretty good."

What kind of question was that, did she like hamburgers? She hadn't come to this country on a boat. Not that she praised them to a man's face, either, or he'll get in the hamburger habit. "I'm sure they're delicious," she said. "And I'll bring the dessert."

"Great." Les gave her directions to his place in Mount Vernon, which seemed like an odd location for a bachelor. He was obviously sucking up to George Washington.

Now, what awesome dessert could she make for Les and his boys tonight? Chocolate mousse was classy, and she'd seen a recipe for that. Yet kids make fun of fancy foods, especially something with a name resembling an animal.

Cherries jubilee had the prettiest name of any dessert. It was impressive, too. Guests always notice flames. However, Les might not appreciate the alcoholic content in it for his kids.

Then she had it, the perfect dish. It was gourmet and tasty, too—baked Alaska. She would take Les and his boys a baked Alaska they'd never forget. And she'd saved just the recipe, out of a magazine, "for the diner who's eaten it all: Baked Alaska à la Surprise."

The directions were a bit unusual. "Scoop out the middle of a grapefruit." OK. She had one in the fridge for Walter. And she could add maraschino cherries for color.

To substitute for the ice cream that would melt on her trip, she doubled up on the meringue, swirling it into fantastic shapes. There, done, beautiful. She watched it brown through the oven door to make sure it didn't char. People don't ask for second helpings of black food.

When she got ready to go to Mount Vernon, she packed the baked Alaska in the back seat of her car, protected by pillows. And she drove extra carefully, checking it every few minutes. The meringue held up fine.

The sign over the beltway said *Richmond*, as most of them do. And in Washington the word *South* doesn't necessarily mean you're going in that direction. It might mean you will get there. Or, it is a state of mind. Anyway, she missed the turnoff and had to take the exit to Lorton, where the prison was, to ask directions.

The guard sat up in his box with no sense of humor, and on a Saturday night. "Where's your pass?"

Holly told him she hadn't come for a visit but was lost on her way to deliver a dessert to a male friend in Mount Vernon. "It's homemade," she informed him, pointing to the baked Alaska in the back seat. Amber drops of sugar had collected on the meringue, looking so delicious she wanted to skip dinner and dive in. "I would offer you a piece," she told the guard, "but I don't happen to be carrying a knife."

He frowned back at her from the shadows. She showed him the directions to Les's place, which he read at a first-grade level with his lips. "Lady, you're way off. Go back and take the beltway to Alexandria," he said, swallowing with his Adam's apple, actually more of a strawberry stuck in his throat.

With his assistance, Holly made it to Mount Vernon with no trouble, just a couple of stops at service stations. And Les's neighborhood was nicer than you'd expect for a bachelor. The oversized garbage cans out by the curb didn't have a thing dripping out of them. And the red brick houses sat back in beautiful trees.

She drove slowly down the street, watching the addresses get higher going up to his. These places all had

41

curtains, so she doubted that many bachelors lived here. At least the ones she'd known all had something seriously missing in their places, paper napkins, or worse.

But she shouldn't judge Les by other men. She had never known such a devoted father. And the way he'd looked at her, with such blue eyes . . .

Pow, she hit her brakes as a bicycle darted in front of her, ridden by a boy with dark hair. She swerved, she missed him. Oh, Walter. Holly sat in her car shaking.

Backing it off the curb, she eased on down the street to Les's place. There it was, with hedges growing up to touch his porch, trimmed by his own hands.

She parked across the street and checked her lipstick in the mirror. Then as she was fluffing up her perm, a voice called from the upstairs window across the street, "I see you found it, Holly. Come on over."

She got out of the car, smiling and waving at the head up in the bedroom as she crossed the street on jelly legs.

This was just a date, she reminded herself, breathing deep. A first date, not the second one where he's starting to like you. And it certainly wasn't the third almighty date, which could give you a stroke for a good reason.

Meanwhile, her body wouldn't listen and thought that it was going to the prom. Her pulse was pounding all through her.

As she approached Les's door, she panicked, realizing that she'd worn the wrong thing. She had debated between a turtleneck (supposedly flattering) and a silky blouse that makes you feel womanly. They both make their own statement. A turtleneck cries out, "You'll have to pull me the whole way off" (which messes up your hair in a manner that is not the most fun). On the other hand, a slippery blouse goes with the flow. "Easy, one button at a time." She had hunted through three malls to find this

42

blouse she was wearing, of her gold signature color. Now she could see that it was too loud.

The door opened before she touched it, and Les came out. He had on a tan shirt and corduroys that fit. The insignia on his chest was the classy horseback rider, no low crocodile for him. "Don't you look sporty," she said.

"Come on in and meet the boys." Les opened the door with his arms wide.

"Guys, say hello to Holly." Les went in the den where his two blond sons were watching television (so exceedingly blond that their mother must have been an albino). "This is Willard," Les introduced his eleven-year-old lying on the couch, who lifted his big running shoe to say hello. "And that's Rex." For a second Holly looked around for a dog, although she had been told the names of both sons. "Hi," Rex said, still looking at the screen.

You could smell the dinner cooking, although it wasn't any hamburger she recognized. Holly remembered she'd left the dessert in the car, and Les went out with her to get it. "You made it yourself?" he asked, smiling at her magnificently.

"I wouldn't bring something store bought on the first date." She smiled back, meanwhile catching her toe on the sidewalk and almost stumbling.

She went over to her car, still looking at Les, and swung the back door open. "Baked Alaska à la Surprise. Made to order for you men."

Les got a strange look on his face as he gazed over her shoulder.

Holly turned around and stared into her back seat. A wild animal must have gotten in there. Or a blizzard had hit. White blobs of meringue were splattered on the seat and dripped down the windows. The grapefruit was on the floor with its red eyes knocked out and lying in slimy

43

juice. "Oh, dear." She stepped in front of the door to hide the sight, but of course it was too late.

"I'll go get something to clean this up," Les said.

"Don't bother," she told him. "We don't need dessert. Kids never appreciate gourmet food anyway. Let's just go back inside and enjoy your sons."

But here they came, Les's monster children, tromping down the walk and heading for her car. "What did she bring for dessert, dad?" the mean one named Rex spoke up. She wished he were a dog.

"Never mind," Les said, roughing his boy's hair into sheepdog bangs. Unfortunately, he could still see out. Meanwhile, Willard went over and gawked in her car, mashing his face against the back window to snoop inside. "Wow, gross. What's that? So, dad, can we have Oreo ice cream instead?"

"Sure. Come on, Holly. I'll show you the house."

So they trudged back into Les's mansion, where she could admire the many rooms loaded with memories of these children's mother, the perfect cook.

Les led the way into the living room, which definitely did have something missing. No furniture. Just a cherry red carpet wall to wall, which had a stain the shape of a puddle in it. "A spot of red livens up a room," she said, quoting her father in the nursery business.

The dining room was furnished with aquariums, fish staring at you with their bulging eyes. One aquarium had rocks in it instead of water. Les reached inside and brought out a cord curling around his manly wrist that stuck out a quick tongue. "You're not afraid of snakes, I hope. Sandy can't hurt you."

First it was filthy crabs, and now a snake named Sandy. "Afraid?" Holly said. "Why, in the west we have snakes in the home rooms of the schools." Les held out Sandy for her to pet, but she declined, as it isn't necessary to touch all animals to appreciate them. "And we'll be eating soon."

"Look at this." Les pointed to a tiny white mark on Sandy's stomach, the size of a hyphen. "It's the incision where she had her Caesarean."

"You're kidding." Holly looked around the room to see if any of Sandy's offspring were nearby.

"Don't worry. We gave the little ones away at Christmas."

She breathed. But here she was blaming Les again, when he was only trying to be a generous father figure.

They went upstairs and down the hall of closed rooms. And he opened which door? The bathroom. It was papered in an attractive leafy pattern containing fuzz that coordinated with the shower curtain done in a jungle motif. Holly watched to make sure it didn't move, after reading in the newspaper about a man out in Virginia who kept his pet python in his tub. She listened but couldn't hear a hiss.

She focused on the sink to calm herself. Blobs of blue gel toothpaste were splattered there, which at least was normal. You couldn't expect a bachelor to spend his time polishing fixtures. Then something moved in the drain. Bugs. Black bugs came crawling out of it.

"Crickets," Les explained. "That's what Sandy eats. You can get them at the pet store."

"You buy those?" Holly stepped away from the scatterbrained creatures that scared her silly, Warren, too.

"Yup. We got a fresh batch today."

She went out in the hall. "Maybe we should check the dinner," she suggested. "I smelled something special on the way in."

"Sure enough."

They went down to a crock pot in the kitchen, and Les mentioned that they were having stew instead of burgers

45

because they were out of buns. "It turned into a family effort," he said, laughing. He lifted off the lid, and the brew bubbled up with stray bits of pink meat swirling in it. "Willard put in hamburger," Les explained. A strand of underwater foliage floated by. "I told the kids we had to have something green. And the only thing Rex likes is lettuce. So he got smart and threw that in. You know how kids are about the greens."

"My Walter, I'm sure, doesn't care for them either," Holly murmured.

The meal did taste better than it looked, and it didn't leave you stuffed. After dinner they watched a space movie on the VCR, so Holly figured this evening was shot. But as she dozed off during one more battle in the galaxy, Les's voice came out of the heavens, "Want to go for a walk?"

"A walk in the winter." She sat up. "How nice."

Les went upstairs to change, and she could hear him moving on the floor overhead. Was he putting on something wrinkle-proof? Adding a dab of aftershave, she hoped?

Meanwhile, he'd obviously left her here to get acquainted with his boys. "You do have unusual pets, not boring cats and dogs," she mentioned. "My son Walter and I have a rabbit, Warren. They make the neatest messes of any animal." Willard looked at his brother and then back at the screen. She was babbling idiotically, she knew it.

Before the boys could answer, Les appeared in the doorway, filling it with his magnificent racquetball shoulders. He was wearing a turtleneck of a beautiful earth shade and carrying—a blanket. "If we aren't back by ten," Les told his sons, "you go on to bed."

"Ten-thirty, dad," Willard said.

"OK, but that's it."

When they got outside, Holly complimented Les on his disciplined children going to bed by themselves. He laughed and said he was just a single parent trying to do his job. Single fathers do seem to be more laid back, whereas mothers are born for stress.

As they walked out in the cool night air, Les's fingertips touched hers. And when his whole warm hand enclosed her smaller one, it felt so good she almost fell into his flower bed.

"Want to go down by the water?" he asked. She had no idea they were close to a beach. She said of course she did.

They strolled to the end of his cul-de-sac and on into the trees, stepping onto squishy ground. A branch swatted her cheek, reminding her that this remote area was the exact type of place where you'd expect to be attacked. But that happens in normal places, too, such as the elevator at work or the laundry room of your apartment.

And she couldn't believe Les would manhandle a woman, not someone so considerate of his children. If you can't trust a man you meet in a health spa, who makes stew for his kids, who can you trust?

She grabbed a branch and slid on mud. See. There was nothing to worry about. If Les had wanted to drag her to the ground here, he would have made his move by now. Instead, he'd let go of her hand.

They came out of the brush, and she heard a slurping sound. "There's the pier," Les said, pointing to dark water glittering in the light of a slim moon.

He went over and stepped onto the creaking boards, spread out the blanket, and lay down. A warm feeling of trust rose in her for this man who didn't force himself on a woman.

However, being a lady (which is frequently a handicap), Holly didn't rush over and sprawl down next to

47

Les of her own free will, either. She sat carefully a few feet away, wrapping her arms around her knees to keep warm. Finally, when her back ached she did ease down on the edge of the blanket, where she lay as quiet as a board.

Les started in talking about the stars, and his knowledgeability of their whereabouts was impressive. But no lecture pointing out a red star in a warrior's belt had ever helped her see it. She was glad when she saw the Big Dipper, which Les passed over as if it were nothing (perhaps because that ladle reminded him of his stew?). Meanwhile, her body was getting cold as a cube and wondering what it was doing here.

Then suddenly Les stopped talking, leaving such a sexy silence out here in nature that she didn't even want to swallow. Of course, as soon as you tell yourself not to swallow, you do. Gulp.

Finally, when her stiff body had to move, she shifted slightly in the direction of Les's warmth. And his lips were waiting perfectly in the way, the softest lips she'd ever felt, or at least that she could remember. They kissed for a long time. And if she had rolled off the pier into the dark water at that moment, she would have had a happy life.

Then Les was touching her so gently down the sides of her body with his sensitive fingertips that her breath evaporated. But when he got to her belt buckle, she forced her hand to stop him there. If you give of yourself on the first date, men think you're a tramp. On the second date, also.

"What's up?" he asked, as she took his precious fingers and moved them to a higher place on her body.

"Sorry, but I'm not one of those easy women you're used to." (However, if she wanted to be liberated, maybe she should learn casual sex sometime.) "With all respect to your dead wife."

"OK," Les said.

What? "I only meant we should get somewhat acquainted first," Holly explained. "And you must still be in mourning. Were you with your wife when she died?"

"No, Maxine was in an institution." Les sat up and rubbed his hands.

"I guess it is easier having them in the hospital."

"Actually, it was a mental institution." He stood up and gathered the blanket, shaking it out once, twice, done. The poor man, having to live with a fruitcake.

Les walked her back to her car in the chilly air that had the smell of snow in it now. They climbed in the back seat for one last delicious clinch—how handy, there were pillows in there—kissing so sweetly that the air almost smelled sweet.

It was. She touched the sticky seat and remembered her baked Alaska. They got out, and she brushed the soggy cake crumbs off Les's behind, which was fun. He laughed and wasn't mad.

Then as she was about to drive away, Les did the nicest thing of all. He had her roll down her window, and he leaned in to kiss her goodby. A man has to like you if he does that. His hands weren't getting a thing out of it.

"Want to try for those crabs next weekend?" he asked, with the world's softest lips.

"Oh, yes," she sang.

# 8

# *Forbidden Fruit*

Claire rolled over into her pillow, stretching deliciously after a dream she'd had about Rodney and Ramona making out.

Ugh. She had to go to work. Jack had already left. He had so much energy for his job.

She looked out the slats of the Venetian blinds at the gray sky. Maybe it would snow today, and they'd get sent home from work. She closed her eyes, imagining that she had a scratchy feeling in her throat. Yes, she definitely felt sick. The thought of going to work made her sick.

She lay there rehearsing the voice of a deathly ill person and trying to muster the nerve to call the office. She would talk to Holly. She'd be nice.

Claire dialed BelCon and, damn, Bill Moss answered his own phone. He was not pleased when she announced that she was taking a sick day.

But after she hung up it was worth it. Free! Now she could work on *Forbidden Fruit* all day. And if you stay in your bathrobe, you must be sick. OK, where was she . . .

*Ramona's dinner on the* Mango Maiden *with Rodney Rhodes had been a disaster, and not just because the crab cakes he recommended (in opposition to her desire for sirloin tips) had arrived containing cartilage. The cameo appearance of Rodney's female friend had forced Ramona from the table, spilling wine—and before dessert was served.*

*She secluded herself in her stateroom, with strict orders to the steward not to let Rodney in. However, as pale dawn peeked through her cabin window, Ramona realized with horror that her tan was fading. So, disguised in a khaki bikini, she stealthily slipped out to the pool.*

*The sky was clear, and he was nowhere in sight as she found a deck recliner and immersed herself in* Principles of Hotel Management, *committing to memory the chapter on "Restrooms."*

*A shadow crossed the page. She looked up. A cloud cover had emerged from nowhere. Him! She would know that profile chiseled against the sky anywhere, a veritable Van Gogh painting.*

*Rodney approached the kidney-shaped pool. He stuck in a toe. Then his magnificent torso plunged, causing a tidal wave in the blue water and a nose dive in Ramona's heart. Maybe she had been too hard on him.*

*He remained underwater so long she was afraid that he'd hit bottom. Clutching her textbook to her cleavage, she watched for his black head to appear, those lips that could melt granite to bubble up again with life.*

*Here he came, swiveling up like a dolphin. He waved!*

*She jumped up to go. But as she passed the pool, he grabbed her ankle in a shark-type grip and pulled her in—after she'd spent hours doing her hair.*

*She clawed her way out, coughing up chlorination.*

51

"I've missed you, Ramona. Where've you been?"

"Oh, sure," she shot back, spitting a mouthful of pool water at him.

Rodney lunged and pulled her down into the vortex of his macho desire, his moist arms aligning her chaste loins with his calloused ones, although she fought and fought. Electrically, his lips met hers. Then sinking to her jugular, he relayed the super circuit of his three-pronged lust.

The volcanic pressure of this underwater passion released Ramona's clenched fists, strained her inhibitions, and broke the strap on her bikini.

"Stop!" she gulped, thrusting to the surface to breathe and pull up her bathing suit.

Weakly she paddled to the pool's edge and dragged herself up the slippery side. Rodney casually hoisted himself up. "Why do we always have to stop?" he said, shaking the water off his curvy pecs. He obviously lifted weights so he could be a hunk, either that or he used steroids.

"I'm a nice girl," she hissed. And now that her hands were free, she slapped his face. "And you'll probably tell me that blond woman sniffing around you is just a friend."

"No, I won't," Rodney answered darkly.

"Go ahead, deny that she's your lover."

"She is not my lover. Where do you get off, anyway?"

"Miami Beach," Ramona answered, "where I'm a professional at my father's hotel, the Muskmelon Manor."

"Your dad owns that seedy place?"

"That's not fair," she snapped. "We serve chocolate-covered cherries on the pillows."

"Heh, I work across the street in the weather tower."

"You don't! You couldn't!"

"Yup. I'm a climatologist. Natural disasters turn me

on. *Tidal waves, earthquakes, acts of God are my life blood. My favorite one,"* Rodney's nostrils quivered, *"is volcanoes."*

*"So that was your ulterior motive in coming on this cruise—to detect atmospheric disturbances. Meanwhile, you use me for cheap thrills when the weather gets boring."* Ramona stood up on the slimy cement and swung a towel around her. *"And you like that other woman better than me because she has a stormier personality,"* she shouted as she hurtled towards the hold.

*"That's not true,"* Rodney called. *"You're both type A personalities. Oh, come on back, Ramona, and I'll tell you about my problem with women. Have a pina colada and calm down."*

*"Never,"* she shrieked, her voice whistling with twister winds.

*"Meet me in Miami then,"* he hollered at Ramona's twirling khaki body wreaking havoc among the deck chairs lying in her wake. *"I'll be in touch when there's a hurricane. It's quite a sight to see."*

*"That'll be the day,"* she hollered back. *"I look forward to never seeing you again, you brute. All you care about is storms."*

# 9

# *Leonard Pudding*

Leonard Pudding opened his eyes. He blinked them. White bits were floating by. Where was he? He pedaled his chair closer to the window. The rollers on it made the chirping sound of a bird. Cars were already leaving the parking lot. He checked his digital watch. It was only 3:13. Cheaters, cutting out early, and not putting it on their time sheets, either, he bet. Those same guys charged big buck dinners on their expense accounts—when who spends that type of dough if you're paying for your own?

He had turned in his voucher to BelCon for the dinners he ate at Big Boy when he had to work overtime. But they wouldn't cough up.

Snow days, ha. He didn't believe in them. Out in Ohio where he came from there was no such thing.

At least nobody was left here in the office to bug him. He reached in his drawer where he'd stashed the singles section of the newspaper. Those ads to meet your mate nauseated him, but he couldn't stop reading them. He hadn't been on a date for seven years and figured he should try. He'd be forty years old next year. And he never met anyone. The only females he knew were here at work, and he didn't date secretaries.

A few months back he'd gone downtown to Dates 'R' Us and made a tape. First they put you in a booth and make you listen to what other guys say on theirs. They say dumb stuff such as they're dying to go for walks on the beach and have a "meaningful and long-term relationship with a caring person." Bull, when you know what they want is hands-on flesh tonight.

He had stated on his tape at Dates 'R' Us that rejects need not apply. No clerical types, either. His standards must have been too high, therefore, no calls.

The only telephone calls he got at home were from his parents or blind people trying to sell you light bulbs. When the phone rang here in the office, it was somebody on his tail.

He took his clipboard and marched down the hall, checking off the names of people whose offices were vacant. Ned Bird was still here, not that he would give you the time of day if you were the last guy in the building. But at least he didn't rip off the company by not putting in the time.

Leonard stopped outside Claire Whittle's door. She was still in there scribbling away on something. This surprised him. They must have finally given her some work to do. He made a note on his matrix that Claire was here. He wouldn't mind having her job of editing, as long as he didn't have to deal with people.

He went on down to the men's room, where nobody was at the urinals or in the stalls. He noticed a piece of mud on his shoe and picked it off with a paper towel. He dropped the lump of dirt in the commode and watched it turn the water brown.

He prowled back to his desk, nauseated at the sight of his job title nailed to the door, *Junior Analyst*. He was supposed to be a college professor. And he'd gotten his Ph.D. in history. But the teaching profession dried up. While he was looking for a faculty job, he'd worked as a mail carrier for the lousy postal service. But the mailbag gave his shoulder bursitis, and dogs sniffed and bit.

He'd answered about a thousand ads for jobs. Then he finally saw the one from BelCon saying "advanced degree preferred but no experience necessary." That was him. William P. Moss (Bill) had hired him, although Leonard didn't know why. Bill probably wanted somebody around to kid. "Pudding, you lucky stiff," he'd say and slap him on the back. "You must have a ball being the only single guy in Special Projects."

Well, he didn't have any ball. He didn't even flirt with the girls here at BelCon (but, yup, he looked and smelled).

Leonard got up again and meandered down to Holly Prickle's desk, although he figured she'd be gone. The ones with kids always leave early. If he ever had kids—and there was a ninety-nine percent chance he never would—on "snow days" he'd make them do their school work at home.

He strode over and stood behind Holly's chair, looking down where her neckline went. She wore this one yellowish top that was a real plunger. He pulled a Kleenex out of the box on her desk and sniffed it. Yup, perfumed.

Somebody was coming. It was the cleaning lady, hauling trash. "Them're all gone home," she muttered. "Scuse me." She reached past Leonard to snatch the can and dumped it in her hefty bag, giving it a sock on the bottom.

"I never got any memo saying BelCon was closing early today," he told her.

"Government shuts down, we shut," she said, dragging her loot out in the hall.

"It's a waste of the taxpayers' money," he called after her.

As he headed back to his desk, a phone was ringing. It almost sounded like his. It was. "Pudding here," he said, puffing.

"Is this the Dr. Leonard Pudding from Dates 'R' Us?" a female voice asked.

"Speaking," he answered, clearing his throat.

"This is Verbena Tangles, calling in regard to your tape recording. Being a doctor, you're going to thrill my mum. Not that I haven't been associated with numerous professional men. But when you said you wanted a quality person, I knew that was me."

Leonard swallowed through his necktie. "I figured nobody would call."

"You mean I'm the first?" she asked after a minute.

"Yup. I guess my standards are too high," Leonard told her. "You aren't a secretary, are you?"

"No, I'm not. But I would appreciate it if you didn't insult my many friends who are. I personally am in the beauty parlor business," she said. "Managerial, at the Hair Ball. I just got a cancellation in this storm and can't find a soul to talk to on the phone. But I wouldn't walk out on our customers. Somebody might come in needing an emergency shampoo or comb-out. My regular appointments never miss. Not even when that hurricane came through they didn't. One time a lady going into labor stopped by on her way to the delivery room, wanting to look her best for the newborn child. A person's hair is their identity, you know."

"You don't have that dyed pink hair, I hope," Leonard said.

"The Hair Ball has no such tint, Mr., rather, *Dr.* Pudding," she said. "Mauve rose—more or less a type of blond—is a popular shade. You'll just have to see for yourself, won't you. My but you do ask the personal questions. I hope you aren't a perve. Doctors can be perverts, policemen, higher-ups in companies, you name it."

No, he didn't frequent dirty bookstores. He used books from the library.

"Well, aren't you going to ask me out?" Verbena Tangles said. Leonard looked out wildly at the swirling snow, where he could be escaping now if he'd taken advantage of his employer. "I am GD," the hairdresser continued, "if that's what's holding you back."

"GD?" He swallowed. That better not be a disease. The newspaper had a separate singles section for their VD customers. And he didn't have any venereal diseases that he knew of.

"GD means geographically desirable," Verbena explained. "If you're going to be a swinging singles, Leonard, you've got to learn the lingo. A person is geographically desirable if they live close in to Washington. I'm barely outside the beltway, here in convenient Springfield, Virginia."

His gut took a nose dive. He lived close to the Springfield mall, not that he frequented such a place. He didn't go to any mall. "I guess we could go to Big Boy," he said. "That is, when the weather's decent. I don't drive in snow except to work, not with the lunatics on these roads."

"Big Boy?" the hairdresser said after a while. "I guess that could be tasty. By the way, Dr. Pudding, you did say one thing on your tape at Dates 'R' Us that bothered me."

"What's that?" Leonard looked at his watch. It was two

minutes to five. He'd have to tell her it was time to go.

"You said you refused to take romantic walks on the beach. Did you have a bad childhood experience with water or something?"

"I don't swim," he informed her. "Music is what I like. Classical music."

"Oh dear. Mrs. Pomeroy just came in the Hair Ball for her cut and blow dry. Got to run. I'll get back to you, Leonard. May I call you Leonard?"

"Yup."

He left the building and trudged out in the blowing snow, barely able to see his mittens. His stomach lurched, making him sick and excited at the same time. He never should have gotten himself into this. Yes, he should. It's what he wanted. He'd better watch this Verbena Tangles, though, with that eager beaver sound in her voice. Back in his day girls didn't call guys on the phone.

No girl had ever called him.

He high-stepped it through the snow that was getting his pants wet, and wet wool stinks. A cold shot of air blew up his leg, giving it a thrill. He had a girl!

He tromped out to the end of the parking lot where he always parked his car so it wouldn't get scratched by jerks. He'd left his boots in the trunk because the chance of precipitation that morning was only forty percent.

He got in to start up. Click. Crap. His headlights were shining in the drifts. He remembered he'd turned them on that morning. When other guys leave their lights on in the parking lot somebody always comes around the office and tells them. So why not him?

He got out and plowed back to his trunk, hauling out his boots and yanking them on. Then he headed back in the building to call Triple A. One light upstairs was still on. It must be Ned Bird, who was probably glad for an excuse to stay here. Leonard hoped if he ever did have a family, he wouldn't dread going home as much as that guy did.

He pounded on the glass door at the back of the building, where a security guard was supposed to be on duty twenty-four hours. Ha. Anybody wanting to steal what consultants turned out would be nuts. Ninety-nine percent of it should go in the shredder. They had a fancy shredder nobody ever used, a real white elephant.

Leonard plowed on around to the front of the building, with his feet sweating in his boots. He waved in the direction of the receptionist's desk and hollered, "Hello."

Nobody around.

He'd have to hike over to Tyson's Corner and call Triple A from there. Cripes. Maybe he should try phoning Verbena Tangles at the Hair Ball first and see if she wanted to give him a lift after she finished blow drying the lady's hair.

His girl! He almost wet his pants thinking of it. Stepping through the drifts, he remembered the yellow dog pee sprayed on the snow in the neighborhood where he used to deliver mail. There weren't any dogs in this neighborhood.

He hiked down the road past steaming stalled cars and made it on foot over to a phone booth in the mall. Drat, he had to wait in line. He stood there on the lookout for anybody horning in. Finally when it was his turn next, the guy jabbering in the phone booth in front of him wouldn't hang up. And he was laughing his head off in there, horsing around. Leonard shook his fist.

When the jerk finally came out, Leonard crammed himself in the booth with his back to the door. His turn now. He called the Hair Ball, but Verbena Tangles didn't answer. He dialed Triple A a few hundred times. When they got around to answering, they put him on hold and played "Singing in the Rain." In about half an hour a voice came on saying there was an "indefinite" delay in Triple A services due to the storm emergency. He could leave his name, location, and the nature of the problem after the beep. What a rip-off.

He hung up and trudged toward the exit ramp going to the beltway. The cars were sitting in line with their wheels spinning. Maybe he could get somebody's attention here. He motioned to a guy in a pickup, but he put his four-wheel drive in gear and stepped on it. Leonard waved to a female driver in a sports car, whose snooty face wouldn't turn and look at him. He charged around and leered in her front window, at least getting her pouty lips to say, "No."

Hauling himself up the ramp to the beltway, he tramped along the emergency lane, sticking up his thumb to the traffic that was barely moving in the white.

Cars went by. Then he saw the square shape of a van. It was signaling and pulling over. Dope heads with their rock music turned up. But it stopped.

He got in the back and asked the guys to turn down the volume on their tape deck, also mentioning that he needed to be dropped off at the supermarket. He had to get eggs for the meatloaf he was making tonight. He'd already taken the hamburger out to thaw that morning.

He thought of Verbena Tangles as he rode through the white night. A female had actually called him and flirted with him. She'd better be pretty.

# 10

# On the Beltway

Holly looked out at the snowy beltway then down at her gas gauge. It often dropped in the red and then bounced out again. She'd made it home on empty plenty of times before payday, and she could make it to Walter's school today.

The taillights in the blurry white ahead of her had stopped moving. Cherries in whipped cream. Meringue. Oh, Les. She thought of his soft lips. And what a devoted father he was. He'd even had to break their date last weekend because of an emergency PTA meeting. But he had rescheduled for this Saturday, so they would finally get those crabs.

This felt like their third date coming up, considering the one they'd missed. And if you counted the night they met at Spa Baby You, it was. That wonderful third date, when you can let your emotions loose.

She held onto the steering wheel.

By now the traffic was stopped, and people were getting out of their cars in the swirling white, dark shapes moving around to clean off their windshields. The driver up ahead of her didn't get out, though. He looked lonely stranded there. So she decided to go up and say hello. Maybe he would know where the nearest gas station was. She was getting low.

She stepped out in the blowing snow that bit at her ankles and stung her cheeks as she went up and tapped on the window of the car in front of her. The driver turned. His military haircut reminded her of Eddie when he was in the Navy.

The gentleman motioned for her to get in, and Holly bounded around and slid onto his soft bench seats. This was a change, after all the bucket seats she'd climbed over in her life—not that she had any desire to cheat on Les. And this man wore a wedding ring, glistening in the dark. He also had a rosary on his mirror, causing her to stay even further over on her side of the car. "You wouldn't have a can of gas, would you?" she asked.

"I don't," he said. "Are you completely out?"

"Oh, no. Anyway, I make it home on empty all the time. Do you have a long commute yourself?"

"I don't work in Virginia. I'm with the government downtown. I came out today to meet with a contractor."

"A consulting firm?" Holly turned to make eye contact, but she could only see the man's outline in the dark. "I work for the beltway bandits myself, a company named BelCon. We couldn't exist without contracts from the generous federal government. And which agency are you with, Mr. . . . ?"

"Trisket. Fred Trisket. Department of Agriculture." He wiped the steam off his window.

"Really? We're working on a proposal for Agriculture now, the school lunch program. And your *RFP* is one of the best I've read. I like the menus in it—finally something

63

I can understand. Do you write *RFPs*? Oh, I'm Holly Prickle."

"No, Miss Prickle. And USDA is a big place. However, our office does get involved in evaluating proposals."

Holly looked at the cross of our Lord hanging before her eyes and bowed to it. "This is incredible . . . that is, your job must be incredibly rewarding." Somebody was honking behind them. "I'm sorry I don't have a calling card to give you," she explained hurriedly. "I'm waiting to have some made when I get my promotion." More horns were beeping, and a voice was shouting now. "I don't know why it's such a big deal, putting in the paperwork for a person's promotion," she mentioned as she stepped out of Mr. Trisket's car, which was rolling.

"I know what you mean," he said as he reached over to close the door.

Holly scrambled back to her car amidst this honking and hollering, oops, slipping onto her knees. "I'm coming, I'm coming," she shouted to these pushy beltway types.

She shoved the snow off the window and got in. OK. The engine gurgled and died. "Please," she patted the dashboard, *"please start."* And when she tried again, it did.

By the time she got to Walter's school, it appeared to be deserted. He must have gotten a ride with some other parent, a father in a four-wheel drive (as opposed to a certain policeman who couldn't leave his beat to rescue his own son). Holly sat and watched the playground filling up with snow, rising up to the seats on the swings and gradually covering them. Oh, Walter.

Then she saw a dark patch in a drift. It was him. Walter was lying there making angel wings, the kid from California who loved snow.

She jumped out and took high steps over to him, smiling at her boy through the glistening air. It had almost stopped snowing by now, just bits floating down, sparkling.

Walter threw a snowball at her, smacking her on the side of the head. "Great—after I drove through this blizzard to give you a ride," she shouted. The school bus would have delivered him to his dad's place, where nobody was home at this hour, and Walter had forgotten his latchkey. She made a wad out of the fluffy snow and aimed it back at him. But it fell apart in the air and dropped silently into the drift below.

"Come on in, mom. You make good snow angels. You're the one who taught me how," Walter called.

Holly hobbled through the drifts and fell into the pile of white next to her son. It was so soft that it felt warm. She lay back and spread out her wings, flapping them. They tossed snow in the air, making it spray the way skiers do when they turn corners up on the slopes. She and Walter laughed and threw more snow at each other, and she felt like a clean kid.

"Come get in the car, Walter. I'm freezing wet."

"You ought to buy a jeep, mom. Then you could rescue people in these storms and drive them to the hospital," he said, shaking a branch of snow on them. "You like to do nice things."

Holly ducked, but a clump of cold landed on her neck. Little bits of ice water dripped down her spine. "Who says I do? Sure, it would be nice to be a saint. Meanwhile, a person still has to make car payments," she reminded her son, shaking herself off, imitating a wet dog.

"You'll get a raise when they promote you," Walter said. "Then you can buy something better than a yucky Escort. Heh, you could get a van."

65

"Very funny," Holly said, grabbing his arm as her leg sank through the snow into a ditch. "You know I despise those drugmobiles. And think of the cops who'd be on your tail if you drove a suspicious van with no windows."

"Mom, you're crazy thinking dad is following you all the time. He won't always be in a patrol car, anyway. He's trying to get a transfer to the bike squad." Walter kicked the fender, knocking off snow, proving he was tough.

"A hero on a bike now, is it? Your father always did want to be somebody. Now get in and close the door, Walter, it's freezing."

She was afraid the car wouldn't start this time, after sitting in the cold. But it perked right up, and she eased out onto the white road with no trouble.

"Dad's going to let me ride on his bike. Maybe he'll teach me."

Holly stepped on the gas. "Don't even think it. I will not raise a hell's angel."

"Did dad tell you they're getting an RV? With a VCR in it, and a big hideaway bed, king size—"

Holly's foot landed on the brakes. But the car didn't stop. It was sliding, ice skating across the lanes of traffic. Please, God, don't let them become cripples.

"Turn *into* the skid, mom, into it," Walter shouted, "and take your foot off the brake." His hands helped her on the wheel, and she lifted off the pedal like he said. They were sliding in a straighter line now, aiming for a white hill on the other side of the road. Thud.

Her arm flew across the seat. "Honey, are you all right?"

"Wow. That was great."

"Great? We could have been killed. Or more likely maimed. Are you sure you're OK, Walter?" Holly tried moving her toes in her wet shoes, and they worked.

"Sure."

"Oh, Walter." She hugged her son and said thank you into his hair. "Does your neck hurt? You could have whiplash. Then we'd have to go to court."

"And who would you sue? Somebody has to hit you first," Walter pointed out. Next he'd want to be a lawyer.

"Well, that doesn't mean your neck isn't hurt. Check yourself, Walter." They undid their seat belts and found that their body parts still worked. "Did I tell you I've been called on jury duty? Imagine your mother administering justice for a change."

"Neat. Will they have real criminals, murderers?"

"I'm sure they will. Dangerous people, anyway." She tried to start the engine, but it wouldn't make a sound. "That skid must have knocked something loose. Or maybe it's the battery."

"Mom, you're out of gas," her know-it-all son said.

"Do cars really do that anymore? You never see people carrying gas cans along the highway. They might be off at the side with a dented car. Or sitting there reading a map. It could be any emergency."

"Get real. You always drive on empty," Walter said. "Could we leave a message for dad to come help us?"

Holly gripped her key. "And just when do you suppose that man would respond? He's probably out in this weather giving tickets for cars that don't have chains."

"Cops do stuff besides give tickets. They help people."

"Not when you need them, they don't. Your father used to disappear down in the basement to his so-called shop, where he never finished building a thing. A bird house with no door in it?

"We'll do fine without him, Walter. We can walk to the gas station in our neighborhood from here, and the attendants will tow us."

67

"Can we stop at Big Boy, please?"

"What a good idea, so your mother won't have to cook tonight. That is, if I have enough money. Check in my wallet, honey, and see."

Walter found two one-dollar bills and some pennies. "That won't fill us up, will it. Try looking in the back," she suggested. "Sometimes coins fall in those cracks." He barreled over the seat head first to check, for once obeying her.

"Wow. There's gobs of money back here," Walter reported. "Look. Quarters." He reached up to show her a handful. "Who'd you have riding back here, mom, some moneybags hitchhiker? Yuck, why is this money sticky? Feel it."

"Never mind," Holly told her son. "Just be thankful for what is provided. Now let's go to Big Boy. I am starved."

# 11

# *Downtime*

"You could shovel the walks," Bill's wife said as he stared at the *TV Guide*.

"Uh-huh." What do guys do on Sunday after football?

Maybe that's when you help your kid with his homework. Got to get Ronnie boned up for another skills test. "Where'd he go?" Bill called to her in the kitchen, where she was watchdogging a cherry pie.

"You said he could go to the mall," his wife called back.

"Oh."

He went to the window and looked out at the street. It was melted down to where you could get out.

He went to the phone and dialed Ned Bird. "Heh, you want to get going on the school lunch prop? Hope I'm not interrupting your family dinner, kind of thing. Well, grab a chicken wing. Or bring the whole bird along. Just kidding. I might even give Leonard a wake-up call. . . . What, you want Claire Whittle coming in? Hell, let's not make a major production out of this. OK. See you."

Everybody was there when he strolled in the conference room. "Heads up, Leonard," Bill said, striding to the board. "OK, folks. Now, what are we going to put on the cover of this prop? It's got to be something that'll grab them by the eyeballs down at USDA."

Leonard volunteered to make a pie chart showing the basic food groups. "Will it look like a pizza?" Bill asked. "Or how about that chocolate chip bread?"

"It's chocolate *chunk* bread," Holly reminded him.

"Right." His mouth was watering. "OK, now, we need a special gimmick."

"I met a man who works at Agriculture and evaluates proposals," Holly said. "Trust me, Bill. Go with a religious motif. We could have a scene from the Bible—*The Last Supper*—with an inscription, Give Us Our Daily Bread."

That had a ring to it.

"And Graphics can show the starving disciples reaching for BelCon's bread," Holly went on. She was good.

"That's it," Bill said, giving the table a happy slap.

Meanwhile, Leonard was scowling at him. No problem. Leonard always scowled. "Heh, I'm as religious as the next guy," Bill defended himself. "Take that water-into-wine story out of the Bible. That's what we'll be doing, only beefing up your basic bread. And nobody else in town will come up with this holier-than-thou strategy. It'll knock their pants off."

Rita yawned. "I'm off the chocolate, considering my condition."

Holly swung around to face her. "What about the Tootsie Rolls on your desk? It isn't us eating them." She looked over at Bill. He pretended not to notice.

Rita shrugged.

70

"And what condition is that?" Holly asked. "Staying out too many nights with Lonnie Bob?"

"Gals—"

"Heh, I don't mind telling," Rita said, lighting up a cigarette. Bill leaned over to suck up the smoke, now that his wife had him on the wagon again. "I'm pregnant," Rita announced. "I said I'd have a kid before I was thirty, and now I am."

Bill's jaw dislocated. Not that he cared what the girls did outside the office. But a guy would be smart if he only hired single gals past the age of this male-female business. So now what do you do? The Harvard Business School never ran this scenario by you. He looked around for some male assistance here, but Ned was scribbling away on something, and Leonard had dozed off. "You don't say," Bill answered.

"Yup," Rita said.

She was not a looker, a big puffy gal. But she got the job done. And she had clout. OK, think positive. With a new mouth to feed, Rita would be wanting more overtime.

"You modern gals," Bill told them, chuckling, "you have it all, don't you."

Rita wasn't a big one with the smiles, and she didn't smile now. He couldn't get a rise out of Holly, either. Bad sign there. "Super moms," he went on, looking around at the secretaries. "Maybe we need one of those mommy tracks around here. Uh, exactly what is it, the mommy track?"

"No way," Rita said. "You aren't cutting back on our benefits and promotions."

"Uh, I hear you." Bill got a cigarette from Rita and lit up, pulling his gray matter together here. "So, are you saying, Rita, that your . . . uh . . . situation won't be impacting on our production schedule?"

71

"The proposal's due in April. I'm having my boy in September."

"Your *boy*?" Holly lit into her. "How can you know that already? Did you have one of those dangerous tests?"

"OK, everybody," Bill threw in the penalty flag. Then he sniffed. Something was burning. It was his pant leg. Damn. He'd dumped cigarette ashes on himself.

"Bill, you're on fire," Holly shouted.

Ned leaped out of his chair and ran into the hall, calling for an extinguisher.

"No problem," Bill said. His brain was coming into focus now. He took his coffee cup and poured the remains on his smoking knee. Hiss, pouf, and the fancy pants his wife bought him went up in steam. Everything under control here.

"Good session, everybody. We appreciate your input. We'll get Graphics going on *The Last Supper* for the proposal cover. I smell a winner here."

After the meeting, Holly ran into Rita in the ladies' room. She was hogging the mirror and picking at her cheek. "You can't just have a baby because you want to," Holly told her.

Rita poked her chin towards the glass, squeezing it with her fingernails. "I can't, huh? Well, I am."

Holly held onto the sink. "And smoking will shrink the fetus. Your child could be retarded." However, according to the size of Rita's shoulders, her child would be born as a Green Bay Packer.

Rita didn't answer and went over into a stall.

Holly went in the next stall, crouching down to see if she was talking to the right feet. Yup, those were Rita's shoes. Fake maroon leather, cracked where her corns pushed through. "And what does Lonnie Bob have to say about this?" she asked under the partition. He already had a wife and four kids.

Rita answered by flushing the toilet.

Holly flushed her commode also, not wanting to be a phony, coming in here and doing nothing.

She went out to the sink by Rita, who didn't wash her hands with soap and barely stuck them in the water. "Lonnie Bob's been wanting me all along to have his kid," Rita said. "Plus, he's fixing to leave his wife."

A swirling feeling went through Holly. "Well, even if he did, he could go back to her. Anyway, a man will still think about his wife. You don't just erase the person you were married to."

"Meaning what," Rita said, "that your ex-husband is thinking about you now?"

Holly rubbed soap on her knuckles. "Maybe. Sure."

"And I'm not getting suckered into any joint custody deal," Rita said. "No ex of mine is going to come sniffing around. So maybe I'd just as soon have a baby by myself."

Holly kept her hands under the water, letting it get hot. "Eddie doesn't sniff around. And he has his troubles, too, not that I would discuss them in a public restroom. Besides, joint custody isn't that bad, Rita. It gives you the freedom to live the singles life. And I've met a man who is a wonderful father. Plus, his wife is dead."

"Dead of what?" Rita asked, lifting her chin. She wore loop earrings the size of handcuffs, which pulled her earlobes down as if they were soft dough. That must hurt.

"Les's wife died of a stroke. And he'll do anything for his children, even sacrifice his own dates." Holly dabbed some lipstick on and plenty of it. "But to make up for that, he's taking me for Japanese food this weekend. It's one of those nice places where you sit on the floor."

73

"I'd rather sit in a chair," Rita said, drying her hands on the hips of her rat-colored dress. Then she marched out of the ladies' room without even saying, "See you."

Grrr. And Rita would probably keep wearing that ugly jersey stretch dress throughout her pregnancy to show off her baby growing.

# 12

# *A Rat and a Nerd*

"Sugar, he's a rat," Fiona consoled her when Holly called with the news. Les had done it again. "First he invites you for crabs, changes that to hamburger, and then he gives you stew. Next the man cancels because of a PTA meeting on the weekend, *honey*, and now the Japanese restaurant goes out the window because his dad has cancer of the colon in New Jersey. Those things take time."

"Who would lie about their parent's cancer?" Holly pulled the comforter up to her chin where she lay strung out on her bed. "And does cancer of the colon sound made up? The poor man, getting that awful disease and living in New Jersey, too. Les has been through plenty. First, his wife is institutionalized. Then she dies on him. Now this."

"Holly," Fiona said in her southern voice (lady-like, but you'd better listen), "why do you suppose his wife had that stroke in the first place? He drove her to it. The man is a rat and a sick person. Drop him before it's too late."

"Oh, you're probably right," Holly admitted. But she couldn't forget the romantic night by the river with Les, the way he'd kissed her through the car window and other places. If a person is rotten, he shouldn't act like that.

And why would a man keep asking you out if he didn't want to go?

"Not getting Japanese food, though, honey, you didn't miss a thing," Fiona said. "You'd come home hungry from Sayonara City, I guarantee. Those people have a mind set for vegetables. And they undercook them."

Hearing that helped some. And Holly did have the presence of mind after Les called to get out and treat herself to some Colonel Sanders chicken. Then the minute she got home she tore off the new outfit she'd worn.

"And where is Hugo taking you for dinner?" Holly asked. Hugo was the older man Fiona had been dating, a gentleman from the deep South who took her dancing. That is, when he could walk. He had just gotten out of the hospital.

"Thai food."

"Thai food?" Holly sat up in bed. "Fiona, you deserve better."

"I know it, honey. But he was stationed in that part of the world and has this belief that their cuisine keeps the male body . . . well, you know, lively. There he is at the door now. Talk to you later."

"Have a good time," Holly called into the clicking phone. Fiona deserved a magnificent meal after putting up with the smell of hospital food every time she visited Hugo all these weeks. First he had pneumonia. Then it was a slipped disk.

Holly lay back on the bed, exhausted. She was too beat to go out tonight anyway.

The phone rang, and she picked it up. "This is Bruce" a male voice said, sounding like it came from the bottom of a swimming pool. "I'm a C-O-M-P-U-T-E-R."

76

She had heard lines from men but never this one. "And what is it you want, Bruce? This is a Saturday night, when people are getting ready—"

"Have you made plans for your future?" the irritating voice interrupted her. And what a rude question.

"I hope to be promoted to admin assistant, and then keep working up the corporate ladder, not that it's any business of yours," she snapped.

"I'm calling from the Shade Trees for All Memorial Grounds," Bruce droned on, "where you can purchase an individual plot at reduced rates with our limited offer."

What an obscene call. You can't spend one Saturday night at home without having people think you're senile. "I beg your pardon," Holly told him and slammed down the phone.

That felt good. She had always wanted to hang up on a man. Look at her, getting liberated here.

She had barely closed her eyes when the phone rang again. Well, look who was the popular one tonight, after all. "Is this Betty?" another male voice asked, this one sounding like a nerd.

"Sorry, wrong number."

"This isn't Betty Brown?"

"Do I sound like a Betty?" Holly said. "And that's the name of a dessert, not a popular one, either. It's made with baked, mushy apples. And if your Betty is so special, how come you can't even tell if you're talking to her?"

"She's just a friend," the nerd tried to waffle out of it. "Actually, an acquaintance."

"And not a very nice acquaintance, is she, giving you the wrong number to call."

"What number is this, so I won't dial it again?"

"Now you're saying it's a mistake talking to me?" Holly stroked Warren's ears furiously out to the tips. And

77

if he'd been a cat, he would have purred. "As if I have nothing better to do than spend a Saturday night giving free romantic advice—meanwhile letting you tie up this phone line so legitimate callers can't get through."

"You sound sexy when you're mad. But guys aren't supposed to say stuff like that any more, are they. Guess I better sign off."

"What?" Holly leaped off the bed, sending Warren thumping to the floor. She knotted the belt of her robe. She only wished it were a black belt. "I don't believe this, you, the obscene caller, claiming you're hanging up on me."

"I thought you were going somewhere," the little worm said.

"It's a bit late for that, wouldn't you say, now that I've wasted the whole evening talking to strangers on the phone. Meanwhile, you're probably dying to call boring Betty. Well, don't let me stop you, whoever you are."

"Norbert."

"Norbert? Spelled with an *n* as in nostril?" Holly began swinging the cord of the phone as if it were a jump rope.

"Yup."

Stars, wasn't there a man left in this world with a normal name. "Well, I'm Holly. Think about that. It is organic."

"I'll bet you're a redhead, no offense," Norbert said through his nasal passages, "although most guys do favor blondes."

Holly patted her frosted perm, with plenty of highlights still in it, a good job done by the Hair Ball. "Well, aren't you the fortunate one tonight. On the other hand, Norbert, you sound short."

"You guessed it," he admitted. "I also have a moustache. Some women get turned on by facial hair. Heh, you want to go out for Mexican food?"

"Mexican food, now?" The thought of guacamole made the receiver go soft in her hand. Naturally, it would take a nerd to invite you for a decent meal—when you've already eaten. However, the crispy chicken legs she'd gnawed on earlier had not digested well.

"Holly, are you there?"

"Of course I'm here, Norbert. I live here."

"If you don't like Mexican, there's this Vietnamese place—"

"Hold it." She'd had enough of the foreign bit. Of course she felt sorry for boat people. But they don't know the meaning of cheese. And if you want to get technical, Mexicans are ethnics, too. "If your mind is set on Mexican, Norbert, I don't see as I can change it. I could order a salad, maybe just a taco salad."

"Anything you want." Oh, those excellent words, coming out of a male mouth.

She gave Norbert directions then hung up and hurried to her closet looking for something appropriate to wear in the presence of a nerd. She simply didn't invest in that type of clothing. She couldn't find one blouse with a stain or any outfit boring enough. So he would be the lucky one tonight, getting her in her new caramel-colored sweater.

She'd barely gotten dressed and squeezed Warren into his hutch when the knock came at the door. It sounded like a chicken pecking. She swung it open wide, and Norbert hadn't lied saying he was short. His moustache, on the other hand, was barely see-through hairs.

She turned on the overhead light as he came in, which was a mistake, as it highlighted the drooping leaves on her dieffenbachia and Norbert's unfortunate skin.

However, in the candlelight at El Toro's, after her second virgin margarita, Norbert looked almost distinguished sitting down. The flickering flame brought out the bold stitch in his tweed jacket, emphasizing its unusual texture. And when the guitar player stopped at their table (and they do choose the most romantic couple in the room), she realized that she'd missed something here.

She looked at Norbert, past his small moustache. *Hello.* She edged her hand across the table within grabbing range of his. Meanwhile, he was busy loading salsa on a chip. Holly held her breath as he balanced it up to his mouth. Yes, he was going to make it. But the moment before the chip reached Norbert's lip it broke, splashing red chunks on the tablecloth. All corn chips seem to do that. It is so irritating.

Norbert moved his plate to cover the stain, which at least proved he wasn't totally insensitive. A tomato seed quivered in his moustache, and Holly envisioned his lips inside it, spicy and soft.

Look, she had kissed nerds before, and there are worse things.

When they got back to her apartment, this time she didn't turn on the overhead light. She felt her way through the fronds to the couch, tossed a twig out of the way, and smoothed a place for Norbert to sit down. Then she rested her head on the back of the couch and waited for his furry lip to strike.

Norbert found her hand in the dark and was holding it. Here he came, approaching her cheek, tickling it, breathing through his facial hairs.

Something furry landed on her lap. Holly touched it, and yes it had ears. Fortunately, they were Warren's. He really was getting huge. His legs hung down and pawed her shins as he nibbled on her kneecap.

Norbert leaped up.

"It's just our pet rabbit, Warren."

80

Norbert eased back down on the couch, and she had him touch Warren's ears to prove her point. "There's nothing to worry about. I'll put him back in his cage. Sometimes the latch gives way when he leans on it."

Holly hauled her big bunny into the bedroom and stuffed him in his hutch. Kiss, click.

Then she hurried back to Norbert.

But, rats, he'd gone to sleep on her—and after she had worked herself up to letting a nerd kiss her.

Well, he would pay for this. She'd make him wait. Wait and beg. Holly marched in her bedroom, locked the door, and lay down for a short rest.

When she opened her eyes it was light. She couldn't hear anything, no embarrassing sounds coming from the bathroom or anybody messing in her kitchen. No snoring, either, which a large percentage of men do, particularly strangers.

She stumbled out in the hall, not bothering to mash her hair down.

Yikes, the nerd was still there, open-faced on her couch. Could he be dead? Dead in the saddle, dreaming of what he'd missed last night.

Norbert blinked through his glasses covered with fingerprints. "Do you have any coffee?"

Holly darted in the kitchen, patting her chest. "Cream?" she called. What she ought to serve him is sour cream. Then she got a whiff of guacamole off her tongue and remembered the generous burrito platter Norbert had treated her to last night. It was delicious.

She added a donut to his tray and took it out to him.

He gulped everything down and licked the crumbs off his fingers. Then when he finished he didn't get up to approach her but reached for the newspaper, turning to the sports page, what a laugh. After that he checked the

81

classifieds. "I need a better job. I'm not moving up where I am," Norbert said from behind the newspaper.

"I know the feeling," Holly answered.

But if that's all he had on his mind, he could go home and read his own want ads.

She thought of telling him that her boyfriend was coming back. Or she could say she had to go to the office, which wouldn't be unusual on a Sunday at BelCon. Then she thought of a real excuse. "Norbert, I can't spend the day with you. I'm on jury duty tomorrow, and I want to be fresh."

He didn't look up.

"We'll be judging all kinds of criminals—petty thieves, drug lords, arsonists . . ." The comics page Norbert was hiding behind began to twitch, but he still wouldn't get off her couch.

Holly went in the bedroom and let Warren out of his cage. Good rabbit. Go.

Warren scampered into the living room and went over to sniff Norbert's pant leg. "We'll be sentencing cases of abuse, molestation. Hopefully, homicide," Holly added loudly.

The newspaper dropped. "What'd you say?" Norbert shook off the big rabbit attached to his pants and stood up. "Guess I better get going."

She did walk Norbert to the door, although she stayed out of kissing range of that face with an overnight beard on it which was definitely inferior to fur as she could now see clearly in the morning light.

# 13

# Loss of Consortium

"Where is she?" Bill came out of the men's room and looked downfield to his secretary's desk.

He checked in the other offices (doing a lateral past Claire Whittle's door). Anybody around who had seen Holly? Damn, Claire was the only one here. He back-pedaled and peered in at BelCon's editor through his imagined face mask.

*Ramona looked up from her receptionist's desk, shocked to see despicable Rodney Rhodes from the* Mango Maiden *staring at her. What a nerve—when she'd warned him never to show his god-like face in her presence again.*

Bill braced himself and stepped into Claire's office. "Uh, have you seen Holly?"

*No, Ramona had not received a Christmas gift from that man, or even a lousy card. "And if you don't leave this instant, I'll have security toss you out for loitering."*

"Did Holly come in today?" Bill repeated.

"What?" Claire slapped her pen down. "Oh. You're looking for Holly. I thought she went on jury duty."

Cripes, she had said something about that.

*"Don't have me ejected," Rodney said darkly. "It's been a rough week—with zero precipitation, no wind-chill factor in these parts, and fat chance of a quake here in Florida. But a hurricane's coming up the coast, supposed to be here by midnight. Join me, Ramona, to watch her blow in. It'll be a blast."*

"Say, uh, Claire, you want to come down and cover Holly's station while she's out of the office," Bill said in a managerial voice.

*Ramona turned on him with slitted eyes. You'd think in this peaceful resort hotel a person could get something done.*

"Sure." Claire stuffed her note pad in her drawer and locked it.

"I'll give the judge a call," Bill announced as they went down to Holly's desk, "and get her off jury duty. Hell, she is essential personnel."

Holly hurried through the parking lot at the county courthouse. This was a dangerous place. She was surrounded by police cars.

Inside she followed the arrows for jurors and squeezed into a seat in the courtroom just as the judge stood up in his robe. He smiled. "I'm Judge Love," he introduced himself, in a jovial voice you couldn't imagine would send a person to jail. He thanked them for coming, chuckling as he mentioned how many people call in with every excuse in the book to get out of jury duty.

Suddenly a noise at the back of the courtroom caused people to turn around. Two police officers came in shoving a handcuffed suspect down the aisle, a young man with blond tangled hair. Holly sat still as a post, finally breathing when she didn't recognize anyone in that group.

The woman sitting next to her whispered that the alleged rapist in the case coming up had already attacked thirteen other women. "He got the last one on the hood of her car at the 7–Eleven."

Holly stared at the suspect being pushed along, looking like anybody else wearing blue jeans. She could not imagine his mind.

The jurors were then called down to the front for questioning, making you feel as if you were the guilty party. When her turn came, the man looked over his half-mast glasses and asked her without the slightest embarrassment, "Have you ever been in a rape situation?"

"Of course I have, I am a woman," Holly said.

"And your age?"

Who did these people think they were, the DMV? But looking up at the judge's high chair, she loudly said, "Thirty-four."

"That will be all, miss."

"You mean I didn't get picked?"

"That's right," the man answered and waved her on through the line.

How humiliating to be rejected for a rape case. Well, at least she could go back to the office where Bill needed her. Holly marched down the aisle to leave. But a policeman on guard at the door made her return to her seat.

She trudged back and sat down next to the same lady, who hadn't been picked either. "There will be other rape

85

cases," the woman said. "And they aren't all as exciting as you'd think. A better trial was the gal who poured Drano in her boyfriend's face while he was asleep and gouged out his eye. And I'll bet it was a roving eye. When a person does that, I figure she has reasons."

"What an idea," Holly exclaimed. "Who would think of a cleaning fluid. Do you use Drano?"

Judge Love then called them to order and announced the next case: *Larchmont v. Giant.* And yes it was the supermarket chain diversifying into crime.

This time the jurors were asked if they had relatives in the retail food business. "I pay the same prices as you do," Holly answered the man, who appeared to be a representative of the Giant supermarket from the size of him. "And I wouldn't take a piece of candy from your open bins. OK, I've stolen grapes. But only from the ones in my basket while I wait in your long checkout lines."

"You may go up to the jury box," the man said from under his well-fed moustache.

"I'm chosen?" Her nasal passage cleared.

"That's right."

"Great," she said and bounded up into the choir loft. Bring on the guilty parties.

The case of *Larchmont v. Giant* involved a Mrs. Lucille Larchmont, heavyset, who was suing the supermarket for her broken arm caused by crashing into the wall of Giant on her way to buy chocolate frosting for her husband's birthday cake. Lucille and her husband were also bringing suit against the Sanitation Department because of the metal plate they'd installed in the pavement, which allegedly caused the litigant to trip.

When Mr. Larchmont came up on the stand, he proudly looked down at his wife. "All those weeks my Lucille was

86

out of commission with her busted arm," he testified, "I sure did miss the little lady's home cooking. And guess who got roped into doing the housework? Me. You guys don't know the half of it." He looked around the courtroom for male support, but got a woman booing instead. "Housework is a pisser. And the worst was scrubbing the kitchen floor. So I had it carpeted." People in the courtroom laughed at that.

So where were these new men you hear about who supposedly do housework, Holly wondered? She'd never met a woman yet who had actually encountered one. Men *claim* they will definitely "help out" with the chores. But when? If you actually met a man who cleaned the toilet bowl of his own accord you would go into shock.

However, Mr. Larchmont wasn't completely awful, as he did care about his wife.

Lucille Larchmont lumbered up to the witness stand next, sighing as if to emphasize the weight of her arm hitting the wall of Giant.

"At the time of your accident, did you weigh what you weigh now?" the attorney for the defense rudely asked.

Mrs. Larchmont giggled with her jello neck. "I lost weight, but I gained it back again. Size sixteen, that's me."

"Do you fall down often?" he continued to harass her, after already violating her constitutional rights by forcing her dress size out of her.

"You mean, do I fall down regular, say every week?" Lucille looked at him and laughed. "When you're lying sprawled on the floor, it's not something you count up."

"Now for our final charge." Lucille's lawyer strode over to the jury box. He was lean and quick and had a good haircut. "Lucille Larchmont's injury not only resulted in the inconvenience of housework to her husband, but it deprived him of something I am sure is dear to every one of you law-abiding people. Think about it, folks: your connubial rights."

Holly swallowed. This man knew his stuff.

"The evidence shows that due to the obstruction in the pavement resulting in Louise Larchmont's fall, plus the proximity of the Giant market, Gus Larchmont is entitled to compensation for the loss of cohabitational rights incurred during the period his wife's arm was recuperating in a cast and the subsequent sling.

"Members of the jury, we're talking deprivation here— of a basic human right ensured in our Constitution, the pursuit of happiness by the people and for the people in this God-fearing country, and that means you."

Holly's eyes became blurry.

Mr. Larchmont called out from the front row of the courtroom, "And I never cheated on Lucy once."

Holly smiled and waved her Kleenex at him.

Judge Love explained that "in legal terms we refer to this interruption in cohabitational privileges as loss of consortium. In such a case, it is the jury's duty to assess the amount of compensation to be awarded to the plaintiff. Do the members of the jury understand?"

Holly nodded. They all did.

The jury got right down to the loss of consortium business. "I'd say she's worth a buck a night," the man across from Holly said. Nobody laughed. The only sound was his snort.

"Her husband likes her a lot," she answered.

"And this Larchmont guy ought to get reimbursed for doing that housework crap," the man carried on. He had a red stain on the cuff of his off-white shirt, which Holly wished came from a burping baby, although it was probably spaghetti sauce he'd spilled on himself.

"All right, folks," their foreman called them to order. "To determine the amount Gus Larchmont is entitled to for loss of consortium, everybody decide how much you think Mrs. Larchmont is worth by the night. Then we'll divide the total by twelve."

Isn't that interesting how the law works. Holly wrote down a hundred dollars a night for Lucille's company. Then considering the deprivation involved, she added fifty more.

The foreman tallied up the results on his pocket calculator. His eyebrows went up with the result. "The average for a night with Lucille Larchmont comes to $19.50." He scratched his head. "Yup, that's right. The reason it's low is because we pulled a minus figure here."

Poor Lucille. You couldn't buy a bag of groceries at Giant for that amount.

But just then the bailiff came in and announced that *Larchmont v. Giant* had been thrown out of court. As it turned out, the litigant had a foot problem that frequently caused her to fall. The Larchmonts both confessed to it.

The jurors were thus excused for the day, which was disappointing when you're primed up to decide on a case.

However, all jurors were required to return for future trials. There would be other chances to administer justice.

# 14

# *The Rapist of Reston*

BelCon was moving out to Reston in the country, where the Company stressed the many advantages to the employees. Unlimited free parking. Jogging trails. Yet even Bill wasn't excited about the new place. And the secretaries were sick to be leaving the mall.

But if BelCon was moving, they were. So Holly took the corporate capabilities in for Bill to update them. They now stated that BelCon was located within a "convenient fifteen-mile radius of the Washington metropolitan area." Their clients would get a surprise, wouldn't they, driving out to Dulles Airport to find BelCon's new location. But Bill said not to worry about it. Everything would come out in the wash.

That was the same attitude he had when a consultant died who was being used in a proposal they were doing. Bill was standing right there when the memo came around announcing that Dr. Reginald ("Reggie") Mason, a nuclear scientist, had passed away from skin cancer. Holly pulled Dr. Mason's résumé on the spot to toss it, with all due respect. But Bill stopped her and said, "Let's not overreact." So they went ahead and bid a dead man to harness solar energy. Luckily, they didn't win that contract, or BelCon would have seen sun spots.

Bill hadn't even visited the new facility in Reston yet. So one afternoon Holly volunteered to drive out and check the Special Projects offices. She also mentioned to Bill that she would be glad to make office assignments if he wasn't interested. He was talking on the phone at the time and nodded yes.

Fiona rode out to Reston with her on a drizzly March afternoon, all the way out Route 7 to where big frame houses sit up alone on the hilltops, and the happy stores of Tyson's Corner are far behind you. "Holly, if we don't like commuting out here, we could get jobs closer in."

"Quit on Bill?" Holly swerved to miss a pothole.

"Has he done anything about your promotion?"

Holly kept her eyes on the temperature gauge in front of her. If it could remain steady, so could she. "No."

"And now this move to a planned community, with no roots, who can bear it. Reston even brought in their own HUD housing, complete with the delinquent element. And you know the worst," Fiona said, lowering her voice, even though they were inside the car.

"What's that?" Holly stared out through the gray rain at farmhouses but no shops.

"Reston has its own rapist."

"How do you know these awful things? Did I tell you, Fiona, that on jury duty I got rejected for a rape case? It was humiliating."

"Sugar, those lawyers will turn you down for any reason. They probably thought you were too pretty, that you'd want to get revenge on the men who have pawed you."

"I would never do that."

"The rapist out here supposedly frequents the jogging trails," Fiona continued as they entered a wooded area.

"Then it's not worth keeping in shape, is it." Holly wished they could go back to Tyson's Corner and stay.

But they had arrived at the new BelCon facility. And it was a fine looking building, of Virginia red brick, although with a glass front. Inside you could see a stairway winding up out of the lobby, looking as if a southern belle might float down it, instead of beltway bandits trudging up with their attaché cases.

She drove up to the front to park, but all the places were for handicapped. The whole row had those irritating wheelchairs painted on them. "And BelCon doesn't hire anybody crippled," she pointed out. Still, she went around to the back to park, not risking any run-in with the law.

"Holly, don't be hateful to the physically impaired."

"I just said there were too many parking places. The reason you like the handicapped, Fiona, is because of the men you date. Not that Hugo isn't a sweet gentleman, what I last saw of him through his tubes. I just don't understand what you get out of senile men."

Fiona laughed and laughed, showing her pretty capped teeth. "Younger men, pouf. They're in such a rush. Hugo, the little devil, he can go on all night."

Holly felt her face grow warm. "OK, maybe I am too picky about men. But if you could see Les Moore's athletic makeup—and he's such a devoted father—you would know why I date him."

"Honey, I hate to remind you of this, but you've only been with out with him once."

Was that possible? Holly had imagined so many occasions with Les that they seemed real. And he did keep asking her out. Fiona had such a cynical mind.

Holly got out of the car, not one to look for the worst in life. She stepped in a puddle. Crap. Maybe Fiona was right.

As they walked across the parking lot, Fiona stopped and clutched Holly's arm. "Can you hear something in those trees out back?"

She listened. Something was making a rustling sound out there.

They went over and peered into the mysterious black trunks. Here came a jogger trotting through the mist, wearing navy sweats, with his blond hair flying. "Do you have any Mace on you?"

"Just breath spray," Holly said, digging in her purse, getting her hand ready on the cool container.

"Here he comes." They strained to see the man's face, but he must have detected them and turned the other way, upping his pace and disappearing into the brush.

"Honey, that could be the rapist. He runs in these woods. And rapists supposedly look like the man next door."

"Except that my neighbor, Mr. Berry," Holly said quietly, "does look like a rapist. You've seen that red scratch mark on his chin. And his eyes are definitely unfulfilled."

"This is true," Fiona murmured.

"Yet Mr. Berry couldn't be nicer," Holly pointed out. "He never makes rude remarks. All he's ever said to me was that I left my car lights on. You can't ask for a better neighbor than that."

"So, if your unfortunate-looking Mr. Berry is no rapist," Fiona figured, "that leaves the clean-cut men." Holly didn't go along with her reasoning, although it might explain why Fiona never dated ordinary looking men. She even favored Hugo's birthmark, a grape on his neck.

"Rapists are the people you least expect," Fiona said as they edged away from the wooded area. "And think about this. A so-called gentleman we both know has chosen to move BelCon out to this remote spot for who knows what reason. Also he's a known jogger. And blond."

"Not Mr. Johnson," Holly said. He was so professional she couldn't imagine him without his briefcase. She also pointed out to Fiona that Mr. Johnson wouldn't let his hair fly loose the way that jogger's did.

"Maybe he doesn't gel it when he's out of the office," Fiona suggested.

That was possible.

They went in the new BelCon building, feeling more like guests going to a fancy hotel than secretaries checking out their office space. A stuffed leather chair rolled by on its way to be installed, looking much sturdier than the ones Bill used now that broke. Everything in this place was state of the art. Your feet sank into the carpets. Maybe working out here wouldn't be so bad after all.

If the lobby was this snazzy, they figured the snack bar should be great. But they found no cozy cafeteria with comfortable chairs overlooking the trees out back. The rooms all had conference tables in them or were set up for computer terminals.

Finally, in the basement they found a room the size of a closet with a microwave and a food dispenser in it. And it was the rotary type for soup and apples, when all you want is a simple candy bar.

"Food doesn't set with me in these uncivilized surroundings," Fiona said. "I can't digest it." Her idea of superior nutrition was having a male waiter deliver the meal to you. She had a point.

"Maybe they're encouraging us to eat out," Holly suggested.

"Sugar, wake up and smell the coffee break. That's all it is. What they want is us chained to our desks with sack lunches, reduced to nothing but hired help. Well, I refuse to sink to that level."

Holly didn't remind her friend that they *were* hired help. Certain factual ideas did not sit well with Fiona's disposition.

They went up the grand stairway to the Special Projects offices on the second floor, which were tiny little rooms, although they might look bigger with furniture in them.

She and Fiona agreed that Leonard Pudding definitely should not have an office with a window in this place. For some reason he had one where they were now, and from across the street you could see him slumped asleep in his chair. They found the perfect cubicle for Leonard here, next to his favorite place, the men's room.

They also agreed that Ned Bird would need one of the big corner offices at the front. They picked the one with a rubber plant outside the door, which might hide the sight of Rita. "And Bill should have the office facing the woods out back," Holly said. "With the stress he's under, he needs nature to sooth him."

"Holly, Bill Moss doesn't give a hoot about nature," Fiona argued. "In his office now he turns his back to the window so he can watch people in the hall. And, stars, it isn't fitting for the head person to look to the rear. What kind of a face does that put on for our clients?"

Holly stared at her friend. "In these new buildings, the back is practically the front. And Bill *is* in charge of Special Projects and deserves a view of the trees. Your boss, Fiona, can have that other big corner office in front, which is more prestigious."

Fiona put her hands on her hips. "Honey, the man I work for is a southerner, for heaven's sake, and knows the meaning of trees. And may I remind you he is the senior member on our staff."

"You don't have to be old to like trees, Fiona," Holly told her. "I practically worship foliage, coming from California. And I'll bet Mr. Johnson chooses that upstairs office looking out back, himself. Bill is trying to get his own promotion, you know. And he needs the same view as our CEO to get on his wavelength."

# 15

# *Pineapple Chicken Breasts*

## MEMORANDUM

TO:      Claire Whittle
FROM:    John E. Johnson
         Chief Executive Officer (CEO)
         Beltway Consultants (BelCon)
RE:      Employee Input Luncheon (EIL)

Your name has been selected through the Company lottery to represent Special Projects at a corporate employee input luncheon (further referred to as the EIL). The EIL will be held in the CEO's office at corporate headquarters in the new Reston facility on March 15, at 11:45 A.M.

Your CEO looks forward to touching base with you and other staff individuals at the EIL, following a seminar he attended in Rio de Janeiro devoted to the Japanese style of management, i.e., probing an organization from the

97

bottom up. BelCon is calling this new thrust its Peon
Pushup Program (PPP).

In sponsoring the EIL, BelCon—who, as you know, is
intimately acquainted with the Equal Employment
Opportunity ideology—is making every attempt to expand
the prong of the Company's growth potential beyond the
boundaries hitherto encompassed by the small business
scenario in today's multifaceted society.

In conjunction with the above, the following menu for
the EIL is affixed for your information (FYI).

MENU
Multicultural Fruit Cocktail
Salsa y Doritos
Chitlins Divan
Fowl Hawaiian
Baked Alaska à la Maraschino
Third-World Blend Coffee
Southeast Asian Tea
Bagels

*Ramona opened the envelope on her desk. It was an
invitation from Rodney requesting her company at a
hurricane watch that night. He wanted to be there "when
Helga baby blows in." But he hadn't even mentioned
dinner, and she despised cheap dates.*

*Then something jumped out at her.* Limo. *Rodney was
calling for her in a* limo. *The delicious four-letter word
sent ripples of desire surging through her virginal system,
after riding in Ed Ward's vulgar van and propped up in
convertibles as the Tangerine Queen—drinking so much
juice she felt that she* was *agent orange.*

*"I know you have a problem with this other woman
business," Ramona read on, riveted. "Don't. I'm even*

98

*prepared to confess my . . . hangup to you tonight—not that this may in any way be taken as a commitment on my part.*

*"Think of the wind! The waves! The incredible undertow! I've enclosed a printout of the weather forecast for your information (FYI). Say yes, Ramona, and I'll be the happiest weatherman who's ever looked in the eye of a storm.*

*"Your potential true love, Rodney."*

*Ramona lay down the quivering invitation and slapped up a DO NOT DISTURB sign, shuddering with anticipation. If Rodney's kisses had melted her to a pulp aboard the* Mango Maiden, *imagine what they could do to her in the back seat of a limousine.*

"Welcome aboard," the Vice President for Corporate Affairs addressed the specially selected BelCon employees seated in Mr. Johnson's office around a table draped with a peach tablecloth.

Claire looked past the corporate heads out to the trees behind the building (furious to be stuck at this lunch when *Forbidden Fruit* was calling). A cloud cover shrouded the nude limbs, swollen with buds about to burst, but not yet. The dark branches swayed in the brooding breeze. Good. A storm was on the way.

Mr. Johnson arrived with his blond blow-dried hair in place and carrying his attaché case with the lump in it. He smiled with teeth reminiscent of a rabbit's and nodded for the meal to begin. The fruit appetizer arrived, fuzzy kiwis and tangerine parts garnished with curlicues of coconut. Claire made a note of these things.

Utensils were raised around the room, but nobody took a bite until Mr. Johnson began. Grinding his spoon into his dish, he ladled a green slice between his mini lips and spoke. "You've been selected," he slicked his tongue over his teeth, "as one of the Company's most valuable commodities. And feel free"—he swallowed, spitting out a seed and marching on with his words—"to say whatever is on your minds."

The corn chips were passed to him, but Mr. Johnson shoved the basket aside, reinforcing his image as a health freak, also a known jogger. Patting the juice from his corporate lips with his linen napkin, he sailed on. "As you know, BelCon has experienced a phenomenal growth curve since our inception. We were recently cited as one of the fastest-growing organizations in northern Virginia and the civilized world."

The chap sitting across from Claire gave a loud clap at this point, which resounded like a single gunshot. His face turned the color of a cranberry, almost to the point of disguising the drop of blood stuck to his throat, but not quite.

Claire kept her corn chip poised in midair until this moment passed. Then she bit into it with a loud crunch. Tasty. She took more chips and made more noise.

"In the interest of time," Mr. Johnson gazed down at the shrunken chicken breast in front of him, inspecting its halo of pineapple that contained a maraschino bullseye leering up at him, "let's get to the meat of this meeting, your input. Folks, BelCon is in a volatile position with the stock market situation, and merger maniacs out there." He took a gulp of water. "Those big barracuda companies are out to gobble up us little fish." Jab, jab, jab, he stabbed at the gray item on his plate, which by a process of elimination Claire deduced was chitlins. The entrée skidded across his plate, almost sliding onto Mr. Johnson's lap before he nailed it with his fork. Securing the mysterious meat, he sawed away at the gristle, then raised the dripping morsel

100

to his mouth and chewed and chewed. Eventually, his jaws locked. And with a frantic motion of his wrist, he beckoned for someone to *get this plate out of here.*

"True, our annual report does indicate minor reversals in the last quarter," he said, taking a drink of water. "But we have every confidence that our incomplete success in the numbers arena will reverse itself and BelCon will surface in the winners column." He reached down to cuddle the briefcase propped against his calf. "Meanwhile, since we've hit bottom, we called this meeting as a last resort, to pick your brains."

A piece of chicken was stuck between her teeth, and Claire probed it with her tongue, wishing she had the nerve to use her fingernail. The pineapple halo had not tenderized the fowl Hawaiian.

"Or," Mr. Johnson muttered (to a room that was now so quiet you could hear the chicken breastbones pop), "you might have questions for us."

The young man across from Claire spoke, picking at his throat. "What is BelCon's target in the coming fiscal year?" he asked.

"Excellent question," Mr. Johnson answered, his lips igniting in a smile, although its fuse was short. "In the ebb and flow of the business cycle"—his hands began to move in waves—"our growth swole up in the early years," he explained, enlarging his undulations, to the extent that he almost knocked over a glass. "Show them, Fred." His right-hand Vice President lurched out of his chair, produced an opaque projector on the spot, and a gigantic column of numbers appeared on a screen.

"However," Mr. Johnson continued when the lights flicked back on, "meeting these figures under the pressures of today's upheavals in the market will call for everybody's two hundred percent effort. The consulting business is

101

high stress, nobody denies that," he stated, stretching down to stroke his attaché case. "And the way the economy's going, this is no time to pamper ourselves with thoughts of bonuses and fat. But by implementation of the latest state-of-the-art management techniques, we have every confidence that we can stay afloat. And you will all be rewarded in the long run, believe me."

Claire raised her hand (oops, put down the knife). "And when will women get promoted into management positions around here?" she asked.

Mr. Johnson's spa-tanned face evolved from bronze to burgundy. Moments passed before a muted answer issued from his throat. "I'm glad you brought up that exact point. Mrs. Whittle is it?"

"Ms.," Claire said.

"Ms. Whittle," he repeated, having difficulty pronouncing the word through his rabbit teeth, or perhaps it was just his male mouth. "We are happy to report that the company intends to include this identical matter in a future agenda, which should bring us up to snuff with any and all regulations. Isn't that right, Dick? Tom?" Mr. Johnson asked, snapping his head from side to side, and they snapped back.

"And?" Claire pressed on.

"Nevertheless," he explained, "under the present set of circumstances, you do have to realize what we're up against. BelCon is based on the military mentality. Even if we did bite the bullet and target certain managerial slots as areas of female infiltration—pardon me, integration—we just don't have the qualified females on board. I refer to officer training, infantry experience, latrine command—"

"Just a minute there," Claire caught him.

"We're talking about life in the trenches, Mrs. Whittle, which is what consulting is."

"In Special Projects where I work," she pointed out, "we do nonmilitary jobs, such as the school lunch proposal we're working on now. And the Project Director we're bidding is a male whose wife fixes his lunch, and he doesn't even know what he's eaten," Claire said, with surprising vehemence in her voice. "What's more, Dr. Bird is bid for a hundred percent of his time for every project we have at once! See if you can make that compute. Sure, BelCon hires professional women. But they get stuck doing research chores and are never heard from again, much less promoted to management where they belong."

Mr. Johnson's eye contact had lapsed early in Claire's speech, and he gazed at the window, where the rain was pecking at the glass, at him. "We'll . . . get back to you on that," he responded from a distance. "But you do admit BelCon has hired a number of top-flight women. Analysts, isn't that right? Dick? Tom? You see them all over the building." Clutching his dessert spoon, he turned to his henchmen.

Dick and Tom nodded.

"Backbone of the company. The woods are full of good support people," Mr. Johnson intoned, extending his arm toward the impending storm, which answered with a distant growl of thunder. "And we salute them. So I really don't see any problem here."

# 16

# Men-Anon

"Holly, there's a place you can go for your problem," Fiona said.

"Which one?" Holly asked, biting down on a buffalo wing. They were at the Grazing Garden, Reston's only decent happy hour.

"Your addiction to men." Fiona picked the fried crust off her broccoli hors d'oeuvre and flicked the green part away. "The way you let Les Moore walk all over you. And his latest move hasn't taught you a thing. Anyway, I thought you were through with him."

"I will not go to a shrink because I believed a man wanted Indian food when he said he did," Holly told her. "You would cancel a date, too, if your basement flooded."

"Sugar, that rain was barely a sprinkle, nothing to spill into a person's basement, even over in Mount Vernon," Fiona answered, licking the salt off her margarita glass. Holly almost wished she drank alcohol tonight. However, nausea did not cheer her up. "I didn't say anything when you took the man a baked Alaska on the first night," Fiona

104

went on, "which could happen to anyone. And I suppose his father could have had cancer of the colon in New Jersey, with the pollution they have up there. But canceling on you for the Calcutta Kitchen the last minute, leaving you waiting in your sari, *honey*—"

"I know," Holly moaned. "But every time Les calls back—and he sounds like he wants to see me—I go ahead and say yes. I forget."

Fiona held out her fingernails, painted with fresh fuchsia polish (meaning she'd had a good night with Hugo). "I'm not saying to go to a therapist, although it wouldn't hurt. I'm talking about a support group. It's for women addicted to men. The name of it is Men-Anon."

"That sounds interesting." Holly finished her virgin Mary on the rocks. "And will you come too?"

"Stars, no, not after working through my dependency problems with men years ago." Fiona laughed. "After you've demeaned yourself for two husbands, you do learn something."

"What did you learn?"

"Well, as you can see, Hugo can't do enough for me now. Nobody walks on Fiona." She stirred her margarita with the plastic stick. "And you can be cured, too, Holly. Think of it. You'll be able to listen to love songs on your car radio and not drive into things. And no more down on your knees begging for a man to call. Once you find your identity, it will be the other way around. Men will be down on their knees to you."

"*All right,*" Holly answered. "You bet I'll go."

The Men-Anon meeting was held in a church on Monday nights, in a crowded room where the women mingled around a table piled with books such as *A Step Program for Weeding out Men.*

105

They sat in a circle, and the first woman introduced herself. "I'm Charlene, and I'm a compulsive men-aholic."

"Hello, Charlene," everybody answered back.

"I've been addicted to men all my life. I got pregnant when I was fifteen, and if that wasn't dumb enough—not that I don't love my little girl—a year later it happened again. You must be thinking what a moron. You're right. I'm thirty-five now, with four kids and divorced. And guess what? I haven't changed that much. In the supermarket I still get in the checkout line behind a guy with good-looking buns. I had a fight with my ex-husband over his missed child support. Then what did I do afterward but jump in bed with him. And here's the sick part: I enjoyed it. I mean, I *really* enjoyed myself. They say your sex drive slackens off when you get married and have kids. Not me. All Frank has to do is touch me."

The women smiled at Charlene's story, although you weren't allowed to chime in.

The next speaker was Lucille, married twenty years. She announced herself as a compulsive pleaser. "Take yesterday. I was ironing Herb's shirts. He came in and saw one on the hanger that still had a wrinkle in it and wadded it back in the hamper. So I immediately trotted the shirt downstairs on the spot and ran another load of washing. As I was pouring in the liquid Tide, I knew that I was crazy. But I couldn't stop myself.

"Herb wakes me in the night to fix him snacks. I've made waffles, chili dogs, even mincemeat pie, you name it. Naturally, I keep stocked up on anything he might want. Then last night he comes up with a new one. At 2 A.M. I get this hiss in my ear, 'BLT.'

"So up I jump, stumbling into the kitchen looking for the Wonderbread. But we're out of Canadian bacon. So I throw on my raincoat over my nightgown and drive across town to the all-night Giant, with never a worry about getting a ticket as I fly past police cars. All I'm thinking about is Herb's BLT, how I'll cook the bacon perfect, extra crunchy but not burned. And somehow I'm imagining how he'll appreciate it, when he never does. Why do I keep doing this? That's the sickness."

People were laughing now, and Lucille joined in until she was wiping her eyes.

"I'll tell you this worst story, then I'll stop," Lucille continued. "It was during a power failure, and Herb calls me from the Bingo Barn where he plays. 'Lucille,' he says, 'bring light.'

"And I did. I found a generator in another neighborhood and took over the lamps from our living room so the men could finish their game. What I don't understand is that the more I do what Herb asks, the more it seems to irritate him."

By the time Lucille finished, the women were dabbing their eyes. This was the finest meeting Holly had ever been to in a church.

When it was her turn to talk, she didn't think she had any funny stories to tell. "I just have a problem with a man who breaks dates," Holly explained. But as she related the reasons Les gave for canceling every date, the women began smiling. "You have to understand, Les is an unbelievably nurturing father," she added. "He sacrifices for his children every time. He cares about pets, too."

One lady was laughing uncontrollably by now. And Holly could see the humor of her situation—waiting in a sari for Mr. Nobody to take her to the Calcutta Kitchen.

"I know the man," a woman in a business suit said afterwards, somebody you wouldn't think had these silly problems. "I call him the new daddy. He's a by-god saint."

"You've met somebody like Les?"

"Yup. So there are worse things than traditional men."

Holly agreed that this was probably true. And she was relieved she wasn't the only nitwit in the world, being taken in by the perfect male.

At the end of the Men-Anon meeting, everybody stood in a circle and said this prayer:

"Give us the serenity to live with the men
   we cannot change,
The brains to change the ones we can,
And the guts to chuck the rotten apples."

"Keep coming back," the women chanted as they went out. Holly repeated the words all the way to her car.

She felt clean and cured of her addiction, free!

She drove home in the fast lane, zooming in front of a convertible, whose driver tooted his expensive horn at her. But did this cause her to faint into her dashboard? Not at all. She smiled. She waved, although not to the point of giving the man her phone number, which you sometimes do when you're stuck in boring traffic. However, men are terrible lip readers.

Then as she went in her apartment, she got down on her knees among her plants. "Thank you, Lord, for helping me be cured of my love addiction." Tears of joy fell into the mulch. "I will follow in Your footsteps forever."

# 17

# *Head Hunt*

Ned Bird tapped his pencil on the desk as he waited for his wife to come on the phone at the elementary school where she taught. He went back to writing his technical plan for the proposal, inserting fresh analyses in the margins. The secretaries ridiculed his small handwriting, but he felt it was compact. "Well, get Mrs. Bird out of the classroom," he told the person at the other end. "This is her husband calling." Why did his wife have to work anyway?

His secretary should be handling this detail, but Rita was out sick again. It was this pregnancy situation she'd gotten herself into. He'd thought she would be a safe person to hire, not an attractive woman, rather resembling a linebacker, who wouldn't have boyfriends to interfere. He had been wrong.

His wife came on the line. "Joan, this is Ned. Could you be at the house today when the phone man comes to put the extension in the bathroom. Sorry I forgot to mention this when I saw you. . . . Yes, I realize your school is in session. But they must have substitutes in these emergencies. Thank you, Joan."

Ned hung up but continued to feel agitated. His wife had not sounded pleased. Over the years she had become a more efficient manager of their home. But she still frequently became hysterical, and they had considered sending her for professional help. Due to the chaos in the house, he felt disoriented spending large blocks of time there. And he hadn't counted on the noise level of three children when he considered marriage.

His first two children had been girls, leaving their paraphernalia all over the place and constantly giggling, Ned feared, at him. The plan had been to have just the two children. But he had thought that one would be a son. Then his wife had pressed him to have another child. So when he came across a study correlating time of conception with gender, he agreed to let her try again for a male.

The study turned out to be valid. Their third child was a boy.

However, Ned Jr. was not the son he had expected. The boy ran wild. They grounded him until he could discipline himself and clean his room. But he remained recalcitrant, refusing to develop good work habits.

Ned stared down at the data he was trying to comprehend. Blast it, he couldn't concentrate on his job with these personal problems nagging him.

His family had also been hassling him to go on a vacation. They'd pressured him to the point where he'd given in and agreed to go this year. He did make it clear that there wouldn't be any trip until BelCon's proposal season was over.

The thought of lounging on a beach for a whole week made him nauseous. He'd written entire proposals in that time frame. At least maybe he could get something done in the hotel when the girls went shopping. He had found that was the best strategy to get them out of your hair.

Bill paced past Holly's desk. "You're going downtown with me to meet these female subcontractors," he muttered. He aimed a wad of paper at the trash and missed. "I've got my handles on your basic minorities, but these new female types are going to want to input."

"I'm riding down to Georgetown with you?" Holly said. "Great." This was looking good for her promotion.

"You want to grab me some coffee, first?" Bill asked.

"Not when you've already drunk a whole pot."

"Right. Well, then, go tell Ned we're ready to leave."

Holly gladly went down to inform Rita about the meeting. But she wasn't at her desk, probably out with morning sickness one more time. Rita had been in the office, though. You could smell her smoke.

Holly went to Ned's door. Then she stopped as she saw him inside in a strange position. He was crouched down going around his desk. Ned was *down on his knees, blowing on it,* what in the world? He might have been kissing a document he'd written. But his desk was slicked off as usual. Ned was blowing at imaginary dust.

"Pardon me," Holly knocked and went in, pretending not to notice that their Sub-Deputy Director was kneeling at his desk.

Ned stood up, stiff as a broom.

"Bill says we're ready to go to Georgetown."

"Good." Ned's thin lips twitched, almost in a smile. He put his writing pad in his briefcase, ready to go.

Bill drove them in his station wagon down the George Washington Parkway. It was Holly's favorite road, overlooking the Potomac River. A canoe bounced along with

111

oars the size of toothpicks paddling it around a rock. And across the water the spires of Georgetown rose up through the trees. The weather forecast had been "sunny with showers." And as shady spots moved in the road, yes, drops came glittering down through the sunshine.

But who could notice such things with Bill speeding along here like a maniac. Holly didn't understand his rush today; he'd avoided meeting these women subcontractors so far. Now he hunched over the wheel as if he were in a demolition derby, shooting past a silver Mercedes, whose driver turned her smooth blond hairdo to stare at the dented station wagon roaring by.

"Bill, slow down," Holly said. A policeman can crop up anywhere. But he hurtled on, shooshing past a limousine with diplomatic license plates and the dark windows that once in your life you'd like to ride inside.

"Say, uh, Ned, you see any of those construction johnnies along here?" Bill asked, when of course there were no outhouses on the parkway.

Suddenly they were bumping off the road onto the median. Bill stopped and leaped out, heading for the bushes, running as if he had to catch a pass. (However, on television the football player doesn't undo his belt as he dances into the end zone.)

Meanwhile, Holly was stranded with the most uptight man in their office, who was also naturally married. And now a patrol car was pulling off the parkway. Great.

She slid down below the dashboard, spying on the officer from there. Good, he was too fat to be Eddie, standing with his arms folded as he watched the lunatic galloping across the median into the trees. Traffic was slowing down, too, so the drivers could stare.

Bill came out of the bushes, zipping up and grinning. Then he moseyed over to make friends with the cop.

During all of this, Ned didn't say a word sitting there. He did nibble on his fingernails.

When Bill finally finished his conversation, he came back praising Officer O'Boyle. "And his jurisdiction needs a software package to track parking ticket offenders. So how about our data base for smoking out delinquent student loan people?" he raved on as he revved up to get them out of the ravine. Then they speeded all the way down to Key Bridge.

"Which lane?" Bill asked as they swerved onto M Street, cutting in front of a Volvo, whose driver beeped at him. The Harvard Business School obviously didn't teach them driver's ed.

"Left," Holly said, also pointing the way, since Bill's directions got confused when he was under stress. They drove blocks looking for a parking place. And they were already late for the meeting with their subcontractors, Rodman & Clark.

Dr. Ramona Rodman, known for numerous successful projects with USDA, also post-graduate research in nutrition, stood up slowly at her desk as they came in. Bill greeted her with a jovial "Hi" and unloaded his things on her conference table. Holly explained that an emergency on the parkway had caused their delay.

Dr. Rodman's associate was a former nun, Ms. Wanda Clark, who had gained her expertise in nutrition by supervising the meals in her convent. Her résumé also mentioned a vision she'd had telling her to take her talents out of the cloister and into the hands-on world. Wanda had curly red hair, which Holly was glad to see had been liberated from her habit.

Dr. Rodman got the meeting started, while Wanda delivered a plate of donuts, smiling with her full glossed lips—not worn down by years of kissing insignificant high school boys and men you never see again.

Bill grabbed a donut. "You want to run your nutrition projects by me again," he said, with a piece of coconut dangling off his lip.

Dr. Rodman's lungs expanded, causing her bow tie to tweak out of line. Bill did this to people. "We sent you our project summaries weeks ago," she reminded him. "Our Analysis of the National School Lunch Program According to State meets the exact specifications of the *RFP*."

"Uh, right. You've got to be responsive on these deals," Bill said, sampling another donut. He grinned when blueberries spurted back at him. "And you can plug in our management plan anywhere."

Dr. Rodman's blouse was tightening. "Bill, cut the crap. And our question to you is—how do you plan to win a nutrition contract when BelCon is a defense contractor?"

Bill licked his palm. "Uh," he looked around, "we've got a great team of professionals. And we're putting some of that logic stuff in this proposal, right, Ned?"

Ned answered by reading statistical material until Holly was falling asleep. But she woke up when she heard Wanda ask, "Is your word processor compatible with our DOS environment?" Bill was installing a new computer, just in time to crank out the school lunch proposal.

"State of the art," he said. "It should hook into any model you've got. Say, do you have any more of that coffee?"

Holly looked over at the former nun and made a *no* with her lips. The holy woman understood.

"You all know we're on a tight time frame," Bill explained.

"And he promised he wouldn't leave everything until the night before the proposal is due," Holly pointed out.

"Yup," Bill agreed, going for the last donut, a powdered sugar one.

After the meeting he fumed, "Dang those gals for putting that plate of donuts in front of me. I finished the whole pile, didn't I."

"You have some sugar on you," Holly said, pointing to white fingerprints on Bill's lapel.

"What's a nun doing in this business, anyway?" he complained, shaking off his suit. "And that Rodman woman ought to be home with her kids. It's these latchkey kids who get into drugs and crime—"

"Stop," Holly said, "that isn't fair." But she couldn't help thinking of Walter lying in the snow waiting for her, on a day when he didn't even have his latchkey. What if Walter became an addict, or a drug lord? He had always loved to sniff the things she cooked, that is, back in the days when she baked and was a decent mother.

"So," Bill said as they walked down the clean brick sidewalk of Georgetown in the late afternoon sunlight. "You want to stop for a bite, since we're here with these great restaurants?" A spicy smell came out of a doorway they passed. Indian food. *Yes.* "Unless Holly has to get home for a hot date."

"Are you kidding, on a Monday night? Anyway, I'm through with men," Holly said. "I'm going to focus on my career." She looked over at Bill to see if he might be thinking about her promotion. Not yet.

"I do have a meeting tonight," she mentioned. "It's a support group. But that's later. And I wouldn't miss a dinner with you gentlemen in Georgetown for anything."

# *18*

# *Fruit of the Loom*

Before the Men-Anon meeting, Holly had time to run a load of laundry. Somebody's clothes were in the drier, so she piled them on the table there. A pair of peach jockey shorts leaped out at her. They didn't belong to anybody in the building she knew, certainly not Mr. Berry from upstairs. His wash came out gray.

She folded the person's things, smoothing out the male articles and several cleaning rags. As she dug down in the pile, she didn't see a single woman's item. This was too good.

She was holding up the last warm piece of underwear when the door opened behind her.

A strange man came in, tall with dark blow-dried hair. He wore an avocado Polo shirt and washed blue jeans fastened with a Gucci belt. He smiled at her through lavender-tinted glasses that made his brown eyes big.

The hot trunks fell out of her hand.

"You folded my things? Well, thank you," he said, smelling good.

"They wrinkle," Holly answered, experiencing short-ness of breath.

"I'm Laurence LeFever. Just moved in across the hall."

"I live upstairs," she answered like a moron. Of course she lived here or she wouldn't be using this laundry room. "Holly Prickle on the third floor."

She stepped over to the washer and tugged out her towels. The little holes in the side of the machine made bumps on the wet cloth matted there, goosebumps all over it. She untangled a bra wound around the middle part of the machine and tossed it gaily into the drier. The hook caught on the top of the inside, and the bra dangled there, unbelievably. She stepped over to hide this view, reaching behind her to undo it.

"I used to do my wife's laundry," he said. "Now we're divorced. She was unfaithful. And I still believe in the marriage vows."

The bra came unhooked in Holly's hand. She let the door of the drier suck shut, and it started up, making a moaning sound. "I like that."

"Louise got me good. One day I came home from the supermarket, and she was out front in a jeep kissing her boyfriend. They were doing it in a jeep."

"I've never liked jeeps, either," Holly murmured. "You deserve better, Mr. LeFever. Everybody does."

"Call me Laurence. But not Larry. I think the name Larry is low." Holly agreed. She had been out exactly once with a Larry, and that was the exact word to describe him.

"I stayed with my parents that night," Laurence continued, wiping off his forehead in the heated room. "Then the next morning when I went back to get ready for work—I'm with the Department of Interior, a GS-9, although my boss, I work for a lady, is trying to get me promoted—"

"You work for a woman?" Holly said. "Good for you. I'm supposed to be getting a promotion, too."

"And a sweet girl like you deserves it. You're nothing like my ex-wife Louise," Laurence said, lining up his dark socks and knotting them. "So the next morning, you know what Louise had done? Changed the lock on me."

"They can do that overnight?"

"She locked me out after eleven years of marriage. She abused me physically, too. I'll show you." He pulled up his pant leg, revealing shin marks the color of raspberries. "That's where Louise kicked me with her pointed shoes. I'm glad to see you aren't wearing those spike heels, Holly. I gave her everything. My problem is I spoil a woman."

The clothes in the drier went around thump, thump.

"My ex-wife also drove me into bankruptcy."

"I thought you had to be rich," Holly said curiously. He obviously wasn't or why would he be working for the government?

"Anybody can file. You could," he told her. "And you've been hurt, too. I can tell by your aura."

Holly looked around. "My ex-husband would never have abused me. Not that he didn't have his problems," she said. "Eddie went to Vietnam."

"Disabled?"

"No. He was never in combat. He got stuck in the harbor the day the war ended, making bombs they never used."

"Then he gave up a nice person like you."

Holly swallowed. She couldn't tell if the pounding she felt came from inside her or the drier. Then she realized that she'd put her lingerie in there, and it melts. "And what do you do for Interior, Laurence?" she asked, stopping the machine and scooping out her damp garments.

118

"Research on endangered species—buffalo, snail darters." He took off his glasses and wiped away the steam. "Extinctions are my specialty."

"My son Walter and I love animals. We have a rabbit named Warren," Holly mentioned, feeling something warm on the front of her blouse. She was hugging her wet clothes.

"Louise wouldn't have children with me." Laurence put his glasses back on, and his eyes grew. "But I have a pet. That's why I moved into these apartments, because they let you have lap pets. Most rental units discriminate against pet owners any more."

"Which lap pet?" Holly asked, trying to remember the last time Warren had sat on her lap, and she could not.

"A ferret. Laura. She belonged to Louise, but I got her in the divorce settlement. That's what I would have named a daughter, Laura LeFever. Ferrets are the in-pet, you know. Want to see her? I'm just across the hall." Laurence gathered his folded clothes to go, and his fingertips were trembling. Either this man had a health condition, or he liked her.

"Sure, for a minute," Holly said.

She did feel at home going in his apartment, which had the same floor plan as hers, although Laurence had more furniture and boxes still to be unpacked.

They sat down on an expensive-looking couch covered with a satiny material of black and melon stripes. As they sank in, you could hear a munching sound. "That's her," Laurence said excitedly. "Give her a second, Laura's coming out."

A lump pushed up under the upholstery, the shape of a fist coming at Holly. "Watch out," Laurence cried.

She leaped up, barely getting out of the way as the moving knuckles disappeared under a throw pillow. The

119

shape shot up the back of the couch, and a nose poked out the top. A fur piece flew into the room, and Laura landed with her paws scraping the wooden floor. "There she goes," Laurence called out as the ferret scrambled for the bedroom. "Better let her go. She bites." He held up his finger to show where Laura had left teeth marks.

"That must have hurt."

"I'm used to pain." Laurence sucked his finger. "Say, can I get you something to drink, Holly? Or I'll cook you dinner, anything you want."

It is so nice when a man does that (although stew containing lettuce for his children doesn't count). "I was supposed to go somewhere, but—"

"You probably want to wash up first," Laurence said, showing her where the bathroom was, although she already knew. "I like to clean," he said, stepping over a pile of rags on the floor and pointing to his shiny tub. Holly took a step inside then stopped herself. No more barging into a bachelor's bathroom without checking it out first. She inspected the sink for bugs and didn't see any.

She complimented Laurence on his polished taps. She had no idea you could get the faucets in these apartments to look that good. And this man didn't know the meaning of grock.

"I like housework," he said.

She felt faint.

"I feel so close to you already." Laurence came over and stood by her next to the commode. "Now, I better go fix the dinner I promised you. Anything you want. Do you like spaghetti?"

"I do."

He went in the kitchen, but immediately came back out. "Darn, I forgot, no sauce. We'll have to go to the store," he said with a big smile.

He was a goofy guy. She could see that. But he seemed kindly and honest and she felt so happy. "I have spaghetti sauce upstairs," Holly volunteered, her mind racing through her freezer thinking of what else she had that they could use. Yes, ground beef. And enough Oreo ice cream for at least one serving. "We could cook up there if you want to, since you are still unpacking."

"Are you sure? Great," Laurence said and followed her out.

"It'll be a housewarming party," Holly said, dancing up the stairs and opening the door to her world of plants.

"You're the nicest girl I've met," Laurence said, wiping his feet on her mat. As he came in she got a whiff of his delicious aftershave and almost sank down on the rug right there. Imagine living this close to someone you date. You could hug in the hall at any time. (And he couldn't lie and say his basement was flooding if you were on the premises.)

"I appreciate this, Holly. Most women won't cook for you anymore. And to be honest, when I cook, I spill. But as I said, I'll do all the housework."

She went in her kitchen, what a lovely room, looking up at the shining handle of the freezer as if she'd never seen glowing chrome before. Inside she found bread, good bread, patiently waiting stored in plastic bags to be thawed out for an occasion.

Soon the hamburger was sizzling in the pan, giving off the delicious smell of frying meat that makes your nostrils want to live forever. And Mr. LeFever, being human and not a stick, didn't stay sitting in her living room reading a magazine but joined her in the kitchen, close up behind her, and asked if he could help. She had him get a can of olives off the top shelf, which she added to the bubbling sauce, shiny and black, alive.

121

"I should pay you for these ingredients," Laurence said, taking out his wallet, "since I was going to cook for you."

"Heavens, no. I enjoy doing this," Holly said, stirring, was she ever stirring.

"Darn, I don't believe it. I'm out of cash." He showed her his empty wallet. "Well, next weekend will be my treat. And I know where I'm taking you. It'll be a surprise. And you can bring your son along. He'll like this place."

# 19

# *Hurricane Helga*

Claire kissed Jack in the car as she dropped him off at Dulles Airport for the flight to his electrical engineering convention in Miami. She could write while he was gone. And in Florida Jack could visit his parents without her.

"I'll miss you," she called as he headed into the terminal.

Jack turned around and grinned. "Put it in your book."

He was such a love, Claire thought, as she sped home to *Forbidden Fruit*. Now, how was she going to work up the bile she needed for her characters?

She remembered a fight she'd had with Jack when they first got married. He'd expected her to match his socks— every damn one of those dark socks—because that's what his mother had done. Claire could still feel the venom of that day. She smiled and hurried in to her computer.

*Rodney Rhodes stood by the sudsy sea, the waves washing his toes, then his ankles, as Hurricane Helga surged up the shore and mounted his higher parts.*

*Ankle deep herself in sand, Ramona faced Rodney. She was furious, but not at the storm. It was the emotions churning in her virginal heart and other pristine parts that tormented her, the cycle of attraction-repulsion brought on by this divine brute she'd kissed passionately against her will in the back seat of his limousine coming over to the water's edge.*

*"Tell me your problem with women or take me home," she demanded from the depths of her beauty queen lungs.*

*"You forget my professional calling," Rodney answered blithely as the air quality got worse. "I'm here to register the force of this hurricane, not talk," he said, reminding her of his important mind, thus causing Ramona's own brain to shrink. He was, after all, the strong and silent type that every nice girl dreams of.*

*"Are disasters all you think about?"*

*"Check out that breaker, wow! Oh, all, right," Rodney said, reaching for her.*

*Ramona staggered away to the safety of a rock, oops, a slippery one. "You think that getting physical changes everything, don't you," she gasped, picking herself up. "But we don't communicate. We have to talk. Tell me about your problems."*

*Rodney's face grew dark as a thunderhead. "Oh, all right."*

*"Let's go inside," she suggested, "where I can hear."*

*"No." Rodney shook his sopping hair. "I'm into nature. OK, I have hang-ups about women," he shouted over the surf. "Commitments."*

*"Which I suppose excuses your callousness about my parents' wedding anniversary on the cruise," Ramona recalled bitterly. "You can't even cope with family, can you. Obviously that cheap woman of yours isn't somebody you would take home to your mother."*

*"Watch it," Rodney growled.*

*"You're still involved with her, aren't you?" Ramona said tightly, picking a sand crab off her leg and throwing it at him.*

*"All right, she is part of my problem," he admitted. "I'm bound to her, my flesh, my blood, my messed-up psyche—"*

*"Spare me the details. I'm a nice girl and a queen."*

*"She has this effect on me because," Rodney glared up at the black bosom of the sky, "she is—my mother!"*

*"No!" Ramona's mouth stayed open, collecting rain water and a palm frond that blew in. "You aren't having an affair with your own mother, Rodney. No wonder you wouldn't tell me your problem."*

*"Of course I'm not," he snarled. "But she's had me on a leash for my whole life. Last night she even tried to get me to do the dishes! And I'm warning you, Ramona, housework is one thing* this *dude doesn't do. As if all her marriages and divorces aren't humiliating enough."*

*"How many?" Ramona asked, gulping.*

*"Let's see." Rodney held up a hand. "Five. That's right. The cruise was my mother's fifth honeymoon, and she had to drag me along. How many stepdads can a guy go through? So you can see why long-term relationships scare the hell out of me. And I hate divorce. It's digusting. Embarrassing. Expensive!"*

*"Thank heavens for that," Ramona replied faintly. How could she have so miserably misjudged this poor man, who was the victim of multiple broken homes—and abused by a mother who was a love addict!*

*"Oh, Rodney." She went over and massaged his magnificent shoulders, accentuated by the stylish cut of his sport jacket, although it was soaking now and shrinking out of shape. "I thought you just wanted your*

125

space. How can I make it up to you?" she asked fervently. "What do you want most in this life?"

Rodney looked out through the sheets of falling rain and smiled. "I want to become a top world volcanologist. And now with Helga under my belt," he said, leaping up to embrace the gusting winds, "I'm leaving on assignment to Vesuvius tomorrow. I suspect rumblings."

Ramona stared. How could he? A minute ago he was practically human, spilling out his sick gut to her. And now these cruel, insensitive words. "You vile and awful man!" she shrieked, throwing a handful of seaweed at him. "Putting me through this stinking storm so you could split as soon as you kissed me.

"Well, don't expect me to be waiting here when you get back. Nobody puts the Tangerine Queen on hold," she yelled. "Get out of my life, Rodney Rhodes. Out. And this time I mean forever, do you hear me?"

# 2 0

# *The K-2000*

It rained the whole next week, often torrentially. Holly worked late but did run into Laurence LeFever out by the dripping dumpster, where he smelled as good as he had the night they met. They hugged by the trash bins, looking forward to Saturday night.

The new computer had been installed at work. It was a K-2000, said to be virus proof and have a super memory. While the secretaries waited for the proposal to type, they practiced on it by writing their own memos.

One afternoon Holly wrote what she was thinking to Laurence. "You looked so sexy when we met. What is that aftershave you wear? It's exciting to think we could meet in the hall at any time."

"You write real good," Fiona said, reading over Holly's shoulder. "But maybe you should use a name from the office in case somebody walks by. Not that your Mr. LeFever doesn't sound nice, although you did meet him in a laundry room, honey. I just hope you don't go overboard. You know how you do."

127

Overboard? Because she was happy to have a great new neighbor? However, Holly did take Fiona's advice and replaced Laurence's name with the most ordinary sounding one at BelCon, John E. Johnson.

And here came Bill to check out his new toy. Hurriedly Holly punched several keys to delete her document. "Got her mastered yet?" he asked, striding up to the screen with her embarrassing words on it. Then as Bill reached out to the K-2000, the screen gave off a big spark, which sizzled down to a pea, and everything went dark.

"You shorted it out." Holly laughed, relieved. "You and your big shoes on that rug."

Bill grinned and lifted up his sole to look at it. "We didn't knock out the proposal, did we?" he asked, dropping his foot.

"You haven't given it to us yet," she reminded him.

"We'll get going on it this weekend. You gals can bring in your sleeping bags."

"Not on Saturday, *please*," Holly said.

"I'm indisposed over the weekend myself," Fiona added in her most southern voice, "with a sick friend."

"Holly, we need you, pal." Bill gave her a disappointed look. "How about if you have Sunday off."

Saturday was her date with Laurence, although he had said Sunday was OK, too. The man was a saint. And since Walter was coming along, they might as well go on a wholesome Sunday. "Oh, all right," she agreed.

Leonard Pudding came huffing up as they stood around the K-2000. But for once he didn't stop to find out what other people were talking about. He was definitely headed somewhere, and looking almost awake. "Heh, Leonard," Bill called, "do you want to work on Saturday?"

"Nope."

"Nope?" Bill laughed. "You really don't?"

Leonard never kidded. He swatted at Bill's cigarette smoke and kept on marching. "I've got something Saturday," he said, hurrying in a trot towards the men's room. Leonard better be careful with that attitude or he could lose his job. Fiona had already predicted that somebody here would be fired before the proposal season was over.

Down at the Department of Agriculture the IBM typewriters clattered away in the Food and Nutrition Division where the school lunch proposals were due the next Friday by 3:15 P.M.

Suddenly it got quiet. Fred Trisket checked the time. He waited, and when it was exactly five o'clock, he said goodnight to his secretary, Sara Lee. He prided himself on never keeping his people overtime. If you were efficient you could get the work done in the allotted time. His own record for meeting deadlines was impeccable. All of his credentials were.

Yet here he was, still a GS-11! Not that he wasn't qualified for his GS-13. But job promotions were frozen throughout USDA.

Like most federal employees, he had considered going to work in the private sector. The consulting business, for example, where you could advance more rapidly. But they work awful hours. And you could be fired.

It wasn't that he disliked his job here, especially when there was enough to do. He looked forward to having all those school lunch proposals coming in next week for evaluation. But it would be nice to be rewarded for your efforts.

What really bugged him was the deadwood in this office. Namely, the guy who sat at the next desk, Clint Boyle. That is, the guy who *should* be sitting there now instead of goofing off somewhere. Because of Clint's incompetence, he was down to analyzing only one commodity. Chocolate. That's all Clint had to cover. *Chocolate.* And he didn't even know that the Mars candy people lived in the Washington, D.C., area.

Yet Clint was GS-13 and lorded it over him.

Down, boy, Fred told himself. Watch the hypertension. *But everybody knew he was a thousand times more qualified than that bum Clint.* Their boss wouldn't do the paperwork, though, to get Clint fired.

Fred's phone rang, and he looked at the clock. It was 5:05, so he didn't have to answer. But for some reason today he picked it up. "Trisket, Food and Nutrition."

"Mr. Trisket, this is Holly Prickle calling. We met in a snow storm." Who? He got a scared feeling. He had never cheated on his wife or even met a woman to cheat with. "I sat in your car. I was running out of gas," she said.

He breathed. "Yes, Miss Prickle."

"I'm calling for directions to your office for when we deliver our proposal next week. My boss tends to run late, and those government buildings are huge." She laughed, and it was a nice sound coming into the quiet office. "Also, would you know of a place to park down there?"

"A GS-11 doesn't get parking privileges," he informed her sharply.

"I'm sorry."

Fred looked over in Clint's direction and added with satisfaction, "A GS-13 doesn't get parking privileges either. That's what I'm qualified to be, a GS-13, but there's a department-wide freeze on advancements," he went on, wondering why he was telling this to a strange woman. True, his wife was sick of hearing him harp about the promotion he deserved.

"The company where I work seems to be frozen, too," Holly said. "I'm supposed to get my promotion, 'as soon

130

as we win a big one.' Not that I'm trying to influence you, Mr. Trisket. If you could just please give me directions to your office. And you might refresh me as to your looks, since I couldn't see you very well in that storm."

A warm feeling went through him. He told her how to find his office and that he wore a gray suit. "And I'm fit. I keep fit by jogging on my lunch hour. I jog around the Tidal Basin."

"Maybe I saw you running around under the cherry trees," she said. "My boss Bill should get in shape. He eats M&Ms all day while he talks on the phone. He thinks because they're so little they don't count. Did you know that the people who own M&Ms live around here? Back in the trees along the George Washington Parkway, so I've heard."

"Yes, I was aware of that." Fred smiled, swirling his chair around to face the mess on Clint's desk.

"I look forward to meeting you again," she said. "And it will be a relief getting this proposal turned in. Thank you."

Fred went out to the bus stop with a jaunty step. A warm breeze greeted him. The trees were sprouting green. Where had he been, not noticing any of this?

His bus pulled up, and he looked at the humiliating number eleven on the front, which usually made him feel dark and angry inside, reminding him of his job status.

But not today.

He got a seat by the window. And as they rode out into Virginia in the diamond lane, he looked down on the traffic and felt so glad he wasn't in a car pool any more. Somebody always has an overtime emergency. Then you have to listen to people complain. Or, the worst is getting stuck with a guy bragging about how well he's doing at work.

131

They passed the Pentagon, and pride soared up in him for serving his country in the military. And it was a good thing for the Gulf war. It gave men in uniform some respect again.

Holly Prickle was a talker, wasn't she. He hadn't seen her real well in that storm. Blond hair, he thought. Curly. He did recall the scent of her perfume in his car, which he explained to his wife Mildred as soon as he got home.

Maybe next week with everybody coming in delivering those school lunch proposals he ought to wear his other suit, his good blue one. You don't want people to think you have just one. You don't want them to think that bureaucrats lead completely boring lives.

# 21

# *Leonard Pudding's Date*

Leonard did not put on a special suit for his date with Verbena Tangles, the beautician who phoned him from Dates 'R' Us in the winter and he agreed to take out in the spring. He was picking her up at six o'clock on Saturday so they wouldn't have to wait at Big Boy.

He stood in front of his steamed-up mirror, wiping it off with his fist. When his face came into focus, he notched his tie up to his dry throat. He'd forgotten how much he hated going on dates. No wonder he hadn't been on one for seven years.

He considered shaving a second time that day as he peered at his dark whiskers starting to grow back in. But nope. His regular time for shaving was the morning when his beard was stiff and not limp from the hot water. Being a beauty operator, his date would likely notice facial hair. So what. Miss Verbena Tangles would have to take what she could get.

He left his apartment in plenty of time. And it was a good thing he did, as he had to make an emergency stop at the men's room of a gas station.

What a dumbo, getting himself into this. He didn't want to live it up on a Saturday night. He'd rather stay home and listen to classical music. Beethoven was his favorite, with the volume turned up. For special occasions he played the Ninth Symphony. It got him so excited he danced around the room pretending he was the conductor.

Well, he wouldn't be doing that tonight now he'd put himself in this noose.

The neighborhood where Verbena Tangles lived over by the Springfield mall was one he did not frequent. (He didn't hang around any mall.) The yards had toys in them, and he kept his foot ready on the brake watching for brats darting out in the street. Through the windows of the houses he could see TVs turned on. If he had kids they wouldn't be allowed to watch the boob tube. As he passed one place, the bedroom curtains yanked shut. He couldn't imagine himself in any bedroom with a woman, or doing it in the kitchen, either, which some guys brag they do.

He counted off the numbers on the houses, going up to the hairdresser's address—905, 907. There it was, 911. His stomach was getting sick. The lawn was not well cared for. It had brown patches in it. A doll lay on the walk, and he remembered that Verbena Tangles had a kid, a daughter from her marriage that had failed.

He felt like he was going to explode as he went up and punched the bell, hoping the door wouldn't open. Then he felt disappointed when it didn't, and he rang and rang.

Suddenly there she was, standing back in the dark hall, where he could sniff her scent easier than make her out. His head was pounding to think that a woman would put on perfume for him.

She came out in the light, and her hair was not the pink color he had dreaded. He didn't know what color you would call this, an orangish shade such as you might see on a doll. But it was long, hooked back behind one ear. Leonard liked long hair. The other girls he'd had dates with all had short hair.

"You must be Dr. Pudding. I'm Verbena Tangles." She reached out to shake his hand, and her fingers felt like a rubber glove.

"Yup."

"You want to come in." He followed her, following that scent.

She went across the living room to where the curtains moved. "Come on out, honey, and meet the nice man." Out came the daughter, a four- or five-year-old kid, what did he know. Her hair must have been from the father's side. It was black. "Dr. Leonard Pudding, this here's my daughter, Chastity."

The child hung to her mom's skirt and wouldn't look at him. "That's a funny name, Pudding." She stared at him.

Having people ridicule his name was nothing new to Leonard. The guys in his school used to holler when he came along, "There goes jello."

"Honey, it isn't polite to make fun of a person's name," Verbena whispered to her child. "They can't help it."

Hrumph. "You ready?" Leonard turned around looking for the door, then he shrank back as he saw another female in the room. She was lying on the couch watching television. "Hi," she said with braces on.

"That's my sitter, Barbie," Verbena Tangles said.

It occurred to Leonard that getting a baby sitter every time would cost.

They left and made it to Big Boy on schedule. But a Greyhound bus had pulled in and was letting off senior

135

citizens in front of them to foul things up. Maybe he ought to go to another restaurant, but he couldn't think of one. So he hustled up and got in line, beating out an old guy coming with a walker.

"I must have been born to stand," Verbena said and laughed when she saw that they would have to wait. "But your legs give out in the beauty parlor business. About when you hit forty they do. My friend Darlene, also an operator at the Hair Ball, called it quits one afternoon when her veins acted up. She took her last lady out of the drier and said right there, 'I retire.' The next week she ran off with the service man for the Coke machine."

Leonard looked up from his digital watch. He was timing how long it took each party to get into the restaurant. At this rate he calculated that their wait would be approximately thirteen minutes. "I don't drink those diet drinks," he said.

He was right about the time: 12.9 minutes later they got seated in Big Boy. He proudly told Verbena that he'd been right in his calculation. She nodded and looked around at the pictures of the burgers on the walls.

Leonard told her she could order anything on the menu (hoping she wouldn't pick the double-digit item, the steak). He recommended the meatloaf.

Verbena took her time reading down the list of entrées, squinting to the point where Leonard worried she might be illiterate. She finally picked chicken "croak-ettes" because they "sounded gourmet," which was OK with him. Just as long as he didn't get nailed with the price of the sirloin.

"Where do you practice medicine, Dr. Pudding?" Verbena asked, taking a Band-Aid off her finger and staring at the wrinkled skin.

"I'm not a medical doctor," he informed her. "I have a Ph.D. It's in history. It's a doctorate."

"What does a doctorate person do?" she asked, sucking her sore finger. "Burned myself on the curling iron. I was trying to get those stubby hairs in the back."

Leonard's neck began to itch. "I was supposed to be a college teacher," he stated, hating this question about his life. "Now I'm what they call an analyst. That's the title they give you in consulting when they can't think of anything else."

Verbena's painted-on eyebrows moved up. "There you go again, using those words that mean nothing to the normal person. At least I can describe what I do: I work on hair." She leaned across the table and stared at Leonard's head. "Have you ever thought of growing sideburns? I could give you a trim and get them started. Guys do come in the Hair Ball. It's usually early in the morning so nobody will see them."

"I always go to the same place," Leonard told her. "Barber Bob."

"Hmm. I don't know that one."

"It's not around here. I drive out because it's cheaper." He scratched his neck.

"Oh," she said.

When they walked out of Big Boy it was still light. Leonard looked around, wondering what you do next in these situations. "I guess there are movies," he said. He saw a marquee across the parking lot and made out the word *Beethoven* on it. His favorite! *Misty Beethoven* was the name of the show. He hadn't heard of it. "You want to see that?"

Verbena Tangles acted as if he'd slugged her. She stepped up on the curb with her high heels, making a loud click. "You're inviting me to see filth? I should have known better, when you weren't a real doctor."

"It's a dirty movie, out here in Virginia?"

"All guys know *Misty Beethoven* is porn," she told him. "Are you sure you aren't a pervert, Leonard? And is your name really Dr. Pudding?" Her eyes became slits looking at him.

He thought. He had gone to a dirty movie once downtown. He'd fallen asleep in it.

The hairdresser strutted back and forth in her tall heels with her angry arms folded. It surprised him that you could get in a fight with a girl you hardly know. "I don't need this," she said in a mad voice. "I'd as rather be home playing with my little girl."

And he'd rather be home listening to classical music, lying on the rug. He could save the price of the movie ticket, too.

A happy, jumpy feeling started in his stomach as he realized maybe this date could soon be over. "You wouldn't have to pay that sitter so much, I guess, if we went back now," he mentioned.

Verbena looked at him with her slit eyes, and he waited for her to say something mean. Then she surprised him. She smiled—right at him—and looking so pretty he could have pounced on her. "Yes, *I'll* pay my sitter, Leonard. Come on, let's go."

On the way back to her house they got to talking almost as if they were friends. And when she got inside her screen door (still smelling good), Verbena Tangles smiled again. "At least you didn't paw me," she said, fastening the latch. "And I meant it when I said I'd give you a trim to get your sideburns going." She was staring at his head again, but this time his neck didn't itch. "You might even look sexy with sideburns, Leonard." His bowels were suddenly ready to move, and he stepped away to get out of here. "Here's my card," Verbena said, pushing it to him through a torn place in the screen. "Call me for an appointment any

138

time. I might even give you my ten percent discount if you're nice."

Leonard nodded and stuffed her calling card in his trouser pocket as he strode out to his Ford Taurus. He got in and turned on the radio to the good music station, getting Rimsky-Korsakov.

He gunned it on the way home, beating out a Bronco trying to cut into his lane. It wasn't a bad life, being a bachelor. You can go out on the town—then come home where nobody hassles you. That's the part he liked best, coming back to his own place.

He could still listen to a little music tonight, then get some extra shut-eye to gear up for Monday morning. This week was going to be a grind, getting that school lunch proposal out.

# 2 2

# *Paws & Feathers*

"Mom, why do I have to wear a suit?" Walter asked. "You don't even know where this guy's taking us. And it'll get wet in the rain."

"It's misting, Walter, misting," Holly told him, putting down her watering can. "You look so handsome in a jacket, honey, with that dark hair of yours. Laurence is nice, and he's our neighbor. He also likes to do housework."

"Yuck, a wimp. Why do you have to go with wimps?"

"You are so critical," she said, adjusting her cactus so that its best side faced the door. "Shush. There he is now."

Laurence came in smiling and showed them his new raincoat. "I bought it for you." The coat was stylish, with flaps that buttoned on his chest. "Hello, Walter. Your mom is lucky to have you for a son. I have a ferret."

Walter peered over the top of his monster comic book where he sat slumped on the couch. "Right."

When they got outside, Laurence had them guess which vehicle was his. "The new Mazda?" Walter asked, perking up. It was shiny enough to be Laurence's.

140

Not to put pressure on her date, Holly chose the beige Buick next to it. "Nope," Laurence said. "Over here," and he walked towards a van. He drove a tan paneled van.

Walter yelped. "Mom hates vans. She won't ride in those drugmobiles."

"Honey, that was before," Holly murmured. The van was well kept, and the space in back would be perfect for Walter.

"A van wasn't my choice, either," Laurence explained. "My ex-wife's father owned the franchise, and she had me trade in my Saab for this. Holly, I've never smoked marijuana once."

"I believe you, Laurence."

They drove through the drizzle all the way into Maryland, but Laurence still wouldn't tell them where they were going, although Holly asked him several times. He said he had a bad ear on her side and made her repeat.

Finally, they took a side road and came to a sign that said Paws & Feathers. That was an unusual name for a restaurant. Then up close you could see the smaller words in the peeling paint: *pet interment*. "It's a pet cemetery," Laurence said excitedly, "since we are all pet lovers."

"People put their cats and dogs in here?" Walter asked, stumbling half asleep out of the van.

"Other species, too, birds and rodents," Laurence said, hurrying down the muddy path to the cemetery as the rain picked up speed. "My pet gerbils are buried here, Samson and Delilah. She was the first to go, flat on her back in the cage. A week later he was dead of a broken heart, hanging from the feeder. They're over by that wall. I'll go find them." Laurence trotted off through the squishy grass.

They watched as he bounded across the plots and got down on his knees groping in the wet grass for his gerbils' graves. She and Walter went over and helped him look, but nobody could find Samson and Delilah.

Laurence raised his stricken face. "They're gone. Somebody's dug them up and stolen them. And I know who did it—my ex-wife Louise."

"Why would she do that?" Holly asked, astounded at the trouble people go to.

"To get back at me. You've seen the scars on my legs from her pointed shoes. Here, I'll show Walter." Laurence reached down to pull up his dripping pant leg.

"That's OK," Holly told him. "We'll be looking around at the graves, if you need us. Good luck."

As they walked away, Walter turned to her with his dark kid's eyes. "Mom, you've got to dump this guy."

"Look at this inscription, Walter. 'Goodby, Sweet Prince. Killed instantly by a tractor trailer.'" A collie was carved in the headstone, down to the full detail of his Lassie tail. Nearby, a woman was on her knees scrubbing an unmarked stone with a toothbrush she dipped in Clorox. "So what are you trying to say to me, Walter," Holly asked, "when I'm having a good time?"

"Anybody can see," he grumbled, motioning back to Laurence LeFever crawling in the rain. "My mother is out with a weirdo. OK? It's embarrassing. And you actually like him, don't you."

Holly lifted her chest and breathed. "He's a sensitive man. You just don't meet that many who are."

"*Mom*, this guy's dipstick doesn't meet the oil."

"All right, he's not the smartest boyfriend I've had. But since when does the child tell the mother who she can date?"

The lady cleaning the tombstone put down her toothbrush and said, "We never had children of our own." Her husband arrived bringing a gift wrapped in foil with a bone attached to it. They opened Prince's present, a red ceramic hydrant, which they placed at the foot of their deceased dog's grave. "We drive sixty miles every Sunday to visit him. This other plot is for his sister when her time comes. Jennifer will be buried next to Prince."

"Oh, Walter," Holly said as they walked away, her eyes growing moist, but not from the bleach. "What would I do without you for a son?" He gave a noisy sigh. "Come on. I was going to let you pick out a plot for Warren here," she went on. "His ears would look beautiful laid out on satin."

"Mom, that's sick. You can't afford it, anyway. You can barely make your car payments as it is," Walter reminded her in his know-it-all, nine-year-old voice. Her son may be sensible, but he was very, very rude. "So, are you going to ditch him?" he said. They looked over at Laurence, who had crawled to the end of the wall without finding his gerbils. "That is gross."

"Oh, go look at the graves, Walter. You have no heart," Holly told him. He ran off, playing hopscotch on the headstones as he went. Then he stopped and turned back to her, grinning. "Guess what's buried here? A turkey. 'Larry: Not Meant for Thanksgiving.' Speaking of food, when do we eat?"

Holly smiled and waved back. "Soon, I hope." She thought of the turkeys she had roasted, realizing only when you see the whole bird sitting on your counter that it was once a living, gobbling being. On the other hand, you feel heartless when you cook with turkey parts.

Laurence came back across the wet lawn with soiled knees. Maybe Walter was right and she should break up with him. Her smart aleck son did usually know what he was talking about.

Laurence looked up at her with foggy glasses. He smiled and said one word, "Holly!"

143

Her lips forgot what they were supposed to say.

"Let me show you my favorite headstone," Laurence said, taking her hand. They found the burial place of Ranger, a German shepherd, laid to rest by a tree stump.

"He was my eyes," the carved words said. "Lord, bless the beasts and singing birds who have no words."

Holly looked at Laurence. His eyes were shining in the mist. And then they were kissing.

# 23

# *Looking for Rodney*

Ramona could not wipe Rodney's ravishing kisses out of her mind, certainly not at the Muskmelon Manor, where she was forced to watch couples go up to their rooms.

And after experiencing Hurricane Helga with Rodney Rhodes, dating Ed Ward was excruciatingly boring. He took her to an outdoor concert, and the little wimp wanted to leave when he felt the first raindrop.

But how could Rodney have poured out his heart to her—then run off to visit a stupid mountain?

Thud. The mailboy dropped a load on Ramona's desk. But what was the point of making room reservations for other people?

What was the point of living now?

She saw an envelope addressed to her, in a magnificent masculine scrawl. With trembling fingers she stroked the stationery that carried Rodney's signature, and his scent!

Tearing the letter open with her teeth, she paused to let her lips caress the sticky flap that her true love's tongue had touched. Oh, Rodney.

"Could I sign in, please," a senior citizen croaked, reaching a claw-like hand across the counter for a pen. Grab, grab, grab, these people and their obsessive demands.

Ramona shoved the register across the desk and stalked off to the ladies' room to enjoy Rodney's letter in peace.

She settled in a stall and read, "Vesuvius is spectacular! If only you were here in my arms, Ramona, on the brink of this cauldron. My desire is such that I've almost considered coming home.

"However, I will be detained."

Detained? Ramona sat like a stone. She needed him here! A stupid mountain could wait.

"But mother nature is about to blow. Speaking of mother, I appreciate your virginal position, Ramona, considering the morals of these liberated women today. Up to a point. However, I must communicate this to you in person.

"I want you, I need you, I may erupt without you, woman.

"From the crater, Rodney."

Ramona let the air seep out of her plentiful lungs. She flushed the toilet, furious at Rodney's copouts. She flushed again and again.

Then she realized he needed her. She got down on the cool tiles. "Rodney, forgive me. I do understand about your career. After all, I have one of my own."

She stood up and wiped her knees, suddenly knowing what to do. She would go and be with Rodney at the volcano. How silly to be jealous of mother nature, when she could join her instead.

And what could be better than Hawaii, a hotbed of volcanic rock? That is where Rodney was, wasn't it?

146

*Racing back to the house phone, Ramona booked a flight to Diamond Head that night.*

The phone rang on Claire's desk just as Ramona received her boarding pass. Damn.

Claire stuffed her manuscript in a plain brown envelope. Now where could she go hide to work on this?

Of course. The ladies' room.

She snuck down to the handicapped stall of the restroom. Nobody saw her go in. Good. She sat on the toilet and spread *Forbidden Fruit* on her lap. Perfect.

*It was a long flight to Hawaii, but thoughts of Rodney kept Ramona awake. As she deplaned, a swarthy native attempted to horn in and yoke a lei around her neck. She deftly ducked his aboriginal kiss, which landed on the passenger behind her, a nun, who religiously kissed back.*

*Hurrying to the nearest hotel, Ramona checked the register for Rodney's name. No listing there, although he could have signed up incognito. Many do. Anyway, he would be off at the volcano.*

*A tour bus was pulling out, and she raced for it and leaped aboard.*

*The view as they circled up the mountain was magnificent. On the beach below the white-lipped waves sucked up to the tourist-dotted sand, spitting up seashells as indiscriminately as hickies were being implanted on the necks of the promiscuous sunbathers there.*

*The Aloha Mobile pulled in to a pit stop, and as the other passengers debused and rushed for the restrooms, Ramona raced up the hill.*

*There he was! She would recognize those blue jeans bending over in the palm fronds anywhere.*

"Rodney I'm here, I've come," Ramona sang, yanking off her spike heels and scrambling up to him. "Forgive me for thinking you were a cold-hearted climatologist when you were just doing your job." She planted her arms around his cuddly waist, more cuddly than she'd remembered, in fact. Hawaiian fruits must have calories in them after all. "It's OK that you left me for a volcano." She buried her face in the back of his familiar white tee shirt and stroked his blue-black hair, which had grown out unbelievably.

He swung around. And he now had a moustache. Ramona gasped, seeing that his teeth had changed also. The overbite was definitely not Rodney's. Neither was this person's breath, smelling of fermented fruit.

"Don't touch me," she shrieked, recoiling from the impostor (although the dimple in his interracial chin might turn some women on). "You aren't Rodney! I'm looking for my true love, who is here on Vesuvius training to become a top volcanologist."

The annoying native stepped back. "Vesuvius? No place by that name here, lady."

"Well, I'm still a queen," she snapped.

Back at the tourist information booth they informed her that Hawaii's volcano was Kilauea. Supposedly Vesuvius was located in Italy, Europe.

Boy, was her high school geography teacher a flop.

Ha, but no little detour would hold her back. After a quick stop at the Luaus 'R' Us gift shop, where she picked up some Hawaiian briefs for Rodney, Ramona boarded the next flight to Rome. The Vatican was there, wasn't it? And if the Pope and his pontiffs couldn't help her find her true love, maybe the mafia could.

So what if she hadn't been to mass for years. Those priests don't know squat about confessions of love. All

148

*the Hail Marys up their sleeves couldn't make a dent in the anguish brought on by romance.*

*But all that would be behind her soon. She would meet Rodney on the mountain, present him with his aloha wear, and then . . .*

Claire stopped in the middle of the sentence, a writer's technique to give yourself a jump start the next day. And embracing her note pad, she swept out of her "handicapped" quarters, gratified by her day's work.

Good heavens, it was after five o'clock.

Holly met her in the hall. "Claire, I've been looking for you. Did they bring you those chapters of the proposal to proof?"

"Why, no," Claire said. "I haven't seen a soul."

# 24

# *Delivering the Proposal*

"Leonard, don't bother me." Holly kept on typing as he huffed up with his whiskers growing out from being in the office all night. "The proposal *is* due this afternoon. So you can forget that Red Team review business." Everybody in Special Projects had worked all night. Rita pranced around with her hair in rollers to show that she didn't get her sleep. Even Claire Whittle was in her office working away on something.

But the proposal still wasn't done, at least not BelCon's part. And the subcontractors were not thrilled with Bill dragging his feet. He just laughed and told Dr. Rodman and the former nun, Wanda, that "getting down to the wire is the name of the game in this business."

"So, you like the cover?" Bill came down the hall proudly holding up the laminated *Last Supper,* an excellent job done by Graphics. The apostles' outfits were high-lighted in vivid mustard and burgundy shades. And they

150

looked starved as they reached out for BelCon's special bread.

"Impressive," Holly answered.

Leonard came up pestering them for something to do. He thought the chocolate chunks in the bread looked like raisins. "Easy, Pudding," Bill said. "Holly, do you have anything finished to give Leonard to calm him down?"

She looked up from the K-2000 at the bickering men. "With all these interruptions? Anyway, you promised you'd give everything to Claire Whittle first."

"Uh, yea," Bill muttered. "OK. Go ahead and run the boilerplate by her for a quick proofread."

Holly gladly got up to deliver it personally to their editor.

*Ramona looked up from Air Italy's flight 911 to Rome at the shimmering wing of the plane that appeared to flutter, either that or she was having palpitations for Rodney.*

*"Remain calm," the pilot's voice came over the intercom, no doubt a recording, as he repeated himself deadpan—while the aircraft lurched and pitched from cloud to cloud, causing children to whimper and adults to cry out for their last drinks.*

*The plane plummeted wildly, spilling Ramona from her seat belt into the rib cage of the blue-eyed stranger next to her, who introduced himself into her ear as they careened towards the earth. "I'm Cliff."*

*Thump, the aircraft miraculously made contact with the Italian soil in one piece. Still, it was another delay keeping her from Rodney, all because of a faulty fan belt, as it turned out.*

*"Don't get any ideas," Ramona told Cliff, taking his hands off her as they deplaned. "I have a true love, thank*

*you. He's a volcanologist, on Vesuvius now—which could erupt at any time."*

"Claire?"

She looked up. Holly Prickle was standing there. What an unusual color for a blouse. Gooseberry. Claire had forgotten to put that on her list of fruits. She added it now.

"Here's the boilerplate," Holly said. "The technical sections still aren't done. And the proposal is due at 3:15."

"So it is," Claire murmured. "Say, Holly, tell me about this new man in your life, Laurence LeFever, is that his name? It's nice. And what does he do that is romantic?"

"Well," Holly came in Claire's office and sat down, "our first kiss was in a pet cemetery, standing on a seeing-eye dog's grave. It's silly, but I actually get those skipped beats you hear about when I like a man. I'm a known fool for men, it's true. But Laurence is different. Really. Can you believe a man who *enjoys* doing housework?"

"Not silly at all," Claire said, writing something down. "This is good stuff."

"Well, I better get back," Holly said. "Sorry we didn't get the whole proposal to you."

"No problem," Claire answered.

Holly stopped at Ned's office to see if he'd come back. Nope. And where was Rita? Then she saw him down in the parking lot, getting out of his Volvo and marching towards the building with his head leading the way.

Ned's family was also getting out of the car. His two daughters, dressed in matching navy jumpers, followed along. Ned's wife held to the son's hand, but he got away and ran after his father.

Holly waited by Ned's door as he came up the stairs. But when she heard him in a hot conversation with his wife, she ducked into the supply closet across the hall.

152

"Ned," Mrs. Bird said tightly, as she and the children followed him into his office, "you promised us a vacation this year." Ned sat down and started writing. "We want a commitment on that now," his wife continued, her voice low and shaking. "These children hardly know their father, with you working day and night in this place. Give us a vacation date, Ned. We want it now."

Ned kept on writing his minuscule words that ruined people's eyes. Then he scooped up his papers and barged out into the hall heading for the xerox room, with his wife trailing after him. And when Ned Bird makes his own copies, he is hot.

With his father out of the room, Ned Bird, Jr., went over to the window, putting his face against the glass. Careful. Don't leave a smudge. He stepped back and saw something on the shelf underneath, pushed to the back. The boy got it out. It was a picture of him.

The older sister came over to see. "Neddy, what's a picture of you doing here? Better put it back. Hurry, dad is coming." Ned Jr. shoved the picture back where he found it and darted to his seat before his father marched in, his mother, too.

Mrs. Bird sat down, stiff on the edge of the chair with her hands folded tightly. She faced her husband. "So. We're ready for your decision." This woman was the perfect dresser. She wore expensive beige colors that matched, and her streaked blond hair was never out of place. However, today a strand hung across her cheek that she didn't touch. "We aren't leaving this office until you firm up our plans."

(If Rita was any kind of a secretary, this is where she'd come in and save her boss.)

"All right," Ned said, gripping the papers in front of him. "We'll take the damn vacation whenever you say. Just as soon as they award this school lunch contract. But I can't get that transfer to the west coast you want if we don't win." He glared at the window, where rain pinged against the glass. It sounded like gravel, gravel thrown at him. "Infernal rain," he said, angrily biting his cuticle. "Now I *have* to get back to work," he informed his family, taking his pinky out of his mouth.

"Disney World," his wife said, from that place down in the throat where animals start to growl. Slowly she stood up. "We're taking these children to Disney World the day after they get out of school."

Ned's mechanical pencil stopped moving. "All right," he answered. "All right."

Holly took a breath and stepped into the office. "Hello, Mrs. Bird, and you kids. Ned, do you have any revisions ready for typing?" He scribbled a few more skimpy words then handed the page to her, getting a lonely look. Holly thanked him and got out of that family hotbed pronto.

Now who should come meandering down the hall but Rita with a crease mark on her cheek. "Ned's upset," Holly whispered. "And I'm going downstairs to check on Repro."

"It won't be open," Rita said and yawned. "You know those people."

"What a thing to say. It's after nine o'clock."

Unfortunately, Rita was right. Bonita, the head of Repro, hadn't come in yet. So Holly sat down on the floor and rested her head against the wall while she waited. That felt good, after a night on the K-2000.

Bonita's rattling keys brought her eyes open. "You're just the person I was looking for," Holly said, standing up. "We need to run off our proposal. Twelve copies. You know it's due this afternoon."

Bonita's black eyes didn't blink. "You've got to be signed up, same as everybody." Holly knew that. Bill had made the arrangements himself so there wouldn't be a foul-up.

Bonita shuffled over to check her roster. "Nope. It says Accounting is signed up for a deliverable report. The rules is written in that memo on the wall, first is first." She pointed to where the memo was tacked up, signed by John E. Johnson himself.

"You don't understand," Holly said, in a massaging voice. "We're talking about a *proposal*, not some report nobody reads." Bonita got a grape soda out of her tote bag and popped it open. "If we don't win these contracts, we won't have work," Holly reminded her. "You wouldn't want to lose your job."

"I could get another job as same as this," Bonita said, taking a swallow of her soda and rolling her eyes back.

"Of course you could. We all could. But would it be in such a nice facility, with trees out back? And they always have toilet paper in the bathroom," Holly pointed out. "Plus, *your* equipment here, Bonita, is state of the art." The soda stopped in front of Bonita's lips. "Do your kids eat the school lunch?" Holly added.

"Supposed to. Unless they'd rather be sneaking off to McDonald's."

"That's why we're improving the menus for them." Holly edged closer with her materials to be copied.

Bonita's eyes grew rounder. "You're fixing to run off food menus on this copier is what you're doing?"

"That's right. And I'll tell you our special ingredient," Holly said quietly. "You know your Bible, Bonita. *The Last Supper.* 'Give us this day our daily bread.'"

"You're making some fancy new bread, is it? I hope not with raisins in it. My kids, they won't eat the raisins."

155

"My boy Walter doesn't like them either. But he does like chocolate." She eased the proposal into Bonita's arms. They didn't hand it back.

"Chocolate, such as chocolate chips you're putting in the bread, to feed those kids?" Bonita asked. Her eyes were as shiny as hot fudge now.

"That's right, only better." Holly waited as Bonita moved over to the copier and put the papers in the tray. Her dark hand with its white inside reached for the switch and snapped it on. "Our special ingredient is chocolate chunks. They're highlighted on the cover, which shows *The Last Supper*, laminated."

Bonita's back was turned, and all she did was shrug. But the copier kept humming.

"You're a saint. And I'll bring you a sample of the bread. Fiona DeForrest and I pretested it. Delicious. Now I'll go tell Bill that everything is under control down here, also how cooperative you've been."

As Holly went out in the hall, thunder sounded. Wet wind slapped the windows, and the trees behind the building swayed. She barely started up the stairs when the lights went out, as if she'd tripped on the cord. She sank down in the darkness, hearing the awful sound of the machines dying out. "Please, God, not this." She bowed down on the good carpet. "Please let the power stay on long enough to run off our proposal. Your son's picture is on the cover, and looking so handsome."

She had barely spoken these words when miraculously the lights came back on. And the sound of the machines wheezing into operation again made her feel so glad she could have cried.

She picked the lint from the carpet off her lip and was just getting up when here came pressed pant legs down the stairs. It was Mr. Johnson.

156

Holly looked up at the clean white collar cutting into his pink neck, becoming the color of rhubarb. She couldn't believe that anybody who blushed that easily would be a rapist, as Fiona suspected he might be. Just because a person looks innocent doesn't mean that he is guilty.

Mr. Johnson's legs stopped. "Hello," he said. Then he hurried on down, swinging his attaché case with the lump in it.

"Hi," Holly answered, watching as he pushed out the front glass door to where a long white car was waiting in the handicapped zone. Then she hustled upstairs to tell Bill that the copier was working.

Holly paused at Claire's door but didn't bother her for their boilerplate, when she was obviously working as fast as she could.

*"The guy you go with is a volcanologist, on Vesuvius now, the lucky bugger?" Cliff carped to Ramona as they waited for their backup flight to Rome. "I'm only in medical school. Cardiology. I plan to specialize in skipped beats."*

*Ramona grabbed her chest. "I suffer from skipped beats myself. What do you recommend?"*

*"Aerobic exercise can help. But I know a better cure." He reached over and stroked Ramona's ring finger. "Do you like safe sex?"*

*She yanked her precious digit out of this potential surgeon's grasp. "You slime, stop that. Now if you'll excuse me, I'm going someplace where I can be alone."*

Holly caught Bill coming out of the men's room admiring an organization chart he'd doodled in there—which he wanted to add to the proposal at this hour.

"You're kidding," she said, amazed.

157

This was no ordinary pie chart, he explained, but a management concept based on King Arthur's round table. "Everybody will think they're in the loop," he said excitedly.

Holly stared at him. "You're crazy. The proposal is due in three hours. You do remember your little disaster when you came to BelCon."

Everybody knew the story. After working for months on his first proposal, Bill delivered it fifteen minutes late to the Pentagon and got BelCon disqualified. There were many such stories in the consulting business. One employee was flown to Nome, Alaska, to deliver a seventy-million-dollar bid his company was favored to win. He checked into the hotel early but didn't realize that Nome had rush-hour traffic. He didn't make it.

"Uh, right," Bill said, not smiling now. He folded his King Arthur seating chart into his pocket for another time.

*1:00*—Everybody was getting tense and thus pitching in to help. Even Rita got off her behind, at least to boss other people around. "Check the pagination." "Count the graphics." And they did discover that Leonard's person-hour matrix was missing (causing him to disappear to the men's room). So Bill had them plug in a matrix from another proposal.

*2.00*—Done! Now, just pack the copies and deliver them downtown. Going against traffic, there shouldn't be a problem.

But they couldn't find a box. Holly ended up in the basement supply room unloading toilet tissues from a carton that said *Squeeze Me*. Bill wouldn't mind. He would like that.

She thought of sweet Laurence. And tonight she got to celebrate with him.

158

*2:15*—They loaded the proposal into Bill's station wagon and headed down Route 66 in heavy rain.

*2:30*—A horrible sight up ahead. Stalled cars and a flashing police light. Bill sat tapping on his steering wheel for about one second, then he roared onto the emergency lane, passing the polite cars waiting. When he wanted to cut back in, he grinned and waved at the foreign moustached driver at the front of the line—who threw up his hands and let Bill do it. He didn't slow down after that, even to look for bodies as they passed the wreck.

*3:00*—They made it across the bridge into town, still with fifteen minutes to go. There they got stuck at a red light. They sat.

While they were waiting for the light to change, Holly noticed the construction site across the street. A muddy pond in the rain, with a billboard saying HUD. It looked like a playground, with a ramp leading to swings. But the swings didn't have any seats in them. "Remember that million-dollar mistake we made for HUD?" she asked. "Wasn't it a handicapped playground project?"

*3:05*—Bill didn't hear, lurching ahead as the light changed, acing out a metrobus as he rounded the corner and pulled up to the yellow brick building that was the United States Department of Agriculture.

*3:07*—No place to park or even double park here. They dodged a postal truck, with its big eagle eye glaring down at Bill as he stopped in front of a hydrant. "Guess the ball's in your court, pal," he said. By now it was raining so hard you could barely see the gray people moving on the sidewalk. "Sorry about that." Bill got out and unloaded the box of proposals into Holly's arms. "Sure you can handle this?"

"No problem," she answered. Her knees buckled momentarily, but this load was no heavier than groceries.

159

Oops, she'd stepped in the gushing gutter. Out she climbed, shook off her foot, and looked for the side entrance Fred Trisket said to use.

"Go for the jugular," Bill called as he got back in his station wagon. Holly balanced the box on the hydrant and gave him the thumbs-up sign as he splashed away. The rain was falling on her head, but the wind gushed at her back as she surged towards the government building that took up a block.

Her foot bumped something. She looked down. A man was lying on the ground in a cardboard box. She had stepped on a homeless person. "I am *so sorry*." An arm swatted at her, with the elbow poking through tweed threads. She stumbled out of the way, aiming for the revolving door ahead of her, keeping upright with her precious parcel.

She got inside with the kind help of a woman wearing a name plate on a chain around her neck, who stepped out of the way. The elevator across the hall was open. *Please don't close.* And that government door did not. Once Holly got inside the old-fashioned elevator, it didn't exactly leap into action either. Move. Hurry. Go. Her heart was beating against the box, and she didn't dare look at the watch on the male arm next to her. Two secretaries stood there complaining about the slow day they'd had.

*3:14*—She heaved out of the elevator and down the hall with her load, looking for the sight of Fred Trisket with his military haircut, his profile with ears that she recalled. She also remembered the rosary in his car, the dark shape against the white, and wished she had one of those rosaries now.

Hugging her copies of the laminated *Last Supper*, Holly staggered into the Food and Nutrition office, looking for a name plaque saying, yes, TRISKET, there it was. The man sitting behind it was wearing a blue suit, not his usual gray one, but it was him. "Mr. Trisket," she gasped, hoisting her soggy carton onto his desk.

"Yes."

She undid the top so he could see the custom-made BelCon covers with the ravenous disciples on them. His nostrils dilated, she was sure they did, as he picked up on the religious motif. He didn't say a word, but his head gave a little bow.

"I'm Holly Prickle. We talked on the phone," she said, wiping away the water dripping off her chin.

"Yes. Right. Holly." He stroked the box that said *Squeeze Me.* Fred Trisket, of the U.S. federal government, with a GS-11 rating but deserving his GS-13.

He gave a quick smile, though enough to show that he had teeth (more than Ned Bird revealed with his stingy lips). He looked up at the government clock. The big hand twitched and stopped at . . . 3:19. He checked his watch. He scowled. Holly's heart became a dried peach.

"All right," he said. "You can go tell my secretary Sara Lee that you checked in on time with me." He pointed to her desk, which was stacked with punctual proposals.

*"Thank you."*

Holly went over and loaded her wet box on Sara Lee's desk, who checked off BelCon's name on her roster.

They'd made it! Her arms were so free and glad she could have gone over and hugged nice Mr. Trisket on the spot in his best blue suit. But don't worry. She didn't. She usually had control of herself in these office situations.

On her way out, she did stop as she noticed the man at the desk next to Fred Trisket's. He was doing a crossword puzzle.

She backtracked and whispered to Fred that she didn't think it was fair for his colleague to waste the taxpayers' money playing games. It was obvious who did the work around here. Fred had a neat stack of outgoing mail, as opposed to his neighbor's incoming trash heap.

Fred was licking an envelope, and his tongue stopped on the flap. "You noticed," he said. "That's nice."

"They ought to appreciate you," Holly added. "Well, I've got to run. My boss will be waiting."

She soared outside and didn't wait long before Bill came splashing along in his station wagon to pick her up. "How did it go?"

"We made it," she sang, getting in.

"Good girl." He looked at her and smiled the finest smile she had ever seen. "Holly, you're a great gal."

She loved her job! The pouring rain! The people waiting at the bus stop, eager to get home after a day's work.

And soon she would be with Laurence.

Oh God. She'd almost forgotten just how special tonight's celebration was. She counted up how many times they had been together. Yes, this was their third date. So what if she hadn't gotten any sleep. New energy surged up in her for this evening's activities.

# 25

# *Love Ovens*

"Sweetheart, we'll celebrate by getting you a present in the mall." Laurence was waiting when Holly got home, one of those good government workers who arrives on time.

"We made it," she said, falling into his arms, sinking amidst his luscious aftershave. She told him about the wild ride in the rain to deliver the proposal. "But you don't need to buy me anything. Just let me get out of these wet clothes." Her shoes were soaked. They'd been tan that morning but were a different earth shade now. Well, maybe they'd match some other outfit she had. Who cared on a special night like this.

"You deserve something nice, Holly, after what they put you through. Your job description doesn't say you have to carry boxes. They can't make you do that," Laurence told her as they went upstairs to feed Warren.

"But it was exciting. I like being able to help," she answered, filling Warren's dish. The pinging sound brought him scrambling into the kitchen, bumping his fur

163

against her leg. It felt good. Watching Warren sniff up to his meal and crunch those pellets with his healthy teeth made a person want to be an animal.

Laurence found a drumstick in her fridge and gnawed on it. "I just hope they give you a raise for this. What you should do, Holly, is get a job with the government." He held up a chicken wing, stared at the scrawny meat on it, and dropped it in the trash. "They won't abuse you; everything is federally regulated. If you worked at Interior with me, we could go shopping on our lunch hour."

Holly looked at him. "But I love the job I have. And I'm up for a promotion. It isn't just the money."

"I'm not a materialistic person, either," Laurence said, wiping his hands on her dish towel. "You ready to go to the mall? I can't wait to buy you something."

She wouldn't mind putting her feet up for a minute. Yet the eager look in Laurence's beautiful eyes wasn't something you poured water on. "Sure," she said, perking up at the thought of what he might buy her. "You don't mind driving to the mall in rush-hour traffic?"

"Oh, no. I'm used to it."

The storm was over, and as they drove around the beltway the forsythia was in bloom, the first color, yellow, saying spring was here. Soon everything would be green, all green.

Holly lay back on the high seat of Laurence's van, looking up at the white clouds floating away, with pink sky coming through. He reached over and took her hand, and her heart nearly jumped out of her bra.

It was awkward getting across the bucket seat to him, but being tailgated by a gearshift was worth it to sit next to his good-smelling self. She slipped her finger under his collar to feel the smooth skin there. Then she leaned over

164

and kissed the back of Laurence's neck. The van gave a little bounce.

Gazing out his window, Holly saw a strange sight. It was a waterfall, coming out of the middle lane of traffic, golden arches here on the beltway.

"Laurence, slow down," she said, although she hurriedly looked away from the place where the stream was coming from. And she did not make eye contact with the man's laughing face, either. You might expect something like this in New York City. But not clean Washington, D.C.—where people don't drop an apple core in the subway, let alone their pants.

"What is it?" Laurence asked.

"That man, in the truck." She pointed as it zipped into another lane.

"A truck?" he said, holding out his bad ear.

But rather than explain in noisy words, Holly used her lips to kiss Laurence's poor deaf ear. Relief from this stressful day, and other warm feelings, were building up in her. "Laurence, could you pull over."

"Sweetheart, are you sick?" He pulled onto the emergency lane with a jolt. "It must be burnout, all the overtime you've been doing. It can make a person ill."

"I'm not sick, you silly man," she murmured, "just the opposite." They looked at each other, and then they were kissing.

When they stopped for air they both turned to the back of the van, admiring all that delicious space. It was plenty more than foot room. Holly couldn't believe she had never appreciated vans before.

"Will it be safe?" Laurence asked as he climbed out to get in the back.

"I wouldn't do this otherwise," Holly called out to him. Then using Walter's quickie method of getting in the back

165

seat, she barreled over the top. It was roomy back there, and like ninety-nine percent of the places where you can lie down, it felt wonderful.

"What if somebody stops?" Laurence whispered into her perm as they hugged on the warm floor of the van.

"Well, they can see we aren't wrecked. And I don't think we're abusing this emergency lane, either." The front of her blouse was about to burst.

Laurence responded with his soft lips, until their kissing caused the humidity in the van to increase considerably. "We're just a couple of love ovens." He smiled at her. "Honey, we better buy some bedding for back here. We could pick up a quilt in the mall tonight," he said excitedly, kissing her more wildly than ever, until her whole body could hear music.

As she stroked Laurence's clean and well-styled hair, she felt a bump on his scalp. He pulled away. "Sorry," he said. "That's where my ex-wife hit me. Louise got me with her purse." Holly picked up her pocketbook and threw it out of the way, wondering how anyone could hurt this kindly man.

"You're good to me," Laurence said. Then he kissed the back of her neck as she turned it to him, ever so gently, sending a quiver down to her tail. Holly let out a little squeal.

Then she heard another squeal. It was coming from behind them. You couldn't drive out on these roads one time without being hassled by the law.

She sat up stiff as a stump. It would be Eddie for sure this time, riding up to catch her here. She crawled across the hot van floor and retrieved her purse, tossing out a Kleenex, a Butterfinger wrapper, and digging in for her mascara. She checked her lipstick in the mirror. How much older did she look after three years?

Laurence combed himself and squirted some breath spray down his throat. Then as they tensely hovered in the back of the van awaiting questioning, they saw one of the great sights of this world—a patrol car flashing past you to catch the speeder up ahead.

After being spared, they joyfully headed for the mall. Laurence whistled as he found a parking place next to Bloomingdale's. He practically danced around the van to let her out, surprisingly speedy for a man who didn't jog or even do major walking because of problems with his arches. Jauntily Laurence guided her into the store, past the perfumes, and on up the escalator to the more expensive floors that he said she deserved.

They didn't stop in women's ready-to-wear. Darn. However, towels make nice gifts, too, Holly thought, as they approached bathroom furnishings. But to her surprise Laurence didn't stop there, either. He hurried on to housewares, arriving at the gleaming pans, pausing to caress his favorite, copper. "But I'm not a selfish person; we didn't come to buy for me." He guided her over to crock pots (please, don't remind her of stew). "How about a Cuisinart?" he asked, pointing to the contraption that reminded her of a garbage disposal.

Holly looked down into the blades and prongs that take hours to wash. "Oh no, it's too extravagant. Just let me look around." Then while Laurence was checking on a stainless steel ice chest, she slipped over to a counter of cutlery. What she really needed was a good paring knife. A very sharp little knife.

She found a model that felt good in her hand and approached Laurence with it. "I couldn't buy such a cheap gift for my girl," he said. "How about this deluxe knife sharpener? Isn't it a beauty."

"But I don't have all that much to sharpen."

"Or, look at this." Laurence guided her over to a pot with a dome lid on it, where their heads swole up in the reflection like balloons. "Holly, you need a wok."

"A what?"

"A wok. It's for making Chinese food. Stir fry. Look, this one's a combination model. It has a skillet and a steamer for vegetables. You could cook gourmet tonight. A sweet girl like you wouldn't give her man frozen micro-wave dinners, I know."

"I guess not," Holly murmured. "But it is an awfully big pan. I don't know where I'd put it."

"I buy the best. And see what it says: 'This all-in-one vessel suits virtually all your cookware needs.'"

Holly walked around the arching pot, the wok. "Does it make egg rolls?"

"Anything you want. And I'll keep it polished." Laurence took out his checkbook. "Don't worry, it won't bounce," he told the clerk. "I get paid by the government on Monday, and they're reliable. My check will clear by then. I always do it this way. Isn't that right, Holly?" Laurence called cheerfully over to where she was investi-gating barbecue tongs.

"I believe you," she called back, for she had never known him to lie.

Laurence carried the wok out on his shoulder, a trophy hoisted up. "Isn't this fun. I feel like we're married already. And I do want to remarry, don't you, Holly?" he said as they stepped on the escalator.

The moving floor picked up her foot, almost throwing her. She supposed she might get married again sometime. Still, the only husband she could imagine was Eddie, even if he had been a dud.

That word *marriage* did put her in a daze as they shopped, and it wasn't a bad feeling. According to the women's magazines, the men of today will not commit. And certainly not this soon. Well, they hadn't met Mr. LeFever, had they.

"I would be a faithful husband to you, Holly. I'll do all the housework, you know I will. Our bathroom fixtures will be immaculate year-round," he promised as they left the store, with the clerk waiting to lock up.

Laurence proudly put the wok in the back of the van, along with the king-size paisley comforter he'd also found in Bloomingdale's. "Can we get in the back again?" he asked her with shining eyes.

Holly took one look and said, "You bet." She smiled and jumped in.

And if you think Laurence was romantic parked in the emergency lane of the beltway, that was nothing compared to his passionate nature that emerged inside the paisley comforter as they stretched out next to the new wok.

Yes, they did celebrate to the fullest extent possible on this occasion in the back of the roomy van, with a view of Bloomingdale's.

And as they lay there, it wasn't in their imagination that they heard church bells ringing at that moment. They pealed out from the chapel next door to Tyson's Corner, conveniently located for shoppers exiting the mall who might wish to pause and give thanks for life's many blessings.

"Holly, we are so compatible," Laurence said, hugging her to him inside the comforter. "And I'll be the same when we're married as I am now. I'll be a good stepfather to Walter, too. So—when should we tell him about us, sweetheart, this weekend?"

# 26

# *Volcano*

Claire gave a grateful sigh as Jack left for the hardware store on a hot Saturday morning in May. He was going to get a part for their broken air conditioner. And, bless him, he liked to shop alone.

As the door clicked shut, she hurried to her Macintosh, brought up the smiling face on the screen, and opened the file for *Forbidden Fruit.*

*Mount Vesuvius was hotter than an oven as Ramona climbed, quaking with the thought that she, the Tangerine Queen, must trudge up a molten mountain to apologize to a virtual stranger. But if he's your true love you must. The skipped-beat specialist she'd met on the plane couldn't compare with Rodney, although he was cute.*

*Suddenly Ramona stopped, glued to the ground as she spied a clue proving that Rodney had been here. It was a used stick of the dynamite he took along to volcanoes as a backup plan. "When nature drags her feet, a little TNT can knock the pants off her," he had told her. She listened for* detonations, but all she could hear was the sizzle from the deep throat of the crater.

Or was that the sound of her broken air conditioner? No, Jack had turned it off. Claire wiped her wet face. Just her imagination working. Good.

*As the hours wearily wore on, Ramona's Reeboks were wearing out. The soles had melted down until the tread was gone. Rodney deserved to be a top volcanologist coming to work in these conditions. Plus, making the earth move is not an easy task.*

*As Ramona approached the summit, the ground began to shake.* Boom! *A boulder shot out of the top, hurtling over a cliff and bounding down directly in her path. It must be a message from Rodney saying hi.*

*She dodged the rolling rock and responded by throwing back a handful of gravel as far uphill as she could. The only answer was steam hissing out of a huge pothole, a sound that reminded her of the depressing substandard housing project she was forced to visit as a queen. A piece of pumice landed at her feet, and she snatched it up for Rodney. Ouch. She let it cool and then dropped it in her shopping bag, which also contained the undershorts she'd bought for him, embossed with coconuts. She did enjoy shopping for a man.*

*Hours passed, and Ramona climbed. Then through the fumes, interspersed by tongues of flame, she saw a sight that made her heart skip more than one beat.*

*There, with his magnificent male shoulders chiseled against the sky, tapering down to his fine-tuned male hips (and perfect buns, which she would grab if she were lower class), Rodney sat.*

171

*"Oh, love,"* she cried, stumbling forward. Then she began to slide back down the precipice, barely saving herself by clinging to a fortuitous twig. Otherwise, her life and this relationship would have been taillights.

*"Ramona? Is that really you?"* Rodney set his laptop computer down and bounded over to where she hung.

*"Rodney, forgive me for getting mad,"* she pleaded into his igneous eyes as he hoisted her up. *"I know you only want to advance in your career, the same as every-body else."*

*"No problem,"* he said in a voice drowning with passion and volcanic fumes. Hot magma rose in her.

He took her in his molten arms, and they fell to the scalding earth, drawn by the magnetism of a gravitational breast bigger than both of them. Stroking her auburn hair spread out on the scorched ground, Rodney murmured, *"And I always pictured myself with a blonde."*

*"I could be,"* Ramona answered responsively.

*"Your hair is fine in its place,"* he whispered duskily, tracing her dove-white neck with his charred fingertips, then moving up to the high cheekbones that encased her remote control, Ramona's brain.

*"Relieve me of this pressure,"* he pleaded. *"Experience the eruption of my body, now."*

The earth heaved under them, spewing hot ash that fell like acid rain on their writhing forms, causing Ramona's off-white shirtwaist, although it washed well, to show the dirt profusely now. *"Forget your rules, Ramona. When will you stop being forbidden fruit?"* he moaned, crushing her to him.

*"But my virginity is my identity. A nice girl saves herself for the man she marries, or at least someone who cares."* And she deserved to give of herself on the satin sheets of a bridal suite, certainly not the sordid ground.

172

Rodney rolled over hotly on his back. "Being a tease is not a pretty sight, Ramona. You shouldn't lead a guy on this way. It's like holding a glass of that damn orange juice up to a parched man's lips and—"

"Tangerine, I'm the Tangerine Queen—"

"And pouring it in his lap," he said sarcastically.

"Rodney, it's not that I don't care. Here, see," and Ramona handed him the shopping bag with his aloha wear, unfortunately with a charred hole in it now. "But you don't consider a woman as a person. All you care about is her bod—"

She was interrupted by the roar of the volcano regurgitating filthy billows that snuffed out the last rays of light. "Rodney?"

"Ramona," he called back, "All right, I think I . . ."

"What? What do you think, darling?" she cried, loving Rodney's mind.

"I think I . . . care for you," he said faintly, hidden in the sooty air. "Now get me off this roller coaster ride."

Her heart skipped several beats. "And I care for you," she groaned, reaching out to touch him.

But the day had turned to night, with no chance to seize it or even to see him. And this wasn't your everyday dark and stormy night but the utter darkness of a supply closet without a door.

Well, she would find a way out of this black hole somehow. Nothing on the earth or inside it could keep Ramona from her true love now.


The door clicked open. Claire jumped up. "Jack. You're back from the hardware store. Oh, Jack, it's so good to see you," she said and embraced him.

# 27

# *Roller Coaster*

Holly heard Walter pound the door and ran to get it. Then she stopped, afraid. But no. Eddie never delivered his son in person. She opened the door. "Walter, just you, oh good." She hugged her favorite human in the world to hug, not that any hug is bad, unless you hate the person.

They were going away for the weekend, just the two of them, since Laurence had been called on an emergency fact-finding mission out to the Dakotas. Walter was studying Thomas Jefferson in school, and she was taking him to Monticello for the hands-on experience the teacher praised. This would also give her a chance to tell Walter that she and Laurence were engaged.

"I've missed you, honey, with that hay fever grounding you for the last two weeks." Holly looked into Walter's eyes, but they didn't look watery to her. Supposedly he'd been affected by the high pollen count here in Washington in the spring. There are so many blossoms that people cry.

Well, Walter's "hay fever" hadn't come from her side of the family. He must have picked it up from the shrubbery

174

on his father's property. Eddie never had learned the first thing about plants from her father, although that is where she'd met Eddie, in her dad's nursery, The Green Hand. Seaman Prickle walked in with his dark sexy eyes looking for something that wouldn't die.

Maybe Walter's so-called allergy didn't result from foliage at all. You didn't see him sneezing in her apartment with all the plants here. It was probably a reaction to the excessive vegetation on the dinner table at his father's place.

"Hi, mom." Walter dropped the ball he was carrying and tapped it with the inside of his foot across the room into a fern, knocking a brown frond on the rug.

"You don't do that with a kickball in the house." Holly went over and picked up the debris.

"It's not a kickball. It's for soccer. That's what everybody plays, even the girls. You want to learn, mom? We could stop at the field on our way tomorrow."

"Maybe briefly. But it's a long way to Monticello."

Walter lay down on the rug and perched the ball on his forehead. "Can we go to the movies tonight, please, the barforama?"

"What is it?"

"A barforama. They're showing all the movies with barfing in them." Walter rolled the ball down his body and balanced it on his knee, spinning it, making her dizzy.

"That's sick, people buying tickets to watch somebody throw up. Can't we just go to a normal cop show or something?" Holly said, fanning herself.

"First you say you hate violence," Walter complained, "then you want to see cop shows."

Holly went in the kitchen and got her watering can. She hadn't realized she did that. "Well, in real life officers aren't necessarily violent," she reminded him, returning to

175

her plants. "Most policemen go their whole lives without using a gun, you know. Your father often mentioned it. Besides, police violence in the movies is nothing compared to the gore of those horror shows you like—people's faces turning into wolves, slime oozing out of the walls. What is it with this slime, Walter?"

"It's neat stuff. Heh, did dad tell you he's getting a promotion on the force?" Walter said. He held his ball still.

Water leaped out of her can and drenched the cactus, the least greedy plant she had. "Well, isn't that nice for him. But men do get promotions easier. It's practically automatic. At least when your father is rolling in money, maybe he'll buy you some decent clothes. Look at those Levis." They were ripped all across the legs, with threads hanging down.

Walter lifted his leg and bent it to make his knee come through. "Mom, lighten up. This is how they make them." His foot thumped back on the floor. Then he picked up a comic book with a lime green monster on the front and hid behind it. What *do* kids see in horror?

"Have you heard about yours, mom?" he asked from behind his monster face.

"My what?"

"Your promotion. As if you didn't talk about it all the time."

"It isn't just talk." Holly gave her tiger fern a shot of mist that went too far and wet the wall. Shoot. "OK, now, let's discuss our trip to Monticello."

"That weird guy LeFever isn't coming, I hope. It was gross, him crawling in a pet cemetery looking for nonexistent gerbils."

"Maybe they biodegraded. And he is a caring man." Holly smiled to herself thinking of Laurence's lips, his whole affectionate body in the back of the van. "But, no,

176

he isn't coming with us. Mr. LeFever is traveling out to the Dakotas for Interior."

"Yahoo. But if he's so great, how come you don't even call him by his first name?" Walter rolled his comic book into a telescope and peered up at her through it.

"I do, too, call him Laurence," Holly said, finding it impossible to make eye contact through a tube. "Never Larry, though. We both think that name is low. At least you should appreciate the nice gifts he's given you, Walter."

"A cashmere scarf for a kid in the fourth grade, when the weather's hot? Give me a break. Now, come on. You said we could go to the movies."

The next morning Holly's body was in no mood to chase a soccer ball—not after a night of dreaming about people upchucking cherry pits into her potted plants. But she had told Walter she would, so they stopped at the playing field on their way to Monticello.

"Use your instep," he called across the slippery grass as he whacked the soccer ball to her, whereas she insisted that toes were made for kicking. She tried to follow Walter's instructions but slid on her Reeboks and splatted on the ground, staining her clean jeans.

Walter also claimed that you weren't supposed to use your hands in this sport. He said to pretend that hers were tied. And they call this a game? He kicked a high one to her. "Bounce it off your head," he shouted, "or your chest."

That was it. "We're going to Monticello now."

"OK, think historical," Holly said as they drove. "And this is no little excursion to Mount Vernon where everybody goes—and I promise we won't be visiting again, nothing against George Washington. But Thomas

177

Jefferson's place is more of a family home, since he did have children of his own." Good, here was her chance to bring in Laurence. Holly put a Life Saver in her mouth and sucked on it. "Walter, wouldn't it be nice if we lived in more of a . . . family environment ourselves?"

"Heh, look," he said as they came to a sign for King's Dominion. "Can we stop here, please? For just one ride?"

"We always go to amusement parks. It's time to expand your horizons, son. To grow." Meanwhile, Walter's hands were expanding around hers on the steering wheel and guiding them onto the King's Dominion exit.

"Oh, all right," she gave in. "But just one ride. Then no more stops until we get to Monticello," she said as they drove in.

"One safe ride," she called, as Walter barreled off through the parking lot heading for his favorite roller coaster. They tell you these rides are safe. But would a roller coaster called the Dragon Tongue put you at ease? She could barely look at the contraption rearing in the air and keep her dinner down. It circled around in a complete loop with no concept of gravity. Plus, she wasn't exactly receptive to any reptile the day after attending a barforama.

Holly watched to see that Walter made it through the turnstiles. Then she went over with people milling around looking the other way. She barely got there when her favorite voice called from behind her, "Mom?"

She turned around, sure she'd given him enough money. "Walter?" He was waving at her, leaning over the railing with his dark hair, and looking so much like his father she couldn't stand it. "Come ride it with me, mom. It'll be fun." Holly looked up with narrowed eyes at train tracks rising in the sky.

"All the other kids have somebody to ride with," he called out to her. And if there's one thing that makes you feel like a lousy parent, it's having your child be deprived. Poor Walter, with no brothers or sisters to play with (and his father not likely to produce any). "You'll stretch your horizons, mom. You'll grow," he hollered. He was a rotten kid.

She stepped away from the sight of mustard being squirted on a hot dog next to her. "Oh, all right, I'm coming," she muttered. And keeping her head down, she marched towards Dragon Tongue.

"Great," Walter said, bounding over as she walked up the plank to buy a ticket for this skydive to her death. "There's nothing to be afraid of. They strap you in. And the centrifugal force will keep you in your seat." Naturally, she was proud of her son using fancy words when it came to parents' day at school. But having him get brainy on her at a theme park was not cute.

They were herded in a line, and Holly said goodby to the good world. They sat down on hard seats, and a bar was locked across their laps. So how were you supposed to get out in an emergency? She looked down to see how these seats were fastened to the floor. Little bolts, no bigger than nails!

A whistle screeched, and she sat stiff as a pole. She moved her toes and found that she could lift them off the floor. So what was to keep your body from flying out?

The rails started moving under them, and the tracks climbed up in the sky, if you like looking at that type of thing. She would never live to get her promotion now, never see her son grow up.

Whoosh, they took off from the ground. "Yahoo," Walter hollered. Holly looked over at this stranger next to her squirming around to wave at the children behind him, who were also laughing ridiculously. With Walter in a great mood, this would be the time to tell him she was getting

179

married. However, when your stomach is going like a Cuisinart, the right words might not come out.

The riptide was coming up in her, rising to her neck brace, and her legs were hooked to the ceiling of the cubicle. She hung to the handlebars with her eyes shut, wondering where in life she had gone wrong.

Suddenly, her head yanked into place, and she noticed it was still fastened to her body. They had landed back on the ground, on her favorite planet, earth.

"Mom, wasn't that great?"

"I'm . . . sure it was, dear." She smiled weakly.

"But you had your eyes closed the whole time. If we rode it again, you could look this time."

"Walter, no way." They stepped out on the platform. It felt firm enough, and her knees began to gel. She looked down at the parents waiting on the safe pavement for their children, the scaredy cats. Well, they'd certainly missed an opportunity. Holly smiled. She waved.

"So, can we ride it again, please, please?"

She looked into the black eyes of her child. "Don't be absurd. We're going to Monticello now."

"In the rain?" Walter held out his arm to prove that drops were falling.

"Did a little rain water stop the great Mr. Jefferson from building his mansion, or practicing his violin in it? Storms are a natural occurrence, son, even if we didn't learn that living in southern California."

They drove off in the sprinkle, although the clouds up ahead were black, and cars coming from that direction had their lights turned on.

Drops splatted on the window, big slow drops at first. Then they got faster, smacking the roof of the car, pocketa, pocketa. Little white balls bounced off the hood. And the news on the radio announced a hurricane warning.

"A real hurricane? Neat. Can we drive into it, mom?"

By now she couldn't see the road. However, she did realize that a natural disaster was an educational experience for Walter—and one his father couldn't provide on the pansy plane rides they took.

The windshield wipers worked desperately, but the glass barely got cleared before it became a stream again. A river gushed around their wheels. All she could do was keep her eyes on the blurry taillights ahead of them and hope they didn't lead into a ditch. "Honey, we may have to stop and visit Monticello tomorrow," she told Walter. "I'm sorry. We could discuss Thomas Jefferson in the room."

"That's cool. Can we watch TV?"

"I guess we'll have to. You look for a motel."

Walter spotted a blinking sign for the Shiloh Inn, and they got the last room in the sleazy place. It was artificial brown brick, as compared to snazzy Williamsburg-type resorts with pillars where other parents take their kids.

Still, she'd never been in a motel she had hated yet. All the clean towels, white sheets, and nobody watching you. And when you tear off that paper wrapped around the toilet, you're starting a whole new adventure every time.

Walter turned on the television while she went in and took a hot bath, lying back in the steam, looking at the faucets, thinking of Laurence. She had to tell Walter about their engagement soon. She would do it tonight over a nice dinner, put him in a good mood with a pizza.

But who would deliver in a hurricane? They ended up having junk food from the shop at the Shiloh Inn, which they ate lying on the bed, aiming the wrappers around the room. Bingo, a Snickers whacked the lamp shade.

"You poor kid, not even getting a decent meal on your vacation," Holly apologized, picking a corn chip off the bedspread and munching it.

"No problem." Walter wadded the Dorito bag in a ball and socked it to the ceiling. She should be teaching him manners here instead of joining in with these garbage disposal tactics. But this was her vacation, too.

OK. Time for her son's education. She picked a piece of red licorice out of her teeth and asked him to recite the sayings of Mr. Jefferson.

"There's the 'pursuit of happiness' bit," Walter said, opening an Oreo cookie and licking off the frosting.

"Thomas Jefferson said that? I love this man."

"Mom, you're funny. And everybody knows 'All men are created equal.'"

That sounded good, too. However, it had no relation to the men she'd known. "Do you think men are created equal, Walter?"

"I guess. Not in sports, though."

"That's right. Not everybody is born to be a bully. Some men are quite sensitive." Ah, she could bring Laurence into the conversation here. During the next commercial break, she definitely had to tell Walter they were getting married.

My but those commercials go by in a hurry.

And if you bring up a disturbing topic before bedtime, a child will have bad dreams. Especially on a vacation, who wants to hear those words, "We have to talk." Never in the history of the world has that been good.

Anyway, they had all day tomorrow. So she stretched out with Walter for a relaxing evening of TV, as the wind rattled the windows and water poured down the panes.

Then in about a minute, the lights went out. And this time they didn't come back on.

So this meant she had to tell Walter now that he was getting a stepfather. Actually, it would be easier in the dark.

"Walter?"

"Yea?"

"There is something I've been going to mention. Or we could review Thomas Jefferson's beliefs first. Take that pursuit of happiness idea." Holly smiled in the dark, thanking the great Mr. Jefferson for his fine thoughts. "Think of those wonderful words, 'the pursuit of happiness.' And I know you want your mother to have a happy life, and to create a nice home for you."

"Uh-huh," Walter answered.

"On the other hand, you won't always be with me. And it isn't easy to find a companion you can trust. They are rare birds, believe me. You know the person I'm referring to. And Laurence isn't one of those men addicted to sports on television who won't budge. He likes to go out, say, to the mall at any time. Laurence also encourages my career; he definitely wants me to work. And you've been the one, Walter, wanting to get his ferret together with Warren. Now you'll have your chance." Whew, she'd made it through her whole presentation, and he hadn't said one rude thing. "Walter?"

She could hear him breathing, softly snoring now. Almost the sound of a man.

Holly lay back looking into the darkness, feeling a strange peace. Here they were stranded in a dingy motel, with a hurricane flooding the parking lot, and no TV. But she got to be with Walter. And he didn't seem to mind this trip. *So why not keep on going?* Go live somewhere else, just the two of them. You just put your child in the car and go. She'd heard people on talk shows tell how they did it.

Look, she *was* Walter's mother.

The next morning the sky was clear, and the air had that clean smell that makes you want to leap in your car and drive across a state line.

"Walter, get out the map and see what state comes next."

"North Carolina," he said, without unfolding it.

That didn't sound far enough. "What about Florida? You've always liked the water." Walter was an adaptable child, who could make friends anywhere, such as on the roller coaster yesterday. And as Holly realized she'd ridden the dreaded Dragon Tongue herself, she felt so proud.

"Mom, you wouldn't be trying to . . . kidnap me, would you?"

"What a word to use, Walter. Children often go on extended trips with one parent." And those childnappers she'd seen on TV gave advice about how to avoid the law, and their spouses. *Don't let your child out of your sight. Remain anonymous.* If we did relocate somewhere, Walter, you might have to use another name for a while. It could be anything you wanted. What name would you pick?"

Walter scraped on the window, F-R-E-D-D-Y.

"That creepy maniac? How digusting. Hmm, Freddy Prickle. At least you would rhyme with your father."

She slowed down. She could hear a siren in the distance. "Walter, can you hear that?"

"No, mom. Dad isn't chasing you all the way down here, or at home, either."

"I guess you're right. Son, will you promise me something when you grow up?"

"Here we go again. Wow, look," and Walter pointed to a branch torn off and lying in the road. "It really was a hurricane. We could have gotten creamed in our motel."

Holly carefully drove around a rolling garbage can and made it up onto the interstate, which some people think is a boring road but she did not. "We are blessed, Walter, so blessed. Now, as I was saying, when you grow up I want

184

you to promise me one thing: that you will be a good husband."

"Mom, I'm only nine." He stuck his head out the window and made the gagging sound she detested. "I don't even like girls," he hollered.

"Come back in here. You will. You'll marry some cute little thing, they always do. But at least I hope you stay with her."

"I don't believe we're having this conversation." Walter turned on the radio to rock music. "This is supposed to be a vacation."

"I know, honey." She lowered the volume. "But just let me finish this one idea. When a marriage breaks up, it's the children who suffer. You know they do. Walter, can you forgive me for being a bad mother, that you came from a broken home?" Tears burned in her eyes, coming out of nowhere on this happy trip. And if your child sees you cry he'll be insecure. Thinking of that made her cry more.

Walter patted her arm. "It's no big deal. Everybody's parents at school are divorced."

"No big deal?" Holly blew her nose. "That's easy for you to say. You're just the child."

"You're getting crazy here," Walter told her, edging up the volume of his awful heavy metal.

"I know I've done things that bug you, son. Go ahead, tell me what I've done. Communicate with me," Holly said loudly, over the music. She dabbed her eyes, getting black gobs of mascara on the Kleenex, and who knows what all smeared on her face. Well, if your kid's seen one, they've seen them all.

"OK. It bugs me when you flip for a dork like that LeFever guy," Walter told her. "It's embarrassing."

Holly stuffed her tissue in her purse and zipped it shut. "You just aren't old enough to appreciate Laurence's good

185

qualities. He's a kind person. He cleans the bathroom. And he smells good. Now back to your suffering, Walter. I know that you have scars. And I realize I've been a bad mother. All you get is store-bought cookies, although they are getting tastier, don't you think? But I never nagged you to eat spinach—or broccoli, did I?"

"You never even served broccoli, mom. The first time I tasted it was over at my friend's. It wasn't that bad."

"Not bad, that big plant? Walter, what kind of a child are you?" Holly shrieked. "I was just trying to make your life enjoyable and avoid unpleasant memories. It's called the 'pursuit of happiness,' if you will recall, in your own words. Green is made to look at. The trees. Bushes. God knows what He is doing in the out of doors. So now you inform me you've been craving awful broccoli all your life. I've been such a failure, Walter," she said, and the tears gushed out.

Walter touched her hand. "You're fine. I always liked you."

Breath came into her throat. He'd said the word *like*. Children aren't forced to tell you that. *Love*, sure. They write it on the Mother's Day cards they make at school with the teacher watching (not that Holly hadn't mounted every one). She turned the radio off.

"Yea. You're fun," he said.

"And of all the boys in the world, Walter, I would pick you for a son," she said softly. She had imagined how it would be to tell an adopted child that you chose him from all the babies (when your real child probably wouldn't believe it). But there was never enough that you could tell your real son.

"So, mom, what happened to you and dad?"

Holly sat there in the quiet, wishing now that she'd left the radio on. "He did go to Vietnam, you know, making

186

those bombs that nobody ever used. All right, so that was before I met him. But getting spit on after you've been to a war does affect a person. Your father also has a minor physical problem. Nothing hereditary, I'm sure. However, it did make him especially glad to have you. Oh, Walter." Her chest sagged. "I don't know what happened."

Walter handed her a piece of gum. Then after a quiet minute he said, "Mom, it's OK if you want to kidnap me."

"Really? You sweet boy. Want to go to Disney World?"

"Great." He rolled down the window and lay back, sticking his feet out. "Your boss doesn't deserve you, anyway, if he won't give you that promotion."

"Right." Holly sucked in her breath—at the sight of all the sunny space out ahead of them. That's all she wanted in this world was to be appreciated.

"Could they arrest you for this?" Walter asked. "Not that you'll get caught."

"They could. And your father would be just the one to do it, wouldn't he, coming after us in a high-speed chase. He is going to be disappointed if you don't come back. And I'd hate to have him drag me into court."

*Court.* "Walter, I can't kidnap you. I have to go on jury duty tomorrow." She made a U-turn on the barren road with no trouble, and headed north, where the sky was light. "And I do look forward to being on a jury. Why, I relish the thought of administering justice for a change."

# 28

# *Tarnish v. Sweat & Kick*

The case before the court was *Tarnish v. Sweat & Kick*, a health club also known as SAK. Ms. Latisha Tarnish, an ex-employee of the club, was suing her former employer for sexual discrimination.

The representative from Sweat & Kick, Mr. Wate, was called to the stand. He waddled up and claimed that SAK couldn't be accused of sexual harassment. "Heh, we're a health club. Clean as they come. Steam bath, hot tubs, all of it top of the line."

But you can still meet a snake at a spa, Holly thought.

"This is not a case of harassment," the judge explained. "The matter is sexual discrimination."

Mr. Wate loosened the tie cinched up to his thick neck. "Sorry. I must have got this confused with some other deal," he mumbled. "But if you've seen our ad on TV, the aerobic cat that does high kicks, you can see we don't go in for a sexy sales pitch."

"What was Ms. Tarnish's position in your organization?" Latisha's lawyer asked.

"Aerobics instructor," Mr. Wate answered with a grunt.

"And the alleged grounds for her termination?"

"Incompetence," he maintained. "She'd stopped using those snappy tunes in her aerobic routines and gone to easy listening music. Heck, our clients were falling asleep on the gym floor during their lie-down stretches."

"Did you receive complaints from your patrons?"

"Not as such. In fact, they—" Mr. Wate stopped himself. "But the slow pace of Tish's class wasn't in keeping with our image." He took out his handkerchief and patted his forehead. "Then she wanted to apply for weight lifting instructor. At this point in time we had to let her go."

"And would you describe to the jury the person you hired to replace Ms. Tarnish as aerobics instructor? Isn't it true that this individual had *no* experience in aerobics?"

Mr. Wate reached for a glass of water. "Well, his hands-on experience in the construction business had him in great physical shape."

"*He*? You're saying my client was replaced with a *male* aerobics instructor—who'd never taught an exercise class, let alone to women?" The lawyer looked over at the jury with wide eyes.

Mr. Wate licked his lips. They were the color of peeled plums. "You can't go by gender in your hiring practices these days. The new man we hired passed all our fitness tests."

"Ah, which proves our case, wouldn't you say? By that same reasoning, you can't refuse to hire Ms. Tarnish—*or to let her apply*—as a weight lifting instructor, can you."

"Hell, Latisha's sex wasn't the reason she didn't get the job. Females can't lift the weights men do." Mr. Wate held up his arm in a Mr. Atlas pose. "Sure, the girls can pump

189

the little dumbbells. But as for pressing your regular barbells, forget it."

"And has SAK constructed weights proportionately adjusted for the female anatomy?"

"A weight's a weight," Mr. Wate said. "Ten pounds, fifty, you can't mess with the measures. But why some babe wants to press iron in the first place, I don't get it, puffing herself up with bulgy muscles trying to look like a guy. Personally, I don't find it all that appealing—not that I don't support each and every program offered by SAK and participate in them."

"Thank you, Mr. Wate."

Latisha's lawyer came over to the jury box and looked them in the eye. "Ladies and gentlemen, this is a clear case of discrimination in the workplace. And I'll bet many of you have suffered that yourselves. I'm sure you'll come to the only right and liberated decision. Thank you."

"Next they'll be saying the NFL has to hire females," said a juror whose teeth were the color of carrots.

"What woman would want to be a . . . Hog?" Holly asked (realizing after she said it that such a person existed in her office).

"It isn't just you gals who don't get bumped up to the better slots," a slim but muscular man in a tee shirt spoke up. "Where I work at Hefty Movers, hotshots come in and lord it over us. Don't make no difference how good you handle the men or the loads. It's paper credentials that count to the big boss, not your time in grade or how good you lift."

Everyone seemed to agree.

All except one woman, who introduced herself as Mrs. Quimby. "I'm a housewife and proud of it. And I think this Tarnish woman got what she asked for."

The foreman asked her to explain. His name was Arnie Brush, and he was bald.

Mrs. Quimby fingered her pocketbook on the table in front of her, a square black purse that sat up stiff on its flat bottom. "Why do these new women feel they have to muscle in on the business world, anyway? I'll tell you why: because they're insecure in themselves. My husband couldn't be happier being the breadwinner in our family. He knows his job, and I know mine." She stroked the clasp of her purse. "This Tarnish woman was burned out trying to be a super woman. And no wonder the aerobics students fell asleep. They were beat. Personally, I take a nap every day," she said, patting a yawn, "so I'll be fresh when my husband Harold comes home."

"Some people like to work," Holly said. "And we do have bills to pay." This woman really bugged her.

Mrs. Quimby breathed heavily (although you couldn't imagine her panting). "I can't speak to that. But I don't see why these personal problems have to be dragged into the courts."

Arnie Brush called for a vote, and everybody sided with Latisha Tarnish—all but Mrs. Quimby, not that she would give her reasons why not. She just repeated herself like a message on tape, saying, "I don't think it's right."

So they went back to arguing until the hours wore on and everybody was wearing out.

It was getting close to five o'clock when Mrs. Quimby began looking nervously at the clock. "I have to leave. They have no right to keep us here past dinner time."

Arnie explained that, yes, by law they could sequester a jury as long as necessary. "Don't worry, folks, they let you eat. Some juries order pizza." Holly's lips formed the word *pepperoni*. "OK, now, if anybody needs to make a phone call, the bailiff will take you."

191

One gentleman got up to call his wife. Then everybody looked at Mrs. Quimby to see if she would telephone Harold. She sat there fingering her small worn diamond, pushing it up to her knuckle and back.

"Would you like to make a call?" Arnie asked.

"I always have my husband's dinner ready," she said sharply. "I couldn't bother him at work, phoning to say I've failed in my duties." She levitated out of her chair then sucked back into it, as if she were riding a wave.

Arnie leaned back, with his hands behind his smooth head. "We'll take one more vote. Does the evidence show that Latisha Tarnish was the victim of sexual discrimination in the workplace?"

The same hands went up that had pumped air all day. And Mrs. Quimby's stubborn fists stayed on the table with her thumbs locked inside. She glared at the clock. She chewed her mouth. At last her right hand yanked out of place and stabbed the air. "Oh, all right. I suppose these new women will horn in and win out, no matter what we do."

# 29

# *Diamond*

It was June, and they still hadn't heard about the school lunch contract. Meanwhile, Bill was getting on everybody's nerves waiting for a call from USDA. At least he agreed to play on a Special Projects team being organized and get out of the office. They called themselves the Megabytes.

Their first game was against BelCon's executives, the Johns, on a humid Saturday morning, a true Washington summer day. The sky was white, and not even the leaves on the trees wanted to move in the wet heat. But Bill got everybody out on the diamond, swinging their bats to win.

"OK, move it," pregnant Rita called. She had bullied her way into being the team manager and strutted around the office with a clipboard. Today she wore a whistle to the game.

Ned Bird, in shorts, marched his stick legs out to left field. He was also playing center, so he practiced racing from one position to the other. Leonard Pudding trudged into right field, wearing suit pants that were shiny in the seat. At her post on third base, Claire Whittle gazed up at the cloud cover, probably planning a winning strategy. And primed on second base was Fiona, blowing on her fingernails, ready to go.

Holly jogged out to first base, wearing gold running shorts. She waved up at Laurence in the stands. He was the only man there with the wives and their picnic hampers, that rare man who will come out and cheer for a woman. Laurence waved back with the thermos he'd purchased for this occasion. His trip to the Dakotas had been a success. He'd turned up fecal matter of an unknown origin out in buffalo country.

Walter had also come to the game (as long as he didn't have to sit by Mr. LeFever). Maybe all children are sickened by their potential stepparents at first, and Holly still believed those two might get along some day. Walter lay on the grass next to first base to be her coach and gave her a high five as she trotted up.

No one from the Johns had arrived yet. They must be practicing at a secret site somewhere to keep their opponents off guard. Higher-ups really hate to lose.

Rita hollered for the practice to start, "Batter up," meaning herself. And she'd picked the position of catcher because she was too lazy to move out on the field. Well, if she insisted on playing in her condition, Rita might as well have her miscarriage at home plate.

Bill did a fancy windup on the mound, lifting his knee up to his chin and chewing on something. His arm was cocked to throw. Then he saw somebody in the parking lot and waved. It was Mr. Johnson, getting out of his limo and jogging onto the playing field, wearing a navy warm-up suit.

Fiona looked over and nodded suspiciously. Holly watched Mr. Johnson carefully run, keeping his head

194

smooth. Some people considered him snobby. She thought he was shy.

Vice Presidents swarmed out on the field following their leader, although they didn't sock their fists into mitts or even bring along balls or bats. Was Special Projects supposed to haul the equipment because they were the underlings?

The Vice President for Public Relations stepped out of his BMW and strutted onto the field with empty arms. However, the Head of Acquisitions was getting something out of his trunk. It appeared to be a basketball. No. It had the checkered pattern of a soccer ball. He bunted it across the grass to his pals, black and white, black and white.

Bill saw the ball go swirling past, and his jaw stopped. "Damn." His leg sank back to the ground, and he scratched himself. "Uh, looks like they caught us with our pants down." But he gave Mr. Johnson the thumbs-up sign. "No problem." Then Bill hollered for the Megabytes to get to home plate pronto.

"So we regroup," he told them in the huddle. He grinned. "Hell, that's what being beltway bandits is all about, going by the seat of our pants. One size fits all. Soccer's another game. Right? So get out there and win it."

Rita stood with her arms folded over her growing body. "Anybody here who hasn't played soccer?"

Holly had Walter to thank for teaching her the basics of the game. Ned Bird complained that they hadn't practiced, but he had read a book on the subject. The only person on the Megabytes who didn't know zip about soccer was Leonard, which was not surprising since he wasn't versed in any game. But Holly had seen Leonard kick a tree that dripped sap on his car, and he had a strong leg.

Bill chose Rita, of all people, to be their goal tender, sending that pregnant person out on the playing field where

195

her unborn child could get battered before it was born. And Rita agreed to this child abuse!

Having her as their goalie did make sense in one way, though, since Rita's body would fill up the scoring area better than anyone else's. And as Bill pointed out, Bel-Con's high-level, polite executives would have a problem kicking a ball at a pregnant woman. The Johns might have complained that Rita's baby was an extra player on the field, but they didn't think of that.

The two teams lined up in the heat. The Megabytes kicked off, and the ball swiveled out to the Vice President of PR, who caught it with his eager beaver foot and punted right, left, then pocketa-pocketa down the middle, aiming to score. But the ball veered to the side, where Rita was waiting for it with the inside of her mean foot and *whack*. She had the face of a mother on her now: *don't mess with my kid*. And she was good, that is, if you don't give a hoot about your femininity.

Ned Bird galloped after the ball with his ostrich legs and kick, kick, kicked it in neat little bunts. But his shot didn't have enough oomph going down the middle, and a John stole it with his trigger happy foot, punting it back down big Rita's way. This time she ate it with her whole leg, and goodby, ball.

Holly was enjoying these activities from her peaceful spot out on the grass. Then suddenly the ball was coming at her, kicked by Leonard, who had slipped and fallen on the field. Here the ball came right at her. So she did what any normal person would and reached out to stop it.

"Mom, *no*, not your hands," Walter called from the sidelines. She knew that.

"Penalty," a mean male voice called, and the Johns got possession of the ball. Fortunately, it didn't come Holly's way again before they were allowed to stop and have a

196

swallow of water at the half-time break of this low-scoring game, 0-0.

However, Mr. Johnson's men couldn't relax and take a breather. Those A-type personalities had to get back out in the hundred percent humidity and bash the ball some more. So Bill pumped up his team, patting male butts as they returned to the equator-type scenario of the playing field.

The Johns got serious now, pushing and shoving in a merger manner. But these higher-ups still couldn't get the ball past Rita Staples.

Playing goalie for the Johns was John E. Johnson himself, protecting his team's turf with his tall tan jogging legs. But his hands dangled out of place with no important documents to hold or his attaché case to hang onto. He fidgeted, sticking his hands in his pockets. He folded his arms. It almost made Holly want to hold him still, not that she would lay a finger on a married man, even if she didn't already have a fiancé.

Bill plunged into the mob of pushing bodies and gave the ball a good high kick. Yikes, it was coming at her again. And she couldn't embarrass Walter this time, no matter what. So she stood her ground and held her arms to her sides. "Use your head," her son shouted. All right, she would be decapitated.

The dark ball was dropping down on her, and Holly held up her forehead to be smacked. But it was coming lower. She remembered Walter had said to use your chest. She breathed and lifted herself up. *Whack.* Ouch. However, the ball did take a good bounce off her front and sailed over to where Claire Whittle stood, leaning down and stroking her shin.

Claire looked up. She saw the ball coming. Then she did a strange thing. She threw her arms around herself and called out what sounded like "*Rodney, yes.*" Claire then wound up and belted the ball, whacking it straight at the Johns' goalie. There it went, whirling towards Mr. Johnson, yes . . . smack through his legs. Score! The Megabytes were ahead, humiliating their opponents, 1-0.

The Johns got in a hot huddle and came out kicking up a storm with their high-powered shoes. But they didn't have the clout to get a point past Rita and her unborn child.

The time was up. And the Megabytes had won it, whipping the Johns in a wonderful sporting event.

Bill grinned all over the field, and Holly went over to him, beaming. "I really like soccer."

Now was the perfect scenario to bring up her promotion. But Rita wouldn't get lost, sucking up to Bill in this success situation. Not that Rita was in line for a promotion in her condition. And once she'd had her baby, a normal mother would stay home and play with it.

Laurence came up bringing Popsicles for the team and wanting to take Holly shopping for something special. He had supported them in this heat, and she said of course she'd go.

This time when they got to the mall, Laurence had her hide her eyes. He even blindfolded her with his handkerchief, scented with his latest delicious aftershave. They didn't go up the escalator in Bloomingdale's today, however, but strolled down the main marble corridor of the mall. She missed seeing the palm trees there, but she could detect when they passed a cookie store.

Laurence led her into a place, where she felt along the cool glass counter top. OK, you can look." He undid her blindfold, and his fingers were trembling.

Holly opened her eyes and saw diamonds—big, little, round, lopsided—sitting on satin cushions waiting to be picked. She'd never had a diamond, not that she didn't like the gold band Eddie had given her, which she had thought she would wear all her life.

But maybe diamonds do last forever! And every woman dreams of flaunting one sometime. When you pass a jewelry store, your eyes sneak in. Or if you go in, say, to get a necklace fixed (broken in a passionate clinch if you're lucky), you secretly drool over the rings and imagine the moment when you'll get yours.

There you are in a starlit restaurant looking across the cozy table at the most wonderful man you've ever met. For dessert he passes you the little velvet box. And when you say, "Oh, yes," he gets tears in his eyes.

"What do you think?" Laurence asked. Holly looked at him. His eyes were more moist than usual, gleaming through his tinted glasses, which she had always admired.

"So beautiful." The diamonds glittered before her eyes. Rita Staples would just die if she walked in the office wearing one of these.

"Which is your favorite?" Laurence asked. "Don't worry about the price. You know I don't go in for cheap things." Holly pointed to a nice round one. "What about the pear-shaped one?" he said, motioning for the clerk to get it out. "It's the in-type to wear."

The elderly salesperson held up a small glass to his eye and slowly brought out the precious gem from under the counter. Laurence's fingers quivered as he slipped the pear-shaped ring on Holly's finger. It was still grimy from the soccer game, but with a tug they got the ring on. At first the top-heavy shape looked odd on her hand. But your finger gets used to a ring in a hurry. Your knuckle swells up immediately so it won't slide off.

"Are you happy, sweetheart?" Laurence asked.

Holly looked into his excited, kindly eyes and told him that she was.

199

He nodded at the clerk. "We'll take it." The man reached to return the ring to its velvet box, but Laurence explained that she would want to wear it. And for once he had read her mind. Holly only wished she were left-handed now, although your left one can do most of the important things, can't it—such as eat, turn on the TV, and touch a person or pet.

Laurence opened his wallet and looked inside. He closed it, sucking in his breath. "This is so dumb of me, forgetting they took my credit cards. You know my ex-wife ran me into bankruptcy, and those companies clean you out. Sweetheart, would it be possible—I know I shouldn't ask this when it's your engagement ring—but could you charge it on your Visa card? You know I'll pay you back."

Holly looked down at the pear-shaped ring and wanted to scratch him with it. Or she could smack him in the head with her purse.

Yet it wasn't as if Laurence were selfishly buying something for himself. And why even think of marrying a man if you don't trust him? It was a beautiful ring.

"I guess I could," she said.

And she wasn't sorry she did it. As they stepped out in the mall, she saw a lady she recognized from the super-market and waved at her (using guess which hand).

"Walter's going to be impressed with this, don't you think?" Laurence exuded.

Holly agreed that her ring would definitely make an impression on her son. Unfortunately, they couldn't show it to him that evening because he'd gone with his father to a policemen's barbecue.

# 30

# The LeFevers of
# Fargo

"Walter, see if Mr. LeFever is out of the bathroom yet," Holly called from the kitchen. She stood at the wok trying to figure out the mu shu pork her fiancé wanted for lunch. The recipe made no sense to her. Walter dragged his feet going to check on his future stepfather. Her son was not pleased about their engagement. "Laurence has some news for us when he comes out," she urged him. "It involves you, too."

"The door's still shut," Walter called back from the hall. "And steam's coming out. What's he doing, mom? He's been in there for hours."

"He is thorough with the housework, isn't he," she answered. "Why don't you play with the pets until he's finished. You've been wanting him to bring that ferret over here for Warren."

A racket sounded from the bedroom, the rattle of Venetian blinds, followed by a yelp. Walter ran in and came back staggering with Warren in his arms, grown to the size of a spaniel by now, certainly no lap pet.

But then, what pet will sit on your lap when you want it to? Warren's ear drooped and was inflamed. "Mom, Laura bit him. That creepy ferret attacked him and chewed it."

"Poor rabbit." They put Warren in the sink and ran cool water over his injured ear. "It's nothing personal against our pet," Holly pointed out. "Laura bites everything. Have you seen Laurence's fingers?"

"Really?" Walter grinned.

"Watch it," Holly warned him. She checked the teeth marks on Warren's ear. At least it had stopped bleeding. She hoped this wouldn't affect his hearing. One partially deaf member of this household was enough. The rabbit's pink eyes looked at them suspiciously as he backed under the faucet. "Get him some dandelions, Walter, his favorite." They had scoured the neighborhood to gather a good supply.

Walter got a handful of the wilted weeds out of the fridge (at least one snack that Laurence didn't devour) and spread them on a plate. Warren scrambled across the counter to gobble his feast, so at least his appetite wasn't impaired. The stems zipped away into his rabbit jaws.

When their big bunny had finished eating, Walter eased him onto the floor. Warren hopped to the door and looked both ways, then scrambled into the living room to snack on the plants there. "Let him go," Holly whispered. "He's had a bad day. Laurence will be out in a minute to tell us his news, and then we can have lunch. We should be glad he does the housework, Walter. I promise I won't ask you to do a thing."

"You don't make me do anything now," he said grouchily.

202

"Well, I should. You do like my ring, don't you?" Holly shook a Chinese noodle off her finger and held it up. "Can you see the pear shape?"

"Yes, mom, for the hundredth time."

"Laurence is a generous man—at least he'll give you what he has. And we should be kind to him. His first wife was mean. Can you believe she hit him, actually physically abused this man?" Walter gave a big nod, and Holly whacked him with the dish towel for that.

Just then a crash came from the bathroom. "Oh dear, he must have slipped." She slapped the cookbook shut and went to see. "I hope he didn't hurt anything."

The bathroom door swung open, and Laurence's big dark figure came out in the fog. They met in a moist hug, and he kissed her in a cloud of steam. She didn't mind that Walter saw. A child needs to see what a happy home life can be. "Isn't this wonderful," Laurence murmured into her hair that was getting damp, "being in the same house."

Holly agreed. Then her feet felt water. She looked over Laurence's shoulder into the bathroom. The towel rod was on the floor. And her sea green towel lay in a puddle, the color of spinach now. "I guess I stuffed it in too tight," Laurence confessed. "That was the noise you heard."

"And what is this flood?" Holly asked.

Laurence laughed. "Sweetheart, don't get mad. I've been kidded before about getting more water on the floor than on myself when I shave. I shaved for you." He held out his cheek to her. It smelled excessively of aftershave she thought today, although his skin was smooth, and she touched it briefly. "I'll get this cleaned up now," he said. "You know I wouldn't leave a bathroom until it's immaculate. You've seen my fixtures."

Holly took a gulp of the humid air and let it settle. "Well, Walter can't wait forever to hear your news bulletin.

He already had to use the neighbor's bathroom because you stayed in here so long."

"What?" her fiancé asked, holding out his good ear.

"Walter had to find a toilet elsewhere, *Larry*," she enunciated, swooping down to pick up her sopping towels and wring them out.

Warren hopped up to the bathroom door, twitched his nose at the swamp, and scampered away.

Next here came Laura, not bothering to look where she was going. She swished in between Laurence's legs and flopped over the edge of the tub, making a splash landing. Then she soared out of the tub in a spray.

"Leave it for now, Laurence," Holly told him, standing up from her mopping. "Come tell us your news, and then you can finish. You can't keep a boy waiting around all day to have a talk."

They all sat down on the couch, and Laurence put his moist arm around her. "We have so much to look forward to, the three of us," he said, giving her shoulder a wet squeeze. Walter pulled up a pillow over his face. "Your mother and I have a lot in common," Laurence continued. "I'm with Interior; and she's into plants." He motioned to the foliage around the room and sneezed. "And, Walter, you can come to me with any problem." Her son then made a sound, a *grrr* coming from behind his barricade. She had raised a wild animal for a child.

"You'll get used to me," Laurence said. "I grow on people."

Walter's eyes looked over the top of the pillow, blacker than Holly had ever seen them. He jumped up as something shook his pant leg, causing the raggedy threads of his Levis to quiver. Laura was nibbling at him. The nasty ferret was snooping under Walter's cuff, trying to climb his leg.

"Ouch," he squawked and charged after the flying fur piece, which sailed over and dived behind the curtain. Walter shook the drapes but couldn't get Laura out.

"Come back and sit down, son," Holly said, reminding herself that material things shouldn't be important, although the curtains were new. "Now, Laurence, get on with your news."

He cleared his throat. "Well, it means a pay raise," he said, giving her knee such an encouraging pat that her shoe fell off.

"Congratulations," Holly said with relief. "Isn't that great, Walter? They appreciate Laurence on his job." She looked down at the lovely engagement ring he'd chosen (and promised to reimburse her for in the next two pay periods). Maybe now she would get a lump sum.

"The adjustment is a step increase within my GS-9 rating," he explained. "I should be getting my GS-11 before long. But this new job does involve a relocation. Redirection is what they call it. So, you see, a person doesn't always get stuck working for the government. The Department of Interior won't let you stagnate."

"They're sending you away?" Walter sat up.

"And guess where?" Laurence said. "I'll give you a hint. It's a long way."

"California?"

"Are you kidding? I wouldn't live in that plastic place. You ever hear of the big sky, Walter, the badlands?" Laurence took off his glasses and polished them (so at least he couldn't see Walter's expression at the moment, which was similar to the one he got when he cleaned Warren's hutch). "And you've seen those faces carved on the mountain out there," Laurence continued. "Your mother tells me you're an excellent student of our nation's presidents."

205

"You're going to Mount Rushmore?" Walter threw up the pillow, barely missing the hanging tiger fern and causing its tendrils to wave wildly. "What extinctions this time? That is what you do, isn't it?"

"You remembered." Laurence smiled proudly. "Well, this work is along those lines. My recent trip yielded unidentified fecal matter, and they want me to comb the buffalo habitat for more."

"You've got to be kidding." Walter gave a big grin.

Laurence moved closer to Holly on the couch. "No, I'm not. And you'll like it out there in nature, away from this Washington traffic."

"I'm not going," Walter stated. He wasn't smiling now. "Mom, do you really want to live out there where there's nothing? You like your job here. And you'll get your promotion, you will."

"When? They've had plenty of chances to give it to me," Holly said sadly. "Maybe in Fargo I can start as an admin assistant."

"I'll bet you do," Laurence said, wiping off his forehead. "Fargo has a number of businesses. And, Walter, don't worry that I'll keep your mom from working. She's excellent at what she does, and I'm lucky to find her." He lifted Holly's hand and kissed it, his soft lips caressing her ring finger. And she would never find another man like him.

Walter stared at them both with a dark face. He looked over at Laura perched on top of the curtains chewing them. Then he bolted up, getting a broom this time, and chased after her, batting at the ferret who had molested him and bitten Warren. Laura flew across the room, skidding down the hall to the swampy bathroom, where Walter shut her in. Laurence tightened his fists, hearing the click. "Please don't."

206

But Walter wouldn't let Laura out. And he wouldn't come back and sit down with them. He went to the door. "No way am I going out there with you people. I like it here. I can stay with dad," he shouted and ran out in the hall.

"Honey, it wouldn't be full time," she explained, jumping up and following him out on the landing. "You could come to Fargo in the summers, or at Christmas," she called as he ran down the stairs. "Come back here, Walter, this is your mother speaking." She watched as his dark head disappeared. She was a mother with no clout.

"He'll change his mind," Laurence tried to calm her. "Kids never like to move. Do they?" True, Walter hadn't wanted to leave California, either, and that was with his real father.

"When are they moving you?" Holly asked, trying to imagine on the map where the Dakotas were.

"They're giving this redirection top priority. Probably in the next few weeks," Laurence answered, stroking her hand. "You know the government, once they get their mind set. So I'll go on ahead and find us a place."

"That is soon." Holly went over and sat by Warren on the floor, petting his ear. He'd left a few round reminders on the rug due to the tension in this room (which she didn't point out to Laurence, since he obviously preferred petrified fecal matter).

They sat there saying nothing, listening to a gnawing sound coming from the bathroom.

"Oh, sweetheart, by the way, would you mind taking care of Laura while I'm gone?" Laurence asked. "I can't keep her in the motel in Fargo while I'm looking for a place for us. How about a nice little farmhouse? You said you wanted a single-family dwelling. We'll be the LeFevers of Fargo."

# 31

# *Goodby Lunch*

*Ramona stumbled down Vesuvius, picking volcanic ash off her designer clothes. She was lucky to have escaped alive. But how could she have trudged up those scalding slopes, only to have her true love slip through the cracks again?*

*A donkey came toddling along ridden by a rotund native, evidently an Italian taxi. Well, when in Rome. She hailed the low beast for a ride to the nearest ladies' room. She couldn't run into Rodney looking like this. Her peaches and cream complexion was covered with soot.*

*Her mistake. When she dismounted, the driver tried to pinch her! "You swine," she shrieked and smacked him with her pocketbook. Clutching her purse back to her chest, pure alligator, she protected her size C cups. "They're for Rodney's eyes only," she cried. Then she looked around for a bite to eat to keep her spirits up.*

"Claire?" a voice said in an American accent, "don't forget the farewell luncheon today at Bibs and Ribs."

Claire looked up. There was Holly. "You remember Lola Romaine, Bill's former secretary—who quit on him and moved up to Acquisitions? Now she's leaving BelCon to 'better' herself on the outside. So I don't see any need to overdo the praise."

Yes, Claire remembered Lola Romaine, who chewed gum. "Sure. Say, Holly, I hear you're getting married. Let me see your ring." Holly held it out. "I like the pear shape. And when's the wedding?"

"Uh, not for a while. Now about the luncheon today. Remember, you said you would write something to read."

Damn, not now. "Just let me finish this scene—rather, this document, Holly—and I'll get to it," Claire said.

*Ramona ripped off her bib and strode out of the smelly restaurant, looking for the Vatican. If the Pope couldn't detect Rodney's whereabouts with his religious radar and the view from his balcony, who could?*

Claire slid into her seat at Bibs and Ribs across from Bill as he attacked a hearty order of ribs spread across the platter, looking like a corset swabbed with stale ketchup.

Good description. Claire jotted it down. Oops, she'd written on the tablecloth. She poured water around her words and tugged the soggy section off. Discreetly she slid the bread basket over the hole she'd made and casually gazed around the room, sure nobody saw.

When Bill had gnawed his last rib clean, he tapped his glass with a knife to get people's attention. It was the knife he'd used for his ribs, and specks of red sprayed on the table and dropped down through his water. He grinned and launched his speech. "Lola was one heck of a secretary."

Lola Romaine took out a piece of gum. Claire glanced at Holly, sharing a look of disdain, and pleased that she

209

could tune into these office politics with her new sensitivity as a novelist.

"Lola's a great gal," Bill went on.

Holly started tapping on her glass with a spoon.

"Right," Bill said. He finished and sat down.

It was Claire's turn now, and she stood up, with surprising anticipation. "This is a memo to Lola from Bill," she explained. The room got quiet.

She tugged on her cheek to imitate Bill. "Uh, Lola, pal," she mimicked his stutter-step speech. "As I was just talking out loud here, we, uh, figured with you hanging around the pool between jobs you'd be chomping to get back to proposal work. And guess what new market we're going after this time? Mental health! Surprised? You aren't the only one. We're bidding on Analysis of Homicidal Tendencies of Females in the Consulting Business, that is, if we can dig up enough heads with lunatic expertise. And that shouldn't be too hard around this beltway.

"But considering the big bucks these consultants charge, we have to tighten the belt somewhere. So we're asking you gals to cut back on the supplies, all this waste paper we're finding in the trash cans. That goes for the lavatories, too."

Claire looked up. The secretaries were smiling. Ned Bird had a frown on his face, but he was always miserable when he'd been pried away from his primal act of writing. Ah, but Claire understood this now, since she had become a writer herself.

"Uh, Lola," Claire read on, "you've gone through the peaks and valleys with us here at BelCon. And without your input, they wouldn't have booted me up to Head of Handicapped Projects. But that's water over the bridge.

"As a token of our appreciation, Lola, we're making you the lead secretary on this proposal effort. Just pull everything together at the end and get the prop delivered downtown on time. And we'll follow the production schedule, enclosed. No problem.

Proposal Overview
for
Analysis of Homicidal Tendencies
of Females in the Consulting Business

Proposal Length:    2,000  pages
Graphics:                  1   map (with overlay)
                               2   bar charts
                               5   milestone charts
                              15   flow charts (foldouts)
                              47   tables (to be typed and boxed)
Résumés:   Just pull these from our other props, Lola, and beef them up with a homicidal slant.
Schedule:   Day 1 –  All chapters in to typing
                   Day 1 –  Typing completed by COB and rerouted to authors, Federal Express
                   Day 4 –  Corrections and graphics back to secretaries for same-day turnaround
                   Day 5 –  Delivery: Nome, Alaska

"Lola, why are you looking at me like that? Will there be a problem getting the whole prop typed in the same day? Uh, I guess that is running a tight ship. And, dang it, editing got left out of the loop again. What about that?"

People clapped as Claire sat down. This was great. If she could get such a response from a memo, imagine the feedback there'd be when *Forbidden Fruit* hit the stands.

Only Bill wasn't smiling. He chewed darkly on his pen.

211

# 32

# *Hands-on Experience*

Bill closed the door to his office and went over to stare out at the parking lot. He was usually an open door kind of guy, but today he wanted to hide. The business school never warned you about these pushy females coming along. Today he had an interview with one, and he wasn't looking forward to it.

Maybe he shouldn't have advertised positions for this school lunch deal until they'd won it. But you've got to get people lined up. He just wasn't in the mood for a hoity-toity female barging in here to land herself the first spot.

Holly buzzed him on the intercom and said that the Townsend woman was waiting outside. "Uptight," she whispered. "Very."

Bill lit a cigarette and sucked on it. "Just give me a couple of minutes here." He watched the flame eat up the nicotine. She was probably a health freak who choked on smoke. He checked to make sure he had a full pack of cigarettes. Yup, good.

"OK, send her in," he told his secretary.

The applicant strutted in wearing a male-type suit and carrying a briefcase. It irked him when they did that. Her hair was long and slicked down, looking like it was ironed to match the rest of her. Some guys go in for the perfect type, but not him. He liked seeing something mussed.

She looked at him through glasses with red rims. "Mr. Moss. I'm Aubrey Townsend." You might know she wouldn't have a normal name. She reached out to shake his hand. Her fingers were cold bones.

"Have a seat." Bill pointed to the chair furthest away from him and lit a cigarette. He collected the fumes in his mouth. "OK if I smoke?" He let out a puff. "So, you're interested in the consulting business." He grinned. Hell, why was he the one worried here, when look who was in the driver's seat.

"You bet. It's challenging, very stimulating," Townsend said, flicking something off her sleeve, as if she were getting filthy sitting here.

"Guys burn out, though," he told her. She gave him a look of contempt.

Bill swirled his chair around, looking for a pertinent document on the shelf behind him. Gotcha. He swiveled back holding a winning proposal, leatherbound, giving him the great feel of pigskin in his hand. "I understand you went to the Harvard Business School," she announced. "Well, so did I."

He got a sick feeling. "Yea." He shrugged. He stabbed his cigarette at the dish in front of him, making a fat black spot. He liked the messy way it looked. That mess was him. "But we aren't in that white tower scenario here, are we, Miss, or is it Mrs. Townsend?"

She looked at him with barracuda eyes. "You're not allowed to ask about marital status any more, Mr. Moss. I go by *Ms*."

213

*Ms.* He hated that little shrimp of a word, a bit-off sound. More like a hiss.

"You advertised for new blood, Mr. Moss. I can offer you that." New blood? He must have meant male blood and guts. "And I have the credentials for this project."

*The opposition was closing in. Moss staggered back in the pocket. Hail Mary, where was a receiver? Anybody out there? . . . Then he saw a hole, an opening—*

"Oh," Bill mentioned. "Didn't I tell you? We haven't actually won this contract yet. So these interviews are exploratory, type of thing. And BelCon is a defense contractor, so bidding at USDA is a long shot. It wouldn't make much sense for them to award a major deal to some upstart Navy bunch, would it." He lit another cigarette and could feel his brain cranking into overdrive.

"But suppose by some quirk you do win this school lunch proposal, Mr. Moss?" Townsend looked at him through smoke. "You will need specialists in nutrition. Here's a copy of my résumé to refresh you."

She pushed it across the desk to him with a bloody red fingernail. Bill stared down at the neat black words lined up. Tightass was more like it. "I have a Ph.D. in adolescent nutrition," she droned on, "with an emphasis on teenage eating preferences. And I recently had a book published, *High School Appetites.*"

*Thwonk, he'd been nailed below the waist. He felt the ball slipping away. But he hugged it, he hung on.*

"Uh, there is one problem," he said. "BelCon doesn't have its own marketing department. So the guys here have to carry that ball themselves."

"Sounds good," Townsend said, fanning herself. "My project at Harvard was on marketing to the government."

*Damn, the blitz was on him. He looked up at the shoulder pads on the puny body lording it over him. Females shouldn't wear that type of equipment unless they want to take a hit. Where were his blockers—his fans—a paramedic to haul him out of here?"*

"Coffee? Tea?" Holly stepped in the office and put a plate of donuts in front of their applicant, not that Townsend lowered herself to reach for one or take a sniff. "No thanks."

Bill snatched a chocolate donut, Holly went for the jelly-filled, and they chewed—watching Aubrey Townsend sitting with her hands folded. A warm feeling came up in him for his secretary. Holly was a great gal. She was a friend. He should appreciate her, maybe even get moving on that promotion she'd been agitating for. Go easy on the praise, though, he warned himself, or the girls get uppity.

He licked frosting off his hand and gave Holly the look that meant she could file the Townsend application where the sun wasn't going to shine.

His phone rang, and Bill snarfed it up, motioning that this interview was over. "My secretary will be in touch."

Then before he answered he got a choke feeling, hoping it was USDA, scared that it was them. OK. Go for it. "Hello?"

"Mr. Moss? Burt Rand, here, from your son's school."

His heart dropped the ball. What had Ronnie done this time? It wasn't just that his boy failed tests. He'd had an asthma attack and collapsed in class the day they introduced the alphabet. Then Ronnie's bladder problem reared up during recess.

215

"I have good news for you, Mr. Moss."

"You do?" His bowels were jumping. "Hike it to me, Burt."

"We followed your idea of adding sports trivia to our regular skills test, and it did the trick. Your boy squeaked through, and we can advance him to the second grade this fall."

"I'll be damned." Bill wadded the paper in front of him and sailed the Townsend résumé in the trash. "Good man, Burt. You won't be sorry. Like I told you, if we pop this school lunch deal, your school is targeted for the free demo menu. Those kids will eat it up, I guarantee."

He called his wife to tell her their boy wasn't retarded after all. No answer. She must be at the market. He went out to find Holly and brag to her about his brainy kid. She was standing up at her desk, already smiling after listening in on her phone line, good girl.

On to the men's room.


Bill was doing his business there when he heard pounding on the door of the john. It was Holly calling. She even stuck her head inside the men's lavatory, hollering to him, "It's Agriculture on the phone for you."

He bolted out to get it. "Bill Moss, here," he answered, panting.

"Fred Trisket, USDA, calling in regard to our school lunch contract. We've finally come to a decision, Mr. Moss." Bill rocked back and forth sitting on his desk (not risking his swayback chair today). Oops, he knocked the ashtray on the floor, spraying gray powder on the rug. He loved it. "We do have a question regarding your personnel for the project," Trisket said. Here it came. They were nailing him for bidding Ned Bird as Project Director, when he was the PD for all their jobs. "It's about your

216

Plate Waste Analyst. You've listed a Dr. Leonard Pudding here, and we wondered if this was a mistake spilling over from your menu section."

"Nope. Pudding's his name," Bill answered, about to bust. "And you don't need to worry about Leonard. The guy is highly over-qualified."

"Just checking, Mr. Moss. Our deliberations were a close call. But we're awarding the contract to you. Congratulations."

"Yahoo!"

*Mighty Moss hugged the ball, dodging a tackle the size of an outhouse coming at him. He could run it himself, yes, and he scampered on into the end zone—TD— "finally!"*

"What did you say, Mr. Moss?"

"Just feeling good here, Fred," Bill said. "Uh, are you sure it's BelCon you're calling? Good, whew. And while I've got you on the line, do you have any more hot nutritional jobs coming up? Now we have expertise in Agriculture, we'll be going for the gold. I'll be in touch."

He took the phone and kissed it, then charged out to tell the troops.

Here came Leonard. "What do you say, buddy. *We won school lunch!*" Bill pumped Leonard's arm. "Hard to believe, isn't it? So that makes it official, Pudding. You're the new Plate Waste Analyst."

Leonard's face puffed up, then it puffed down. He said grouchily, "There go my weekends." But as Leonard strode away, Bill saw him take a Hershey bar out of his hind pocket and wolf the whole thing down. Tightwad Leonard usually parceled out a square of candy at a time to himself, driving the secretaries nuts.

217

The gals were buzzing around with the news by now, and folks were coming in from other offices to suck up to the big winners here. Ned strutted in, and Bill went over and hugged his friend, old buddy, who had a grin on his face about to bust it.

"Congratulations, sugar," one of the girls called out. Fiona DeForrest. "And why did Agriculture give this job to us?" she asked.

Bill scratched his jaw. Hmm. Trisket hadn't mentioned why. Must have been BelCon's management plan. "Great team effort everybody," he called out over the hubbub.

"Don't forget our bread," Holly said. "And Fred Trisket is a religious person. By the way, Bill, did he tell you he is now a GS-13? He got his promotion when USDA took off their freeze. So, when's the freeze coming off here? When do we get our piece of the pie?"

Bill looked around for refreshments, or maybe somebody coming in the door he should talk to. And here came John E. Johnson himself.

"Congratulations," he said in that smoothy voice CEOs have (and Bill figured he better start practicing). Johnson came over and shook his hand.

"Everybody did a great job." Bill motioned to his people around the room. Meanwhile, he had his eye on Johnson's snazzy summer suit, wondering how many of those he'd have to spring for if he made Division Head.

"So, where are you taking us to celebrate?" Rita Staples hollered. "Happy hour at Pigs in Blankets has all-you-can-eat buffalo wings."

Maintaining a low profile here, Bill ignored her and kept the eye contact going with the big boss until Johnson had to leave for a meeting.

Then Bill caved in and told the gals they could have their party. "But not until COB." They still had time today to write up a capability statement documenting their new hands-on experience in nutrition.

Sure, tonight they would treat the troops to drinks on the house with this type of dough rolling in. And a few beers might get their minds off this piece-of-the-pie business.

# 33

# *In the*
# *Shredding Room*

Holly looked across the office of celebrating people at Mr. LeFever's face coming in the door. "Laurence." She hurried over and took him out in the hall. "How did you know we won the school lunch proposal? Amazing, isn't it. Everybody's a little crazy here."

"I knew you could do it, sweetheart." He hugged her. "I just hope they give you the credit you deserve. Holly, my travel plans got changed, and they're sending me out on a military flight to Fargo tonight. I had to see you first."

"Oh, Laurence." They held each other, pressed up against the fountain, as people streamed in the office to congratulate Bill. The aroma of Laurence's latest aftershave made Holly's knees faint. "I'm so glad you came," she whispered. "Winning gives you this incredibly outgoing feeling. Let's go find someplace where we can be alone."

"Don't you want me to meet your boss?" Laurence asked. "I could put in a good word for your promotion."

He did look extra nice today in a new beige summer suit that set off his red power tie.

"Thanks," Holly said, "but I've already approached Bill. And he's feeling so good. Come on, let's go down to the shredding room. Nobody goes in there."

Their state-of-the-art shredder sat neglected in the corner of the room with its steel tongs primed to gulp whole documents, cardboard boxes, whatever you put in. Fang. "This is a good machine," Laurence said, getting down to check the label. "It's the Cadillac of shredders. Or more like a BMW. I think we should get a Saab, sweetheart." He looked up from where he was kneeling with the beaming face he always got when he talked about or touched nice things.

"A *sob*?" Holly smiled at the sound. "I don't know that car. But you're right, this is a good shredder. Too bad nobody uses it."

"Why not?" Laurence asked, touching the machine up and down the sides.

"The men here love their writing too much to destroy it, even the losing proposals. Not that we need to shred them. Who would want to steal anything from a consulting firm? Ned Bird, especially, is in love with his words. He'll call long distance for us to read what we've typed over the phone. And I swear you can hear him heavy breathing on the line."

Laurence stood up. "Has he been coming on to you?"

"Ned Bird? Women don't excite him. His children are probably test tube."

"In Fargo you can work in a place that's sane," Laurence said, holding her close to the shredder. "Have you told your boss you're leaving yet?"

To be honest, she hadn't even found Fargo on the map or been able to visualize the Dakotas. "Bill has been busy."

221

And she couldn't announce on her boss's big day that she was leaving. The thought that they were winners was so delicious she swooned to the floor with Laurence as they hugged. "We could put down some shreds and make this more comfortable," she murmured. They got paper from the trash and added the sales slips from Laurence's pocket. The machine growled as they turned it on. The steel teeth clamped down, and out came sliced paper.

They stretched out on the shreds, enjoying the delicious reclining position, where a kiss is more than a kiss. It's a whole body.

They were just getting comfortable when the door opened and in came legs. Holly lay as still as a log, watching pressed pant legs come towards her head. Looking up one of the legs, she saw a slim attaché case, which could only belong to one person in this company with that bump in it. "Mr. Johnson." She sat up, grabbing at her button holes. "I didn't know you used the shredder."

Mr. Johnson's face turned the color of lava, and that's the red hot type that flows in tongues. "Mrs. Prickle. Sorry to intrude." He smoothed his bleached blond hair on both sides, although it wasn't mussed.

She and Laurence scrambled to their feet. "We were just celebrating after winning the school lunch contract," Holly explained, picking scraps of paper off her skirt. "Not that I'm trying to get out of work. But that office is so noisy you can't concentrate."

"Yes, certainly. Congratulations to you all," Mr. Johnson said, removing a shredded sales slip that was clinging to his pants.

Laurence knotted his tie and introduced himself. "Not that I work in this consulting rat race, myself. I'm down-town with Interior, where they're relocating me to the Dakotas to extrapolate buffalo remains tonight."

Mr. Johnson slowly nodded.

Holly mentioned how exciting it was that BelCon was now qualified in the field of nutrition. "It's one of my favorite market areas, probably my very favorite. And Bill did work hard to win that contract."

"Everyone will be rewarded, I'm sure," Mr. Johnson said, edging across the room through the debris.

"Holly, there's something I need to ask you," Laurence whispered.

"Excuse me," Mr. Johnson said, slipping out the door and closing it quietly.

"I hope he won't get you in trouble." Laurence smoothed his hair. "Now I hate to ask you this, but I have to."

"Ask away," Holly said, serene with the feeling of success that nothing can touch.

"Could you lend me a little something for the taxi ride when I get to Fargo?" Laurence asked. "I can cash a check when I get there, which should take a week to clear. I am a little pressed, with the expenses of this unexpected trip and all." He centered his red tie.

Holly stared at his new summer suit, observing the expensive slacks that were barely wrinkled after straddling the floor. She envisioned the welts on his shins underneath, put there by his wife. So why not a few more? And she had conveniently worn spike heels today, perfect for the occasion. A modern woman would kick this man on the spot, and she could, too. She rubbed her toe against her calf, getting it ready.

"Easy, sweetheart. I know it's hard on you, having me leave so soon." He reached over and touched her cheek.

Holly eased up on the leather strap of her purse, which was exactly the size of a whip. Suddenly she smiled. "They're really sending you out to the Dakotas tonight?"

She got out her wallet. At least taxis must be cheaper out there. Way out there.

Feeling much better, she tucked a five-dollar bill in the pocket of Laurence's new suit, which she did admit looked handsome on him. And to be civil she kissed him lightly on the cheek, immediately stepping away from his after-shave.

He looked pleased when he saw that the bill she'd given him was a five and not a one. "You're my sweetheart." He reached in his pocket. "And I couldn't leave town without giving my girl a present." He handed her one of those little jewelry store boxes that excite you even if you already have your diamond.

Holly lifted the lid of the expensive box. It whacked back on her thumb. She tried again. Inside were earrings, long yellow crescents. Moons, they must be new moons. This was romantic.

Laurence helped pull the wire loops out of the satin backing and held up his gift. "Bananas, your favorite color."

Fruit. How could he? And her favorite color was not the neon yellow of a ceramic banana. It was more the shade of melted butter, or gold bracelets on a tan arm. "You want me to wear fruit in my ears?"

"They're to remind you of the island honeymoon we'll take once we get settled in Fargo," Laurence explained.

"Oh."

# 34

# *Horror Picture*

"Walter, find a horror movie for us to see now," Holly said.

"You're kidding." Warren thumped out of Walter's arms onto the rug, the parsley he was eating quivering in his lips. "You hate that gore. You hate being scared."

Holly sat staring at her cactus. The more sharp quills the better. "Things change, son. Get the newspaper."

She had just been through a major trauma of her life. Yet look at her, calm as can be. Warren came over and gnawed on her toe. But did she kick her pet? No. She said politely, "Please don't do that." Their big bunny stopped chewing on her. He also left a raisin on the rug. Well, fine. It was the perfect statement for the mood she was in.

"Can we see *Attack of the Killer Tomatoes,* please?"

"Yes. Perfect." Maybe watching the big fruit fight back in this rotten world would help.

"*All right.*" Walter found his shoes under the couch and stuffed his feet in them without undoing the laces. But she didn't say a word. Let him ruin his Reeboks by walking on

225

the rims. What is the point, anyway, of trying to do things right in this world?

At the mall, she pulled into the concrete parking place too close and scraped the bumper. Sorry, car. But that's the way life is. "What's with you?" Walter said.

"Plenty. But we'll get the biggest tub of corn and forget our troubles in the dark."

"You're neat when you're mad," he said as they went inside.

"*Mad* isn't the word for it," Holly muttered. "Come on," and she marched into the dark theater, looking for a seat where she could put up her feet and pretend a certain person's head was there to kick.

"Is creepy LeFever getting to you all the way from Fargo?" Walter asked as they sat down. "You didn't break up with him, did you?" His hand stopped moving in the corn.

"No, I didn't. And would you stop picking on Laurence." Holly took a handful of corn, bit down, and got a kernel on the first chew. This did not surprise her today. "He's a nice man. And he cleans bathrooms."

"You mean he *stays* in there all day," Walter answered, tossing up a piece of popcorn, which he caught by sticking out his tongue. She had brought a frog to the theater.

"Meanwhile, my son is such a polite person. At least have some consideration for Laurence out there trying to find us a place to live." She didn't want to hear another rude remark about Fargo from somebody who'd never been there. "The Dakotas might be nice. And you could have an Indian for a friend. Plus, those faces on the mountain will help you learn your history."

Walter did his barfing imitation into the bucket of popcorn.

226

"That is so disgusting. And there are worse men than Laurence. No thank you to the corn, Walter." Holly pushed it away, refusing to eat another bite of it now.

"Who could be worse than Laurence LeFever?" Walter asked. "The guy who wouldn't take you out for crabs?"

"Crabs are a filthy food, Walter, garbage piled on the table, literally. And they have no taste compared to tuna fish." Yet as she thought of the skinny pink claws reaching out of grime, her eyes began to sting. This was not helped by the extra salt they'd put on their popcorn.

He handed her a tissue. "It's your promotion, isn't it."

"Oh, Walter," and the tears fell out. "A terrible thing happened." Holly wadded the Kleenex into her eyes. If she could only blot out the scenario of yesterday, the worst day of her life. "It's not just that I didn't get mine." Fumes boiled up in her. "I was in the ladies' room, just minding my business, washing my hands—and that's with soap, not the way some people do it, barely sticking their hands under the tap. The temp was at the next sink. Oh, it's awful remembering this part."

"It must be about Rita."

"Honey, you know these things. Well, the temp said to me, 'I guess Rita will really be bossy now that she got her'—I can't even say the word—'since she got her *promotion* to admin assistant.'" A sob gagged out of Holly's throat, and she reached for some corn to plug up the embarrassing sound, "Naturally, I liked the part about Rita being bossy. But how could they promote her ahead of me? And she's having a baby, too."

Holly blew her nose, "So I went in to confront Bill, only I forgot he'd gone on vacation that morning, which shows you where my mind was." She dabbed at her eyes. "So I guess this means I'm supposed to go to Fargo. At least out there maybe they appreciate their employees."

227

"It could have been a mistake," Walter suggested, looking around the theater for friends. "You might get your promotion when your boss comes back."

"That's what I said. But why would Bill rush off without saying anything unless he was afraid to face me?" Her eyes were burning, and she wished they would turn down the lights so she could cry in peace. And a funny movie is good; then people just think you have a cold.

Walter patted her arm with his salty hand.

"Thank you, son." She took a large handful of corn to clear her tear ducts, and it helped. Then as the killer tomatoes bounded onto the screen, leaping off curbs to smack car windows, she felt better. She only wished that one of the giant tomatoes' victims resembled Rita.

By the end of the movie she was cried out, also comforted by Walter's words and the popcorn. She also had puffy eyes, which one dousing from the fountain does not fix. So she put on dark glasses as they went out into the gray day, staying especially on the lookout for police cars in the condition she was in.

That evening she dropped off Walter at a friend's and drove over to see Fiona. She had been out all week with a virus. She was also sick with worry over her boyfriend Hugo's health. This time it was his heart.

Fiona was propped up on a satin pillow, looking much better than when she'd left the office on Monday with her viral infection. "Have some candy, sugar." It was a two-pound box of chocolates from Hugo. "And I'll bet those white ones don't have as many calories."

Holly nodded and took two. "And how is Hugo?"

"Oh . . . all right."

"He'll make it through an operation fine, Fiona. I know he will."

228

Holly then related her story of the awful day before, when she had heard about Rita getting promoted.

"There must be a foul-up somewhere," Fiona said. "Well, at least let's go over to the office and see what dirt we can dig up."

"Are you sure you're well enough?" Holly asked.

Fiona was already up out of her sick bed. "Stars, yes."

So they drove to BelCon on this hot night, following a big vampire moon that slid in and out of slinky clouds, disappearing as they stepped out in the sweaty dark. The only light was fireflies in the bushes, floating sparks. And no jogger could be heard out back tonight. It was quiet there.

The guard let them in, never surprised to see people coming to work at any hour in this place. They went up the winding stairway in the eerie night light, heading first for Rita Staples's station.

"What if she's here working late?" Holly whispered as they crept down the hall. You couldn't see a light, but they got a whiff of rancid food from that direction.

"She doesn't need to now," Fiona pointed out.

Rats, that was right. Rita had gotten what she wanted. And what is worse in life that seeing your enemy succeed?

They turned on the light in Rita's area. And she hadn't cleaned up her station since she'd become an almighty admin assistant. Her desk was littered with an ash tray dumped but never washed, a mug that had her lips on it, and a pile of romance novels that looked as if they'd been chewed. On the floor was a brown grocery store bag stuffed with Rita's clothes. She could at least use a shopping bag with handles.

The article in the bag was Rita's rat-colored dress. Holly held it up. A thread dangled out of the armpit, and she gave it a tug. It wouldn't pull. "And wouldn't you love to tear off these tacky cap sleeves." Holly looked at Fiona, and they both said the same word, "Fang."

"Use it or lose it, honey," Fiona pointed out as they hurried down the hall to the neglected state-of-the-art shredder. "Although I must say, that experience of yours in the shredding room, Holly—"

"I know, I know." Fiona had not approved of her celebration with Laurence among the shreds, though not because Mr. Johnson had caught them. Fiona didn't believe a woman should give of herself in low places such as on floors or back seats. A lady deserves a decent bed provided by a gentleman was Fiona's opinion. Obviously she missed many valuable experiences in life due to this belief.

They turned on the shredder and held up Rita's ratty dress to drop it in. "This won't ruin the machine, will it?" Holly wondered. "Cloth is tough."

"Fang's a big boy," Fiona said, giving the shredder a pat. Rita was a big girl, too, Holly figured, who should learn to take criticism. Still, she did have to buy clothes on her secretary's salary.

"How big of a raise do you think Rita got?" Fiona asked, who herself had been hired as an admin assistant at the top salary level BelCon offered at the time.

"Throw in that ugly dress," Holly said, and they wadded Rita's itchy outfit into Fang's food dish.

The shredder gave a shudder. It made a gagging sound and started to vibrate, going into a rocking motion. The movement got grander and grander until the machine was practically rising off the floor. It burped, and gray tangled threads came out. Goodby, ratty dress. Hello, yarn.

They wadded the remains of Rita's dress and took it back to stuff in her grocery store sack. That should give her a message about her wardrobe.

230

Fiona went to freshen up after this chore, also to check on Hugo at the hospital. And Holly strolled down to her desk to clean up the mess she'd left the day before in her traumatized state.

She went through her mail, automatically looking for Bill's *CBD*. And why was she doing this? She ought to put his favorite publication in the shredder after what he'd done. Then she stared at an envelope with her name on it, typed, not stuck on with a label. When she saw the return address, a chicken bone stuck in her throat. It was from BelCon's Chief Executive Officer, with *John E. Johnson* engraved under that. He was getting her for the day in the shredding room.

"What's that?" Fiona walked up, patting her eyelids with a tissue.

"How was Hugo?" Holly asked, still holding the un-opened letter.

"I hope the by-pass operation works. Or they're talking about putting a pig valve in his heart." Fiona looked away.

Holly handed her a scented Kleenex from the box on her desk. "Really?" she said, putting her arm around her friend's brave shoulders. "I haven't heard of that one. It is amazing how they can fix people's hearts these days."

"He is such a dear coot," Fiona answered. Then she swung around and said with her old spunk, "And what is that letter you're hiding?"

"It's from Mr. Johnson. To me, for some reason," Holly said, feeling sick. "You open it."

"How bad could it be?" Fiona took the envelope. "There's not enough paper on the planet, honey, to reprimand all the people looking for affection in strange places—such as you and Laurence on the floor—if that's what you're worried about." She sliced the letter open with her fingernail. "But, Holly, you'll have to read it."

231

She unfolded the expensive bond paper, the type that easily cuts you, and smoothed out the sharp folds. "Dear Ms. Prickle:" (the *Ms.* no doubt put in by someone in Mr. Johnson's office, who would tell everybody why she got fired). "This letter is to confirm," Holly read in a scared voice, "your promotion to administrative assistant, effective July 1."

The rest of the words became a blur. "Fiona, you read it to make sure."

She took it and looked. "Congratulations! Of course that's what it says. And you deserve it," Fiona said, her own voice a little shaky. She came over and hugged Holly with a sweet-smelling hug. "See, you got your promotion when Rita did."

But that wasn't enough. She had come to BelCon before Rita did.

Then a worse feeling hit. Guilt. "So we shouldn't have shredded Rita's dress."

Fiona laughed her pretty laugh. "We did her a favor getting rid of that unbecoming outfit, child. She's wearing maternity clothes now anyway and will probably never fit back in her old ones."

Holly felt envy swirling through her.

But—how silly to have bad feelings now. "I'm an admin assistant," she said out loud, and the words were wonderful. Why, she never needed to be jealous of anybody again.

It was raining as they drove home, beautiful cleansing drops. And the sound of thunder was music.

"Are you still going to Fargo?" Fiona asked.

Holly felt her car hit mud. "Sure, I'll join Laurence. But he has to find us a house first. And it will be nice. He doesn't like cheap things."

232

The night grew darker as she thought of leaving her friend. "Fiona, will you come see me in Fargo?"

"They do have a summertime in the Dakotas, don't they? Child, of course I will."

"I know it's an icebox out there. But you probably appreciate spring more," she added, although she couldn't imagine enjoying any blossoms more than those here in Washington.

Fiona laughed, as she always could, even with her sad heart worrying. "And has Walter accepted Laurence as his stepfather yet?"

Holly swallowed. "I'm sure he will. You know how kids hate change." But maybe Fiona didn't know this about children at all, since she hadn't been blessed with any. And Fiona claimed that she was glad she didn't have kids—considering drugs and rock music and having them hate you. "But we will have a house and a yard in Fargo," Holly mentioned. "Laurence does spoil a woman, you know. That's what he says."

"So that's what he calls it," Fiona said, looking down at her dark fingernails.

# 35

# *Ramona in Rome*

*Ramona realized how spoiled she'd been by her American escorts as she forged through a mob of Italians outside the Vatican. They shoved and pressed against her as she elbowed up to bow down at the basilica. Then when she got there, a sign said in several languages, you guessed it—No Audience Today.*

*Incensed at the unreliability of the Pope, she marched across the street to the Tower of Pizza restaurant, where she ordered the local lasagna—only to have it arrive on a tilted plate that slid the messy pasta onto her lap. Damn.*

*With oregano on her tongue and Rodney on her mind, Ramona trudged towards the Colosseum to look for her true love there. He did favor acts of God and might consider ravenous lions as one.*

*"Rodney!" she cried out to the crumbling walls, but no roar came back. The maintenance in this place was a disgrace, certainly after you have experienced the immaculate artificial turf of NFL stadiums. She felt homesick thinking of the football tickets her father indiscriminately handed*

*out, which brought men swarming into their home like flies trying to get free seats, and a date with her.*

*A man down feeding the pigeons looked up at her. His raven hair could have been Rodney's, although the Italian's sloping shoulders weren't up to snuff. Ramona did notice such things after her embarrassing mistake in the Hawaiian islands, when she had approached the low native wearing Levis from behind, thinking he was her true love.*

*Speaking of the perfect torso, where was Rodney? Maybe he'd slipped carrying his laptop computer and fallen in the volcano, to be consumed by tongues of lava and digested into a lump of coal or, at best, a diamond in the rough.*

*And the other woman was only his mother, a troubled woman at that, with all those marriages. No wonder Rodney was cynical. Ramona wanted to caress his charred cheek, interface her fingers in his singed hair, and whisper, "I'm OK, you're OK."*

*Outside the Colosseum, she sat on the sun-baked ground to think where to look for Rodney next.*

*A donkey dawdled by, and something sprayed on her. This gave her an idea. She would go to the fountain where you throw in three coins and make one wish.*

*She had to ride a disgusting, noisy bus to the Fountain of Trevi, only to discover that it had deteriorated drastically since the photograph was taken for her travel agency. The statues had turned green in the polluted water, and the goddess crouching there had lost her head. Nevertheless, Ramona made a wish (you guessed it, to be in Rodney's arms) and tossed a lira in.*

*It sank dully to the bottom of the pool. Then a bigger, brighter coin flew in from behind her, possibly an*

*American quarter, glittering through the bacteria-filled water to land on the soiled tiles next to hers.*

*The ripples receded, and a face came into focus in the reflection. Yes—those were Rodney's sooty eyebrows arching over obsidian eyes. A voice behind her said in language she could understand—*

"So, when are you coming to bed?"

Claire jumped as something rubbed her neck where she sat at her computer, causing her hand-held mouse to scurry off the desk and dangle by its cord tail. "Jack. You startled me. Just let me finish this scene, and I'll be with you."

"You said that an hour ago," he said, giving her earlobe a nip. His lips moved to the back of her neck, sending a massive current down her spine.

"*Oh, Jack*. Has it really been an hour?"

"Yup." He massaged her shoulders, activating muscles she hadn't known were there.

Claire swung around to face . . . *her mysterious masseur*— sweet Jack. He was cute. And who would have dreamed that an engineer would be a linguistic godsend, offering the electrical vocabulary that would charge *Forbidden Fruit* with its magnetic juice.

"I'm coming now," Claire murmured. Giving her Macintosh an appreciative pat, that apple beyond compare, she joined the man in flannel pajamas she had so fortuitously married.

And as they glided in to their satin-sheeted bed, she trembled with anticipation for the moment when Rodney and Ramona would fuse their love forever.

236

# 36

# *Hog Heaven*

Holly's engagement to Laurence had come to an end. He'd never found the upscale farmhouse for them in Fargo, although he continued to call and say he couldn't live without her. Fiona finally pointed out the truth: "Honey, any man who writes you asking for money to live on in the Dakotas is trouble."

Holly knew this was true. Still, she missed Laurence terribly. When she passed the door to his apartment, she heard some other couple there. His van was gone from the parking lot. And every time she saw shiny bathroom fixtures, she would think of him.

But when she realized she didn't have to go to Fargo, she did a little dance. And Walter wouldn't have a step-father who nauseated him. The two of them had never gotten along, not since the day Laurence crawled around Paws & Feathers up until his final telegram inviting them out to the buffalo digs, that is, if they could finance their airfare and accommodations. They were also expected to bring their own receptacles for collecting buffalo remains.

"That was scary," Walter told her. "Mom, you almost married the world's goofiest guy." Warren, also, was more relaxed with Laurence gone, particularly in the vicinity of the bathroom.

"All right, I have a weakness for nice men," Holly admitted, getting up from where she was kneeling by the bathtub shining the taps. "But you won't have to worry about any more stepfathers. Walter, your mom is a love burnout. From now on I'm concentrating on my career."

For Fiona's sake Holly did agree to go to a singles bar one Friday night. And what could be safer? It's the last place you'd ever meet anybody decent. Supposedly Fiona was trying to cheer her up after Laurence LeFever. Yet Fiona was the one who needed to get out and stop worrying about her boyfriend's health. Hugo was back in the hospital with more heart problems.

The restaurants Fiona usually picked were the latest happy hour establishments, serving appetizers such as zucchini with tofu dip. (Fortunately they had regular food, too.) Fiona liked classy places after growing up on a farm in North Carolina.

But tonight she had a need for her roots. So Fiona had found a bar out in Herndon called Hog Heaven. It was the last place Holly would have picked, where the men do nothing but watch sports on television and won't say boo to you.

Fiona drove them in her Cadillac, which rode like silk out to where the air smelled country on this warm September night, a southern night with no city lights showing through the trees. Then up ahead they saw the gold neon sign blinking, Hog Heaven, Hog Heaven.

It was a shack with trucks parked out front, and Fiona drove her clean car to the end of the lot to park. But even that far away the smell of barbecue oozed out to them, and it was good.

They went inside and hoisted up on the last two stools at the bar. Holly got a whiff of male fragrance as she sat down, although she doubted it came from the man next to her, whose arms had so many tattoos on them she thought that they were sleeves. The person by Fiona rudely ignored her, talking nonstop to the woman on the other side of him—who must have wanted very much to meet someone, wearing an excessive amount of blue eye shadow.

Holly hadn't bothered with the blush or eye liner tonight, barely putting on mascara. She sat and drank a Coke and felt content, free of all the Les Moores and Laurence LeFevers of this world. She was happy.

Fiona, who wasn't so relaxed, drank a beer in large sips. This helped to loosen her up, although the shade of her fingernails indicated her true mood. And it was worse than dark. Tonight Fiona's nails had been stripped down to a flesh tone that looked nude on her.

For some reason, the men weren't watching sports on the two TVs hanging on the wall tonight. Their games must have been rained out, or it was that tragic time of year for them, between athletic seasons. A movie was playing instead. It was about three girlfriends on a vacation in Rome. What a nice Friday night, to be watching a romantic movie with your best friend.

Naturally, the man sitting next to Holly picked this moment to introduce himself. "Hi, I'm Rodney."

"Sh." She wanted to hear what the handsome Italian was saying to the girls. The tattoos edged closer to her, and Holly got up to find Fiona, who had gone to make a phone call.

There she was down a dingy hallway facing the phone on the wall, having one of those dreaded conversations with a hospital. Holly remembered the call she got when she was working at Star Kist, saying her mother had collapsed and was in intensive care.

Fiona hung up and turned around, her pretty complexion lit up with a color better than makeup. "Hugo wants to see me."

"I'll go to the hospital with you," Holly said.

"Honey, there's no need to give up your evening here. And if one of these gentlemen doesn't give you a ride home, I'll come back and pick you up."

"Don't make me even think of a man tonight, Fiona. I am so relaxed."

"I'm not saying to get all riled up," she answered, marching to the door. "But you might practice your flirting skills, honey, for when you will need them."

"Why even bother in a Hog Heaven?" Holly said. They stopped and looked back into the bar at the tattooed man, whose arm was spread across the counter space she'd left. "Just drop me off at home, Fiona. Really. All I want is to watch TV with Warren."

"Well, if you insist on putting yourself out of circulation," Fiona said with a sigh. "But you might try being detached with a man once in your life."

Holly laughed. "Oh, please. Come on, let's go."

So they escaped from the smoky bar into the warm night.

As they approached Fiona's car across the lot, it appeared to be parked in a pothole. Yup. Flat tire.

"We should have taken that auto mechanics class," Holly said, determined to sign up for it at the community college when she registered there in the winter. "Maybe we could change the tire ourselves," she suggested, getting down to look for a puncture. "You're the one, Fiona, who's always saying we should develop our identities."

Fiona stood with her hands on the hips of her dark shorts, her feet spread out in sandals. Only her toenails hadn't been updated to match the sorrowful mood she was in tonight. They stood out in fluorescent orange. "My identity, for sure, honey, is not getting soiled on the ground doing male manual chores."

"Women out west are not such wimps," Holly told her, running her fingers along the tread to feel for a nail or piece of glass.

Then behind her she heard Fiona say in her most southern voice (meaning a man was on the premises), "Hello."

Holly turned around where she crouched and saw Nikes coming at her, with bright spots of paint on them—yellow, maroon, green. She got up and stood at eye level with a man in a cheap plaid shirt. He had a dark red beard, almost burgundy, which appeared to have a gold fringe around it in this light. But the hair sticking out from under his Redskins cap was straight and brown. Why is it that men's facial hair never matches what's on their heads? No wonder they're confused.

"You ladies need some help?"

Holly would have told him they could call Triple A. However, it wasn't her car. Meanwhile, Fiona sidled over to the man, smiling up a storm. "We surely do."

"I'll get my things," he said and trotted off, going over to his pickup sitting on huge wheels. No doubt it was meant to build him up, but it made him look short instead. Not that he had a wimpy build. Shorter men often do have extra muscles in their arms, and this man did.

His name was Charlie Valley, and he lifted up Fiona's car on the jack as if it were a toy. Holly was in awe of people who can fix things, especially important machines. Anybody who can look into a car engine at the coiling wires and greasy pans and see what's wrong was a genius in her eyes. Meanwhile, when she stood stranded on the highway next to her broken-down vehicle she almost felt the world had ended.

However, she no longer worshiped mechanics, or went home with them.

*Fiona, where are you going?* Her friend was deserting her, going back inside Hog Heaven to make another call, leaving her here to entertain this stranger. "We do appreciate this," Holly told Charlie. "I'm sure you have better things to do."

"Not really." He went back and got the spare tire out of the trunk, patting it easy on the rubber as he rolled it along.

"Ordinarily, I wouldn't go to a sports bar," Holly said. "I don't care for football. I just came with my friend."

"Too bad," Charlie said, swiveling the bolts off the tire, the muscles in his arm firming up as he gave the first tough tug. Then he smoothly rotated the wrench as if the bolts never had been tight. "You're missing the fun, living in Washington."

"Watching men hurt themselves? I knew someone who never got over what football did to him. He was my . . . an acquaintance of mine."

"What type of injury was it?" Charlie asked, slipping the good tire into place, making it fit snug, so easy in his hands.

"Oh, nothing physical. It was his mind."

"A concussion? Ah. He didn't make the team."

Charlie was right. Eddie had been cut from his high school team for being undersized. "Yes."

Charlie nodded, letting the big car down easy. He kept his Redskins cap on, even though he was sweating. The red squares in his plaid shirt had turned the color of rich wine.

242

"I'll get you something to drink," she said.

He wanted a Budweiser, and Holly gladly hurried back to the bar for it.

As she came out of Hog Heaven with the cold beer in her hand, Charlie stood up in the parking lot to greet her. She knew he was only coming to get his beer. Still, the cool can sent a chill up her arm. Steady, girl. All men—well, almost all of them—know how to act like gentlemen to get what they want.

So she faced Charlie Valley calmly, making eye contact the way you do in the business world, not letting yourself shrink. And as he approached her, his eyes were as gray as the street. So there. That was one color she had never fallen for. Eddie's beautiful black eyes had gone into her heart for good. And Les Moore's blue ones left her handicapped on the floor of a health club. (However, she now believed that he wore contact lenses.) Then brown eyes come along that you can trust, only the person happened to be Laurence LeFever.

But a man with gray eyes, nah. Sure, she'd been impressed for a minute there, watching Charlie change the tire. Yet any sleaze on the highway can do it, raising himself up to be a god for a day with that kindly deed.

Charlie finished his beer, the cool can meeting his lips through his curly beard, with his head tilting back until you could see where the hair on his neck ended. And his skin wasn't all that red. His eyes came back level with hers, and he wiped off his lips and smiled. A small earthquake went through her, although nothing she couldn't handle after growing up on the San Andreas fault.

*Fiona, would you get back out here.*

"What type of things do you paint?" she asked Charlie as they walked back to the car. He had paint drops on his arms to match the colors on his shoes.

"Exteriors, mostly. I also do some carpentry. You need any kitchen cabinets?"

"Doesn't everyone?" She laughed, too loudly in this open parking lot. But shelves, beautiful shelves, who could resist. However, she did remind herself that a man who does home improvements is no more a saint than the one who is fixated on cleaning your bathroom.

"You want to give me your phone number?" he said.

She was ready to say *no*, she didn't need any more hassles with men. So why were her fingers flying into her purse looking for something to write on? She took the foil wrapper off a piece of Juicy Fruit and wrote her number on the back of it. Oh well, he was probably just selling his carpentry products and had no interest in her personally.

"What type of work do you do?" Charlie asked.

"Sec . . . rather, I'm an admin assistant," she answered proudly. "And I hope to keep moving up, although I like the boss I have now."

"He's lucky to have you," Charlie said, in a voice growing more magnificent by the moment.

"Thank you. Not that I bow and scrape the way I used to. You aren't even supposed to bring coffee to your boss any more. But I sneak Bill a cup when I feel like it. I don't see what's wrong with that."

Charlie laughed, a big warm laugh rolling out into the southern night. "No, ma'am. Guys have their problems, too. I opened the door of my pickup for a lady friend, and she called me a chauvinist."

Lady friend, what lady? "Well, that was silly," Holly said, when he was just being nice the way he was tonight changing a tire. But the situations were not the same, she knew. "We would be happy to pay you."

"No problem. Glad I could help." Charlie folded up the jack and went back to put it in the trunk, softly closing it.

Then he walked with her back to the door of Hog Heaven, where she had to go in and find Fiona.

"First, let me see if I can read this number," he said, holding up the little silver paper she'd given him in the golden light. She would be chewing Juicy Fruit all week, she knew it. He read out her phone number correctly in a voice that could have sung operas. Or maybe sound travels better through a beard. It certainly did in this case.

She stood outside Hog Heaven and watched as Charlie went back to his pickup. He was whistling. Oh, God. She'd met a happy man.

Hurrying into the ladies' room, she found Fiona fixing her makeup. "Well?" Fiona said.

"Well, yourself," Holly answered. "How is Hugo?"

"Afraid of having a pig valve put in his heart, not that he'll admit it." Fiona brushed her cheeks with blush until they radiated happiness. "Holly, what if—"

Holly looked at her friend, knowing well those dark goodbys that take the air out of you. "Hugo will live through it fine, I know he will. He's a feisty person, Fiona. You're always saying how much so."

Fiona smiled with her pretty capped teeth, in the bright light of the public restroom that showed the little wrinkles around her eyes. But she took good care of herself, and she was beautiful. "Well, yes, he is a scrappy one. And the little devil claims we're going on a cruise to the Virgin Islands when he gets on his feet. He says he's too much of a tightwad to die and lose his deposit." Fiona shut her container of blush with a snap. "Now tell me about this Charlie, honey. He is cute."

"With that big beard, and paint splattered on him?" Holly said. "Yes, he is, isn't he."

"Did he get your phone number?" Fiona asked as they went out to the car.

245

Holly looked down at the spare tire Charlie had put on personally. "Yes, he did."

"I knew it," Fiona exclaimed. But then in a more somber tone she added, "Of course a man asking for a woman's phone number can be just the male mouth talking. I swear, men are toilet trained to do that. And the ones who never plan to call you back are the worst. They just say they will to get off the hook."

Holly knew this to be true. Ah. "But Charlie didn't actually *say* he would call at all," she answered. "Anyway, if he did, he'd probably just be selling the kitchen cabinets he makes."

"Sugar, you're doing good, making yourself tough this way." Fiona put her arm around Holly's shoulders. "And I know it isn't easy, going against your nature and all. This is not an easy life."

# 37

# *Tightening the Belt*

Claire got up and closed the door to her office. Bill had been pacing by all day, and she couldn't concentrate on *Forbidden Fruit*. If only she could stay home and write. The distractions in this place were giving her writer's block.

OK. Back to the action.

*Ramona stared transfixed at the reflection of her true love's features in the fountain, as the words came from behind her—"You must be Ramona"—in the voice of a bitch!*

*She whirled around, confronting the woman who had hounded Rodney on the* Mango Maiden. *Yes, those were his charcoal eyebrows, although not nearly so attractive on the face of Rodney's mother! And just as Ramona had suspected on the cruise, the roots of her blond bouffant were black.*

*"Mrs. Rhodes," Ramona answered politely (since this witch might be her mother-in-law someday).*

*The chokecherry lips parted, and out came one of the least popular sentences in the English language, "We have to talk."*

"Claire?" A man with dark hair sticking up on his crown stood in her doorway. It was Bill Moss. "You got a minute?" The only person who said *no* to that was Leonard Pudding, who was not in the greatest favor around here.

"Sure," Claire answered, putting her writing in the drawer and locking it.

She followed Bill into his office. Sometimes he sat next to the person he was interviewing, trying to give the impression of equality. He didn't try that little trick on her today. He hurried around to his leather chair.

"Uh," he said, avoiding eye contact (which was the most important thing he had learned at the Harvard Business School). Then he got a paper out of his drawer and pushed it across to her.

It was an official memo from him. Subject: Termination for Lack of Work. She hadn't the faintest idea what that meant. The school lunch project had given them more work than they could handle. "What is this?"

"As you know, Claire, everything in this consulting business is scenario dependent," Bill said and coughed. "Not that we haven't appreciated the wordsmithing you've done, type of thing. But these government contracts don't necessarily include funding for that, as such. And, hell, we can't pay you out of overhead."

"So," Claire writhed, "you plan to keep on making million-dollar mistakes—because you're too cheap to put proofing in your production schedule?" She smoothed the quivering front of her blouse.

"I get your drift. We've got to tighten the belt some-where, though. Bill scratched his stomach. It was a tough

248

management decision letting you go. But a guy's got to bite the bullet," he muttered, gnawing on his pen.

Claire looked back at the ridiculous memo, trembling in her hand. "Discussions with BelCon's CEO reveal gaps in funding of existing as well as anticipated projects," she read aloud, hearing her voice modulate into a higher register. Gaps in funding. That was rich. "In order for the Company to meet its financial commitments, it has come to our attention that an immediate reduction in force (RIF) is imperative." What? She thought RIFs were only for government workers, military personnel.

How could this be? People in her family didn't get fired, much less riffed. They might be unemployable, sure. They were academics. Her brother, who had a Ph.D. in art history, was a house husband. And she'd had a hard time finding this ridiculous editorial position. Still, she'd never dreamed that anybody she worked for would let her go.

"This reduction in force is effective September 15 by COB," she read, in a voice growing increasingly shrill. She looked down at the calendar on Bill's desk. Shit. September 15 was today.

"Your past contribution to BelCon's advancement, Claire, is appreciated. Contact the personnel office for your outprocessing," she hurtled on, "and feel free to call on their assistance in finding re-employment.

"Thank you, and have a good day."

Bill was fondling the *CBD* in his mailbox now, thus indicating that this little meeting was over.

Thunder growled deep in Claire's brain. But as the storm cloud burst against her frontal lobe, BelCon's crack editor arose and holding her head high . . . *she strode away with the demeanor of a queen.*

Back in her office with the door shut, Claire breathed hard.

249

She stared at the résumés she was supposed to pump up for the next proposal. *Tailor* was the word they used. And guess what new market area Bill was going after this time? Cryonics. He was bidding on a cryonics clearing-house at such a bargain price for freezing heads he was convinced they'd win it "with our pants down."

All right, Claire thought. She would "tailor" Ned Bird's credentials to fit the cryonics project perfectly, no problem. She wrote the following to be inserted in Ned's résumé: "Dr. Bird is ultimately qualified to head this or any other cryonics project because his internal organs were frozen at birth."

What fun. But why waste her talents on this trivia? She never had to pump up a résumé again now that she'd been riffed (well, maybe her own). Her energies, her very soul, could be funneled into *Forbidden Fruit*, and its sequels.

As she took out her manuscript, she felt her writer's block dissolve. Words, phrases—paragraphs—pulsated through her fingers, pushing to get out.

*Mrs. Rhodes fanned her heavily made-up face with her blue-veined hand (flaunting a diamond the size of a peach pit) and faced Ramona. "I may not have been a model parent for Rodney, considering my many marriages. There have been five, you know," she cooed, stroking her obscene ring. "But nobody could say that I've neglected my son."*

*Ramona sulked in silence, knowing this was true. Then she thought of Rodney and cried, "We have to find him before the tidal wave from the volcano comes in. You know how he gravitates to acts of God."*

*"Yes, he does," Mrs. Rhodes agreed bitterly. "He has always run off to mother nature to get away from me."*

*Ramona could relate to that.*

250

*They hailed an Italian cabbie, who drove them recklessly out to the raging sea (barely missing a group of nuns carrying picnic baskets). Let's see, which sea was this one? Once again, Ramona was infuriated by the incompetence of her high school geography teacher.*

*The beach was deserted except for Italian litter—pizza crusts, discarded stolen purses—and a group of Japanese tourists taking pictures of each mounting wave as it came in. "I'd better freshen up," Mrs. Rhodes said, noticing the cameras and scurrying off through the sand to find a ladies' room.*

*Ramona pressed on towards the pounding sea, desperately scanning the rugged coastline for her true love's silhouette.*

*Suddenly a god-like figure in charred clothing emerged over a hump of sand. It was him! She would recognize that raven hair blowing in the wind anywhere. "Rodney!"*

*He turned, he saw, and flinging back his blue-black mane, he galloped towards her.*

*"Ramona, where have you been?" Rodney moaned as he trotted up to her, nuzzling her peaches and cream complexion with his charcoal one. "I was afraid I'd lost you in the lava," he said, hugging her. "But tidal waves bring me good luck. Isn't this one a dandy?"*

*Letting her go, he raised his arms to the wave that reared up before them with a giant lip of foam. "Ramona," he cried tumultuously, "if we don't get together soon, I'm going to explode."*

*Getting up off the sand where he'd dropped her, Ramona gasped, "But—"*

*"I know your virginal position," Rodney intercepted her words with a sandy kiss. But this relationship is putting me through a wringer. It's tearing me up. I'm afraid that—"*

251

*"Just what are you afraid of?"* Ramona asked, recalling her former boyfriend, Ed Ward, the wimp, who was frightened by a raindrop.

*"I'm afraid that I . . . love you,"* he spewed it out.

*Choking with emotion and salt water, Ramona echoed, "And I love you."*

*"But I have to warn you,"* Rodney said, putting a finger to her lips and sealing them with seaweed, *"if we move in together—"*

*"Move in?"* Ramona shrieked. He expected her to live with him? No way would she, a Tangerine Queen, clean up after a noncommittal male.

*"When we get a place together, mother will join us."*

*"What?"* She pounded on Rodney's massive chest with her insignificant fists. Then as Ramona stopped to rub her hurting hands, she remembered, *"Your mother is here, right here on this beach. Rodney, she's over in that outhouse now."*

*A thunderhead rose up in his face, although it soon gave way to a grin. "Well, good. We'll show her. Seize the day, Ramona. Seize it with me now,"* and he seized her.

*Ramona tried to fight him off, but her arms had turned to petroleum jelly. "A queen doesn't live with a man."*

*"Oh, all right,"* he muttered. *"Make it marriage then."*

*Marriage? A seismic shock wave surged through her, unleashing a lava-like emotion, of the type that melts mountains, reduces rock, and vaporizes a woman's virginity into a handful of dust. "Oh Rodney,"* she cried, *extending the entire magnetic field of her body to him, at last—*

Knock, knock.

Claire jumped up. "Come in," she said, piling résumés on top of *Forbidden Fruit*.

252

It was Leonard Pudding. He wanted to borrow her editing manual. "Here, take it," Claire said and jammed it in his hands.

"I'll bring it back," he said gruffly.

"No. Keep it as a present."

Leonard looked at her oddly. And Claire stared back at something different about him. His hair wasn't cut as short as usual on the bumpy back of his head. "And you're growing sideburns, Leonard. Looking good."

He turned the color of a damson plum, pressed the editing manual to his barrel chest, and left.

The phone on her desk rang. Damn. Claire took the receiver off, smiling vaguely as the male voice on the other end repeated its vain requests to the wall.

Heavens, it was four o'clock. Only an hour left in this prison. Dummy. She didn't have to stay now. She dashed off the last hot sentences of *Forbidden Fruit* and leaped up to throw her things in a shopping bag and get out of here.

She put in Jack's smiling picture. Then she tossed in a BelCon proposal for the jargon she might use in one of her romances. Her characters could meet in a consulting firm, working overtime. Right. That would make them hate each other. Barriers are good, though. You need them to keep your characters steamed up.

Claire took one last look around. Nice stapler. The cool feel of the metal was titillating to her touch. Why not? She dropped it in the shopping bag with her other booty and stealthily stepped out in the hall.

The coast was clear, and she made it down past the shredding room, a deserted area. Then she slipped into the back stairway, her personal favorite route for sneaking in late after her extended lunch periods.

Yikes, somebody was coming up the stairs. It was the slow, heavy step of a corporate male.

Claire froze on the stairwell, stuffing her shopping bag behind her shaky legs. "Good afternoon, why, Mr. Johnson. We'll be healthier climbing these stairs, won't we," she said. Meanwhile, her bodily functions were approaching the circuit breaker level.

"Yes, indeed," he answered and marched on up the stairs, swinging his slim briefcase with the lump in it.

She made it out to the parking lot and looked up. Sky! Trees! You forget about hands-on nature when you work in cubicles.

Staggering out to her car with her shopping bag, Claire got in and yanked off her high heels. Vaguely she realized that getting fired was one of life's most humiliating experiences. However, its significance had yet to penetrate. Of course she had always sympathized with the unemployed. But maybe they're happy. Well adjusted, too.

The thought of not getting a paycheck did almost cause her to flood her engine. But when *Forbidden Fruit* hit the stands, she could live off the royalties from it.

She sped out of the parking lot, amazed at how light the traffic was at this hour. She smiled, she laughed, she hummed along with "Hail to the Redskins" on the radio. She might even watch football with Jack this weekend. And it would be romantic with all the free time she'd have (once she broke the nasty news to her husband that she had been riffed). She drove gaily past the Imperial Arms Hotel. Good name. She made a note of it as a romantic setting.

And as it began to dawn on Claire that getting fired was a godsend—a mandate for her to write romance novels full time—tears of gratitude rose in her eyes.

Through this reverential blur, she sailed past trailer houses, in a tract called Paradise Park. Ha, there was the last place you'd use for a romance. Paradoxically, though, you could show that true love can survive even in a dump.

254

Aren't writers amazing, using everything they come across, even trash.

As she got closer to home, she envisioned the evening's scenario, when she would have to tell Jack that she'd been fired, drop that little bomb on him. Announcing that he would be their sole source of support was not a funny joke.

All right. She would wear the tangerine negligee she'd bought to test the waters for Ramona's seduction scene. And dim the lights. Ah, no. For an electrical engineer she should turn the lights up. Then she would read in magnetic tones to her husband from *Sources of Electricity*.

As Claire hurtled away from the life of consulting forever, she did have BelCon to thank for this: they had taught her that all things are possible in this fair world.

# 38

# Up the Corporate Ladder

The phone on her desk rang. Holly yawned. She couldn't imagine anybody exciting it could be. Charlie Valley from Hog Heaven, finally? Well, after two weeks, she wouldn't go with him anyway. "Bill Moss's office," she answered in her smooth new admin assistant's voice.

"John Johnson, here." Johnson? She hadn't met a man with a normal name like that in years. Whoops, it was BelCon's CEO. "Oh, *Mr.* Johnson. I'll see if Bill's in."

But he wasn't calling for Bill. He wanted her to come up to his office. To congratulate her on her promotion? Right. He was firing her! If they could get rid of Claire Whittle for no reason, he could easily terminate her.

Holly took the elevator up to the top floor, one of those smoothies that gets there before you feel it move. She stopped off in the ladies' room to make sure her hair wasn't sticking out in horns. Then she glided down to Mr. Johnson's office with the posture of a beauty queen.

Mr. Johnson's admin assistant, Elizabeth Kale, looked up from her post guarding his door. A CEO usually hires a showpiece to represent him, with the long blond hair and knees you can see all the way down the hall. Not Mr. Johnson. Elizabeth's hair was short and gray and combed straight back. Obviously, he didn't fool around with her.

Holly announced that she was expected, and Elizabeth raised her chin to say, *go in*.

She stepped into Mr. Johnson's office. Across the carpet he sat with his hands folded on his slicked-off desk. "Sit down, Mrs. Prickle." She sank into a chair that looked soft but was not. "I appreciated your message."

Message? She hadn't sent him any message that she knew of. It must have been the vibes he'd picked up from her and Laurence lying in the shredding room.

"You might think a guy in my position gets complimented all the time," Mr. Johnson said, taking out a handkerchief that he kept folded as he patted his forehead. "Quite the contrary. Praise is a relatively rare thing."

Holly couldn't have agreed more. But she didn't recall any opportunity she'd had to compliment him personally. "Everyone does need to be appreciated," she agreed.

His face turned a darker shade of tan. "Sure, I've had employees butter me up. But they don't put their remarks in a memo. Your correspondence is obviously genuine."

Memo. Oh, boy. It must be the one she'd written to Laurence on the new K-2000, replacing his name with John E. Johnson. The ad for the K-2000 hadn't lied: "Our memory saves what others lose."

"Mr. Johnson, I'm sorry. But that message wasn't meant for you."

He got out an envelope and removed the contents. "This part where you say it's exciting that we could meet in the hall at anytime—"

257

"Not meant disrespectfully," Holly explained.

"I was touched by that. And your memo came when I was having a bad day," Mr. Johnson said. "It gave me quite a lift. However, your comment saying I look 'handsome in tinted glasses,' well, I don't wear them." He took off the steel-rimmed glasses he had on and held them out to her. "Look. Plain. No tint at all. It must have been the light at the time." He polished them with his handkerchief and set them back on his straight nose.

"I think you *would* look nice in tinted ones," Holly mentioned.

"Think so?" Mr. Johnson's prim lips gave way in a little smile. "I'll look into it. However, I didn't call you up here to discuss my optical options," he said, clearing his throat. "I have a job for you this evening. That is, if you're free."

"Certainly, for work," Holly told him, relieved, and looking forward to the money.

"Good. I'll pick you up behind the building at five-thirty. Now you can go get your things."

Things, what things, Holly wondered, as she wandered out in the hall? Unlike a certain redneck, she didn't bring extra clothes to work in a paper bag. (And speaking of Rita, she still wouldn't admit somebody had fed her rat-colored dress to the shredder. According to her, she'd left it for the trash.)

And what job did Mr. Johnson want her to do tonight, Holly asked herself? Not that working all hours for BelCon was anything unusual. At least she hadn't been fired. And if you're thinking of sexual harassment, Mr. Johnson wasn't the usual type who chases women. In fact, he was so professional that he seemed shy.

Juse before five-thirty that evening, Holly stepped out of BelCon's back door and looked around the corner of the building. She almost expected to see a slinky black limo roll around, with a gloved hand in the back beckoning for you to come over, or else.

Instead, Mr. Johnson's white CEO-mobile promptly pulled up, and he leaned over and opened the door for her himself. She climbed onto plum velvet seats. "Good evening, Mrs. Prickle."

"Fine," Holly answered ridiculously, starting to hyperventilate on the expensive upholstery before they got out of the parking lot. As they drove to the corner, she thought she might faint. If he turned right, they'd be going to the woods. Whew, he made a left. Only now they were heading for the Imperial Arms Hotel just down the street. What an idiot, getting herself into this. Fiona had warned her from the first about this man.

At least the marquee of the hotel announced a convention, Macintosh Madness. Probably more people go to hotels for business, anyway, than to have cheap flings.

And Mr. Johnson brought his briefcase along when they got out, striding up to the front door of the hotel with all the dignity you could ask for in a man of his stature.

They went in the dark bar, where Holly figured they were meeting other people working on their project. She let Mr. Johnson buy her a virgin drink (although swallowing alcohol for no man). He ordered whiskey on the rocks for himself, which he drank rapidly. And he didn't take any goldfish crackers from the bowl in front of her. Nibble, nibble, she ate them. They were one of her favorite forms of seafood, next to tuna fish.

Mr. Johnson put down his drained glass, with the ice cubes barely melted. "Ready to work?"

The last goldfish dropped out of Holly's hand. She flicked the salt off her fingers professionally and nodded that she was.

The elevator stopped on every floor going to the top, but it still got there all too soon.

The room they went to was a suite, not the conference area she had hoped it would be, a silly hope Holly realized now. It had an oversized beige bed with a canopy, which might have been romantic in a story, but not this living nightmare she was starring in.

Trying not to show her fear, she strolled across the room to look out at the view. This place cost; it had a balcony. She tugged at the door until it broke open. She stepped out to see how far she would have to jump to escape from this married man.

The concrete parking lot was way down there. She held to the railing and looked up, startled to see a sunset. It was the color of cranberry, with gold streamers of clouds. Don't go down yet, sun. Off in the dark trees, the BelCon building was lighting up. If only she could be working late there now she would never complain again. Out at the horizon was Dulles Airport with its sunken roof, looking as if it had inhaled to avoid a low-flying bomber. A plane was taking off, a silver pencil, becoming a minnow that swam through the red sky and disappeared in the dark.

"Mrs. Prickle?" Mr. Johnson called from inside the hotel room. Stiffly she went over and looked in at him through the slats of the balcony door. He was sitting on the bed taking off his tie (causing her throat to become a knot). Up until this moment she had still believed in him, that he was a decent person. Then he did a strange thing. Mr. Johnson lay face down on the bed and made a moaning sound.

"Yes?" Holly went inside.

She asked if he wanted some water, that foolish thing you say to your child when you don't know what else to do.

She brought him a drink from the bathroom in the nice cut glass they had there. It was good enough to steal. "And do you have children?" she asked, holding the water out.

Mr. Johnson propped himself up and took a sip. "Two daughters." He took a gulp. "Two little girls."

"Daughters would be wonderful," Holly said, "not that I don't enjoy my son. I only wish I saw him more, although I know joint custody is fair."

"And I'll bet you're a good mother," Mr. Johnson said. "You want to hand me that briefcase," he asked, pointing to where he'd put it on the bottom of the bed.

Her legs were stumps but frightened stumps that moved. Even touching his attaché case gave her an eerie feeling. The secretaries had discussed what the contents might be. They had made jokes at the time. She inched the briefcase across the slippery bedspread to him.

"Go ahead and open it." Mr. Johnson handed her a tiny little key he dug out of his pocket. She was a person who always puts a key in wrong the first few times— backwards, upside down, who knows how—so Holly figured she would have a minute here. Wrong. This key slid in on the first try and turned as if it were oiled. The leather flap of the attaché case eased open, the way you breathe when your belt comes off.

She stood there trembling. It was now obvious that the object in the briefcase was a weapon. It was the exact shape of a gun. Or maybe a knife with a fat handle. Possibly a rope coiled up.

"And have you enjoyed working at BelCon?" he asked.

"Very much so," Holly answered, locating her vocal cords. "Especially getting promoted," she confessed. Fear rolled down through her like ice water.

"Glad to hear it. Now go ahead. Take it out." Mr. Johnson pointed to the place on the bed where her eyes did

261

not dare focus. Certainly she felt *some* curiosity as to the item he constantly carried with him—the same way she was curious about what it is to die.

She inched her hand into the smooth leather case, trying not to touch anything. It wasn't cold metal she felt, or a scratchy rope. Cloth. Soft, cottony cloth. She pulled it out, bulky and white. Maybe it was an oversized hanky such as she had imagined Mr. Johnson might need for the perspiration he shed in his high-stress meetings.

But the white material was no man's hanky. It was a rag big enough to smother uncooperative employees!

"As for moving up the company ladder, Mr. Johnson," her voice rattled on unbelievably, "you know better than any of us how satisfying that is."

He let out a small yelp, the sound of a stepped-on pet. "I'm not as successful as I appear," he moaned. "Sure, some divisions of BelCon are doing great, such as you people down in Special Projects, landing that school lunch deal. But overall we're on shaky ground." He lay back and stared morbidly at the ceiling, pulling the pillow up over both ears. "And as your CEO, I take full responsibility for overextending us," Mr. Johnson said loudly, "getting into those junk bonds. Now the big boys are sniffing around with this merger madness, Holly, giving me migraines. They gobble up little companies like us."

She got an Excedrin out of her purse and gave it to him.

"Good girl. Now, you want to hand me that," and he pointed to the white cloth she'd stuffed under the spread.

She carefully pulled it out, giving it a brisk shake to extract any weapons that might be concealed inside. Good heavens. It looked like a diaper. It was. Pampers, with the adhesive fasteners on the sides. (The poor man had incontinence problems at his age. And to think that Bill envied him.)

But why was Mr. Johnson revealing this embarrassing problem to her?

He got under the covers and was taking off his clothes. *This was it.* All your life you know the moment will come when you'll be attacked. If she could just reach her purse, car keys are supposed to be a good weapon. But she'd put it on the dresser so it wouldn't get stepped on.

"You want to help me get this thing on," he asked, handing his diaper out to her from under the sheets.

Holly took it, thinking back to the moment she first saw Walter. "No, I will not diaper you, Mr. Johnson." The role of mother was already degraded enough. "And do you realize how unbecoming this is for the CEO of a company? Plus, I don't get mixed up with married men." She pointed towards the balcony, where it was dark now. "You'll see me . . . jumping off there first."

Mr. Johnson's face lost some of its tan. He did have the face of a nice, clean-cut man—scrubbed skin, with no fresh nicks in it, or old scars. (Yes, Holly knew, decent-looking men are supposedly the rapists. But not all of them.) "I wouldn't want that," Mr. Johnson said, pulling his Pampers back under the sheets with him. She turned away to allow him his privacy.

"At least do this for me, Mrs. Prickle," he pleaded from the bed behind her. "Spank me, will you? Do it. Spank me hard. You can do it through the blanket if you want."

Holly turned around. Mr. Johnson was deep under the covers with his haunches up.

"Do it as a mother," he begged. "It's what I deserve, believe me I do. You have no idea how much." He pulled the sheet up over his head. "Think of those women's liberation people," he called out from inside his tent. "They would jump at the chance to strike back at male power. Go for it, Holly."

263

He was right about that. And after all her efforts to become a new woman (getting nowhere), the opportunity was being handed to her now.

Holly flexed her fingers and stretched out her palm, ready to administer the swat of a lifetime. She raised her arm as high as it would go. This was going to be great.

"Really whack me," Mr. Johnson called out excitedly. "Remember, I'm not a god, or even a very good man. I've been a competitive, greedy bastard all my life, when all my mother wanted was a Christian son. And now she's gone. So spank me for her," he panted. "Give me the whipping of my life for that poor soul."

She would do it, slap Mr. Johnson for his mother's sake—for the sake of all women wanting to lash out. Holly studied the contours of his buns beneath the sheets to decide where she could hurt him the most. Finally, she would have some clout.

Then her arm, which was aching, and her fingers, becoming stiff, came slowly to rest at her side. She liked her hand and refused to hurt it. Yes, she had failed to find her identity one more time. But she was sick of this silly trying. So she would do what she pleased. "Mr. Johnson, I'm sorry, but I don't like to hit people."

"You don't want to whack away at male power?" he called out. "You're giving me an outright *no* on this?" he said from inside his teepee.

Her heart was whacking, but she answered, "That's right." And since she had lost her job anyway by now, she could say anything she wanted. "Look at yourself, the CEO of a fine company, and with such low self esteem." Mr. Johnson's head came out from under the sheet. "What you need is a support group," Holly told him. "They have them for all kinds of problems. And we'll make a list of steps to improve your self image. I'll write them down."

264

Mr. Johnson looked at her with frightened eyes, as all men do when it comes to dealing with their personalities.

She got some Imperial Arms stationery out of the drawer, heavy duty paper with a manly crest engraved on it. She wrote Mr. Johnson's name in big letters, along with his title. "And if you follow these steps, I'll never mention anything about today," she promised (amazed to be using these blackmailer tactics, which she must have learned from the cop shows she watched).

"OK. Step number one. *Attend a support group*," she wrote, underlining the key concept the way they did at BelCon.

"Step two. *Share problems with your wife,* not other women."

"Oh, Marion would be disgusted by this," Mr. Johnson broke in, "seeing me this way. She gets her status from my, well, my position of respect."

"Then she needs her own support group," Holly said. "But how do you know your wife wouldn't enjoy hearing about your weaknesses? Women love that. Another thing. Call her from the office just to say hello. Bill Moss does that every day. He's a great husband."

"Really?" Mr. Johnson sat up in the bed.

"Yes. Step three. Require all BelCon employees to *call their spouses daily*."

"But I just issued a memo requiring cutbacks on the personal calls," he said irritably.

"Well, you could write a retraction admitting your mistake. People would love that. Not that you aren't well-liked now," Holly added.

"You think it would work?" Mr. Johnson asked, getting dressed under the sheets, making a zipping sound. "I'm always ready to try something that works." He got out of bed, fully clothed. "So, is that it?"

265

"One more thing," she said. "Step four. *Promote Bill Moss to Division Head.* And thank him in person for his services."

"No problem about the promotion," Mr. Johnson said, pulling on his suit jacket, of an expensive material that didn't give a hint as to his activities. "But is that other really necessary? Our official letter of promotion includes a statement of appreciation."

"And it's a wonderful letter to get," Holly answered warmly, remembering the almost perfect day of her life when she got hers. "But people still like a personal touch."

"I guess you're right," he said, folding his diaper to put it in his briefcase.

"Mr. Johnson," Holly said softly, "no."

He looked at her. "Right. I better get rid of this." He went over and dropped his Pampers in the hotel trash can with a slight thump.

"Congratulations. And remember, you want to remain abstinent on this. Now, I really have to run. Tonight I get to see my boy Walter."

# 39

# *Citrus City*

"Rita got her boy," the news came around the office. She had given birth to a ten-pound baby during half time of the Redskins game.

"Well, let's hope she's lady enough to stay home in her sick bed," Fiona said, blowing on her poppy red fingernails. Hugo was being released from the hospital today with the new pig valve in his heart pumping fine.

"Rita probably expects us to rush over and see the baby," Holly mentioned. "And since you are going to the hospital anyway, we could." They did owe Rita something after destroying her dress.

On the way they stopped to pick up a gift for the child who'd gotten Rita Staples as a mother. A cow that mooed and raised its tail was cute, but Rita might take it personally. So they bought a baby's burgundy warm-up suit that would make her drool. And to be forgiven, they bought Rita a matching sweatshirt, on sale, extra large.

In her hospital bed Rita looked no worse than she did in the office, actually better without her pink eye shadow.

Most people put on makeup to hide their red eyelids, not make them look that way. But this was Rita.

The nurse brought the baby in, healthy looking with a big smooth head. He resembled his father, Lonnie Bob, who was going bald.

Rita let Holly hold the baby. "What's his name?" she asked, taking the soft bundle in her arms.

"T. D."

"What if he isn't athletic?" Holly said. "T. D. would be an embarrassing name if he turned out to be a nerd." The little hand gripped her finger, cutting off the blood supply. OK. She was wrong.

"No kid of mine'll be a wimp," Rita stated, helping herself to a cherry chocolate out of a drugstore box, which she didn't pass around, just pointed for them to get their own. So tacky.

"Sugar, he'll get a rash with you eating that," Fiona warned. But Rita ate her candy.

"And a baby is more work than you think," Holly said. "Not just the diapers. They have incredible emotional needs. I don't know how anyone can do it, have a baby and work full time."

"They give you maternity leave," Rita said, picking a piece of cherry out of her teeth. "And with Ned quitting, they have to find me a new boss, anyway. Don't worry. I get my work done."

Ned was quitting? To go where? How irritating to have Rita spreading news Holly hadn't heard. Well, she knew something about Mr. Johnson that Rita would never know.

"Is Ned going to California?" Fiona asked. "I know that's what he's been agitating for."

"Yup," Rita said. "Bakersfield."

Holly smiled. He did want to get away from the rain. And speaking of moisture, T. D. was getting her arm wet.

She passed him back to his mother. "We better get going. Fiona is meeting her love coming out of surgery with a new pig valve heart. Can't you just see the two of them."

"That older guy, right?" Rita said, opening her night-gown to give T. D. his lunch, advertising the menu to anybody walking down the hall.

"Hugo's a gentleman is what he is," Holly answered.

"Rita is so rude," she told Fiona when they got outside.

"I just let it pass," Fiona said. "I let rude people slide right over me. And who can speak to the type of man Rita associates with. I only hope the baby's father sent something on this occasion. I didn't see a flower in the room."

"Maybe he sent the cherry chocolates," Holly suggested, thinking how lonely it would be if the father didn't show up to brag about his new son.

As they went down the long white hall to Hugo's room, Fiona said, "It's a shame you and Eddie didn't have another child, at least at the time."

"It was," Holly said, remembering. "And Eddie's low sperm count was a reason we broke up, I know it was. It took us four years to have Walter." She thought back to the days of taking her temperature and rushing home from Star Kist on her lunch hour. Eddie hurried home, too. "And it was a happy day for Eddie when Walter was born."

After seeing Fiona and Hugo reunited—him looking frail but jolly in his wheelchair—Holly still didn't envy their situation. All that caring and hoping and sexual tension can drain you, especially if the man is an invalid.

She took her time driving home around the beltway, gazing into the trees looking for fall colors. Last year's leaves had stayed brown. Yes, there was a patch of yellow amidst the green, yellow, the first color.

Then she saw something that wasn't so great. The glittering traffic had stopped. And a helicopter rattled overhead to broadcast the backup, so it must be a bad one. Drat. She might have met Fred Trisket stranded out here in a blizzard, but nothing like that was going to happen today.

She got out and learned that a tractor trailer had overturned. The last time that happened, eggs were scrambled across four lanes of traffic. Today it was a citrus spill.

Up ahead she could see the big truck lying on its side, a huge silver box across the road. She hiked on up to see the mess, sniffing as she went, and sure enough, detecting juice. The smell of citrus out of doors made her homesick for Long Beach, her mom's back yard where a lemon tree hung over the wall. When it dropped a big lemon in their yard, they made a pie. Maybe she had boycotted fruit long enough. Her mother may have died bottling peaches, but it was what she liked to do.

Holly hiked up to where the broken crates of fruit were toppled in the road. Cars swerved around the barriers, smacking grapefruits and chasing after escaping oranges. The lemons got out of the way easier, some of them still looking good enough to eat.

Sitting on the ground next to the fallen truck was the driver himself with his head down in his hands, probably wishing this wreck had knocked him out. Imagine calling your boss to report the incident, explaining that you had never dozed off before. Yet now the ton of fresh fruit in your care was spoiled, and miles of commuters sat in their hot cars swearing at you. Or maybe this truck driver hadn't fallen asleep at all. He could have had a fight with somebody before he went on duty. And with the hot words still revolving in his brain, the load he carried strayed into the next lane. Whatever had happened, the man wouldn't be getting his promotion now.

An ambulance came screaming up in the emergency lane, and the medics jumped out to attend to the stricken truck driver, getting him down on a stretcher. He was saying something, and Holly wished she could hear what. Was he begging for a sedative to erase the sight he could never forget? Everybody has those days when they could become a drug addict.

A motorcycle came weaving through the stalled cars up to the accident. The driver was wearing a black leather jacket in this heat and a white crash helmet. A policeman giving a ticket for what? The bike wobbled over to the railing, and the officer slowly climbed off, steadying himself. He was not a large person, standing on legs that stayed the shape to fit his bike. He yanked off his helmet, showing his black hair sweated down. He took a step, and it was a walk that she knew well.

Move your feet, Holly. Now. But they must have been stuck to the sticky road.

He was looking at her. "Holly?" he called across the sweet-smelling road in a voice resembling no other.

She nodded, her face going up and down on a string. Here he came, high-stepping across to her, kicking a squashed orange out of the way with the sharp toe of his boot. He skidded on his heel, almost falling. But he stayed up, he made it, hugging his helmet to his skinny side. "Holly."

He was standing in front of her.

"Eddie, hi," she answered in a voice that sounded nothing like the smooth one she practiced at work. It wasn't Eddie's former wife speaking either but some other new person. "I never thought I'd see you here," she said, "although I always look for you on the highway."

"I didn't expect me here, either." Eddie laughed and took his goggles off, showing those magnificent eyes that

271

could make you forget everything else, such as his scrawny build. Of course, she had loved that too at the time, every part of him. But Eddie did seem smaller than she remembered.

He smiled and still had a tooth missing on the bottom, knocked out by a baseball bat. She felt so glad that no other woman had gotten him to the dentist to have it fixed, either. Maybe Eddie and his wife would get divorced sometime. There was something to look forward to.

"Heck of a mess, isn't it." Eddie grinned, looking across the highway littered with rinds.

"I'll say," Holly answered, managing a small laugh.

He shifted his helmet to his other hand. "How've you been, Hol?" he asked, using the nickname he had invented.

"Fine. Really fine. And Walter's school is going fine."

"So he says. Seems he got both of our brains added up," Eddie said, scratching his hair.

"Yes, he did." She laughed, a real laugh this time. "And congratulations to you, Eddie, for making it to the bike patrol. I know that's what you wanted."

"I did. It's good. The work is good." He pushed his hair out of his eyes and wiped his hand on the leg of his dark uniform.

She waited. "Well, aren't you going to congratulate me, too?"

Eddie gave his holster a pat. "You mean for getting engaged to some guy taking you out, where, Montana?"

"The Dakotas," Holly said. "But that's over. I was referring to my promotion."

"That's good you got it, real good," Eddie said, looking out to where the sun came through the trees, making the yellow leaves bright. He put his hand up to shade his eyes.

"Eddie?" she asked, feeling the question come up in her that always did.

"Yea?"

"Whatever happened to us?"

His shoulders gave a little slump, and he looked over at the truck lying on its side. "Things just happen. Life going along, I suppose it is." He shoved his hands deep in his pockets. "Hell, I don't know, Hol," he answered quietly. "Heh, you want a ride back to your car?"

Holly glanced at the place on his motorcycle where she used to sit on his first bike, hugging him as they sped along. Her hair was long in those days, flying out behind. Maybe it was even beautiful. "Thanks. But I just guess I'll walk. It isn't that far to my car."

He nodded.

Down the road people were getting in their cars. An engine started up, and she took a quick step in that direction. Something squished under her foot, but she kept on going, trying to make her stride look confident, the way you do at work.

"I'm glad for you, Holly," Eddie called. His words, and the warm breeze coming behind her, made her smile. Her whole body smiled. "You deserve that promotion you got. Everything."

She couldn't see the ground by then, but her feet were glad for the gravelly earth that did not give way. The warm scent of citrus rose up deliciously to greet her where she went.

# 40

# *Drop Kick Me, Jesus*

"Mom, a guy named Charlie's on the phone," Walter called to Holly where she was watering her last living fern.

"Hog," she whispered the mantra she'd practiced in case this moment should come. She had even written down her long-term goal: *No more men.*

If you answer, you know what happens. (1) You go on one date and come home crazed with love. (2) If he doesn't call back, you think something is wrong with you. (3) If he does, your child becomes sickened by this potential stepfather. (4) You break up. (5) Life is dirt.

She would just say no.

She went in and took the phone from Walter, holding it against her chest as she explained what she was doing.

"You're kidding," he said.

"I've turned down men before" she whispered.

"Who?" Walter asked.

"A mother doesn't have to explain every man she's refused to her nine-year-old son," she answered, stuffing the phone under a pillow.

"I'm almost ten."

"*Walter,* would you help me out here." OK, Holly told herself. Just speak professionally the way she did when she screened people who were calling her boss.

"He wants to go for a drive," Walter informed her. "You should go."

Is that all Charlie wanted, to go for a drive in the daytime? And after he'd waited weeks to call.

Holly retrieved the phone and prepared to say *no*. Still, you can't run away from your problems. The only way to be cured of men was to be in their presence and then not care. And a person you met at a Hog Heaven would be perfect to practice on.

"Sorry to keep you waiting," she spoke into the phone. "I was just talking to my son. Of course, I remember a person who fixed our flat tire. And I would like to take a drive. But I do have to get back and help Walter with a report he's doing on the bald eagle as an endangered species." Walter waved at her to say no, wagging Warren's ears from side to side, but she wasn't swayed.

"OK, I'll have you back." Charlie asked for her address and said he'd be there in half an hour

"Fine," Holly said in her most casual voice.

It did look desperate, she knew, going with a man on the same day that he asks you. And yet if he's nobody to you, why not?

She got her oldest jeans out of the closet, holding them up to Walter where he was lying on the floor with Warren sitting on top of him. "See these old Levis? This is not what you would wear if you were planning to fawn over a man."

"Just don't freak out over somebody weird like that LeFever guy," Walter said. Then he proceeded to kiss a rabbit full on the mouth.

"Laurence was a good person," Holly said, noticing sand on the knees of her jeans, which she did not brush off. "He just had problems like anybody else."

"Mom, his problems were *not* like anybody else's. Crawling in a pet cemetery looking for buried gerbils that he said his wife stole? And you made me wear a suit for that."

"I'm sorry, honey." Holly turned away so Walter wouldn't make her laugh at her former fiancé.

Realizing that she wasn't with Laurence did help her relax, not that she was tense. In fact, when the knock came at the door—watch this—she didn't budge. Finally, she strolled in the living room to answer it (oops, the long shoelaces on her Reeboks made her trip). Well, that thud could have been anything. She got up and swung the door open. "Hello, Charlie."

"Hi. How're you doing?" His beard had not been trimmed. Mes-sy. This was good. And with those eyes the color of a sidewalk, there was nothing to worry about here. "Does Walter want to come along?" Charlie asked.

Ha, a man might think he's making points by inviting your child to go on the date. Meanwhile, you get grilled when you come home and have to explain why you went out with another loser. "That's OK," Holly said. "He's going to a friend's to watch the football game."

They went out to get in Charlie's truck, up on the big tires that made him look small. This was going to be easy.

She climbed in and settled onto the high seat, so glad she didn't have to talk today. All your life you carry on ridiculous conversations with men, thinking you're a big success if no silences crop up. But not today.

She looked over at the gearshift between the bucket seats, which had caused her so much discomfort crawling over it in the past to get to the driver. She would nibble on the man's ear so he wouldn't be bored doing the driving—when she was obviously the one bored out of her mind.

Charlie did take her favorite road going out to Reston, conveniently close to where she worked, not that it mattered. It was a road winding through trees, where the leaves had turned bright red, apricot, gold, with the sun shining through their veins. "Yes, very nice," she responded to Charlie's raving compliments to the foliage.

He turned on the radio, getting a commentary about the Redskins game that afternoon. They were playing the Dallas Cowboys. "It's going to be a physical game," the announcer said.

"Of course it's physical," she commented. And she had thought football was over her head.

Charlie laughed, pulling on his beard, the way that dumb guys do. "Sportscasters can be pretty inane," he said. *Inane, inane*? What kind of word was that he was using on her? And naturally when she didn't have her desk dictionary handy. He could even have made the word up.

Holly yawned and looked out her window, where a whole tree was lit up the color of a tangerine. "It is such a brutal sport, football." Eddie had never gotten over being cut from his high school team. And now she had seen Eddie again! She pictured him riding his motorcycle through the rinds on the beltway in the citrus spill. He had looked good. "I guess you played football," she said.

"Nope," Charlie answered. "Wearing that heavy equipment to practice in the heat, and they make you do double time around the field. It's murder. Heck, I'm a spectator. I watch it on TV."

He did have the easygoing build of a couch potato. Holly gazed out the window, as the sportscaster now announced that "the Redskins have to get some points on

277

the board today." Really, who needs a paid person to tell you that?

Then as if Charlie had read her mind, he changed the station to country music. And they were playing one of her favorite songs, "You Picked a Fine Time to Leave Me, Lucille." Wouldn't that feel good, walking out on the man for a change.

After while a song came on that Charlie liked, "Drop Kick Me, Jesus, through the Goal Posts of Life." It said not to kick the ball too far to the left or too far to the right but straight down the middle. At least the song taught you more than the sports announcer on the radio. Still, a song about dragging Jesus onto the playing field for your own success, the poor Lord.

Holly lay back and closed her eyes. Having all this control over her life was making her sleepy. Then a picture came in her mind that she didn't ask for. It was Charlie in the Hog Heaven parking lot, though not him showing off his muscles turning the wrench. He was rolling the tire along, patting it easy on the rubber, giving it love taps.

She could feel him next to her now, breathing the same air, as if a magnet were pulling her over to his side, and she was the nut. But don't worry. She wasn't climbing across the gearshift for this man. Look, see, she was holding onto her seat.

Lust, that's all it was. The lust you get from boredom.

She looked over at Charlie's frizzy beard through slitted eyes. Today it wasn't fringed with gold as it had been the night they met.

Then she made the mistake of looking up at his face. And the profile of his nose was so perfect that the swallow stopped in her throat. Not that good looks in a man made her go berserk any more. In fact, men's perfect parts can make them cruel.

278

So what did Charlie do at that moment but take off his Redskins hat, as if to prove he wasn't overly handsome after all. He was going bald. She wanted to reach over and touch his head where the skin was showing, not that she would think of making the first move with a man. Her mother had taught her right and wrong.

On the other hand, if the man doesn't mean beans to you, why not? And the day she could get physical with a man and *then* not care, she would be liberated. She would definitely be a new woman if she could learn casual sex. Her heart came in little jumps just thinking about it.

She would do it. She would seduce Charlie today. And since he wouldn't be calling her back (they never do if you give of yourself on the first date), she could relax and go completely wild.

But what if he did happen to ask her out again? Well, she would turn him down anyway, and enjoy doing it. So she hoped he would call back, please, yes.

"I'll show you my place," Charlie said.

Oh, boy. "Good," she answered, stuffing her hands underneath her legs so he wouldn't see them shake.

They drove into a subdivision of big frame houses painted in pastels. He lived there? But she wasn't that impressed. These places were boring without any landscaping. However, this was a neighborhood where you would expect to have a callous affair. "You live here?" Holly asked, running her tongue across her dry teeth.

"Nope," Charlie answered. "But I paint these places. I have my own little company, you know, and business has been good." Gulp, he was successful. Still, small businesses fail, Holly reminded herself. Most of them do.

"Do you have any unusual pets?" she asked, preparing to look for crevices in his bathroom or openings in the upholstery where strange creatures might appear.

"No. Just a dog. German shepherd."

How ordinary. "I have a rabbit. You'll have to meet War—" Holly stopped herself barely in time to keep from inviting Charlie over on a future occasion, since there wasn't going to be one.

The road got narrower, and the houses along here weren't so nice, with the appliances out in the yards. Yet the trees were beautiful. The leaves made a colored roof over their heads and dancing shadows in the road.

They arrived at a tract of trailer houses called Paradise Park. Charlie must be kidding. He was turning in here. Still, this low-life, transcient place would be perfect for the quickie affair she had in mind. Her heart beat rapidly.

"At least it's mine and paid for," Charlie announced as they bumped down the drive to a lemon-colored trailer in the trees. The yard was landscaped with painted inner tubes that had flowers growing out of them, old roses with bowed heads.

"As you can see, I don't have much of a green thumb," Charlie said, chuckling. (So inferior to her father.) She envisioned Charlie's lips inside his beard as he spoke. And not being a prostitute, she did kiss a man on the mouth. "But if you want something painted, I'm the guy."

They went in the little living room of his trailer house, where the decor was what you'd expect for someone you met at a Hog Heaven. Brown, brown, brown, although not what you would call earth tones. The arm of the stuffed beige chair was just a darker shade than the rest.

Charlie picked up a beer can off a table made out of a barrel and squashed it with one hand. So? All men do that (except Eddie, who used his foot). "I have cleaned the place since Rhonda lived here," he announced. "She wasn't much for the housework, either."

There it was! The man isn't alive who doesn't drag in his other women the first minute to torture you. Well, she could tell a few Laurence LeFever stories to give him fits (or mention Eddie to be really cruel). But why bother to make the other person suffer when you don't care?

It is sad, though, that as you go through life everyone has so much baggage. Yet Charlie *had* said that Rhonda was a lousy housekeeper. So not all baggage is bad.

"That must have been cozy, two people living in a trailer," she said, going over to check Charlie's lumpy couch for holes in the ragged weave. He had claimed that no strange pets lived here. She patted the upholstery, and nothing came out. OK, let's get on with the flirting. Or—why waste time chitchatting in the living room? She got up and boldly walked towards the bedroom.

"I have a surprise for you," Charlie said, coming behind her. Just don't ask her to go in the bathroom, please. He didn't and swung the door shut as they passed it (where she'd already seen a pair of Levis sitting up on the floor, which at least was normal for a bachelor).

"Close your eyes." He put his warm hand around her forehead. The callouses on his fingers tickled her skin, making her wonder how much pleasure you're supposed to have with casual sex. It couldn't be none.

"Ready?" Charlie said so close to her ear that the hairs inside it stood up. He took his hand away. "There it is, my masterpiece."

Holly looked into an amazing room. Everything was done in burgundy and gold. A hog hung down from the ceiling made of maroon papier mâché with a gold foil snout, twirling over the big low bed. The burgundy comforter was decorated with gold helmets that seemed to float. And the floor was painted green. "You certainly are loyal to the Redskins."

"You might say so." Charlie laughed. "I have my fun."

Then when she saw what was next to the bed, she took a big step back. A huge dog was sitting there. "Say hi to Vince." Holly tried to greet the German shepherd cordially, realizing that he couldn't help his enormous size—or that he was trapped in a trailer with a maniac football fan. When the appropriate words wouldn't come, she did manage a small bark.

Vince nodded at her politely and didn't drool. Pet lovers do enjoy having their pets in the bedroom. You miss the warm place at the bottom of the bed when they aren't there.

"Guess I got a little carried away with the decorating, didn't I?" Charlie said. "It gave me something to do with myself last year."

"You did this yourself?"

"Yup. I also do carpentry, you know. So I built the frame for this water bed." He looked down at it. "I read up on how to do it in a book. But I still got it too low."

Yes, *low* was the exact word Holly would use for this entire experience—now that she realized she was standing in a playboy's den. "At least Vince won't hurt himself leaping off a mattress this close to the floor," she said (if he didn't spring a leak and drown them all).

Holly looked at Vince, and he gave her strong eye contact for moral support. She boldly reached over and touched the smooth skin on Charlie's head, which she had been itching to do. Very nice.

"Pathetic, isn't it." He smiled and took her hand. Not pathetic at all. Very sexy, actually.

They sat down on the bed, way down, and she entwined her fingers in Charlie's beard, which felt better to touch than look at, just as the skin on his head did.

He put his arms around her, and the world began to sway.

282

*Keep it casual, Holly. Remember, this is just cheap sex.*

"First," he said, "I want to tell you about Rhonda." That was it. There isn't a man on the planet, is there, who doesn't harp on other women. Rhonda this, Rhonda that. Well, we'll see who gets zapped this time.

Holly leaned over and snapped open the top snap of Charlie's K-Mart shirt. Careful, don't rip the cheap cloth. She touched his jugular, detecting a nervous pulse beat. If she pulled his chest hairs that could hurt. *Rhonda* is it.

Then she had a wonderful thought. If all men harp on their other women, Eddie must mention her. He could be saying her name at this moment.

"I'll tell you about Rhonda now," Charlie began. Holly squeezed his little curly hairs, getting ready to pull. "Then I won't bring her up again."

What? Her entwined fingers stopped what they were doing and became numb against Charlie's chest.

"We lived together for three years. I wanted to get married," he explained. "But Rhonda needed to find her identity, as you liberated ladies say. So she left."

The poor man. And she had made Charlie listen to the words of the song about cruel Lucille walking out on her husband. Holly tried to slip her hands out of Charlie's shirt inconspicuously. Maybe he wouldn't notice that she'd been coming on to him. It is possible for a man and a woman to touch as friends.

Right. She had practically mauled the man. "I guess we are all looking for our identities."

"You're good the way you are," Charlie said.

Oh, God. Holly moved away from him on the swaying bed, praying that it wasn't too late to come across as nice. "I should be going." She smoothed out her Levis, which looked as if they had rolled in dirt. A decent person would

283

have worn permanent press. "I did promise Walter I'd get back and help him with his report on the bald eagle." She looked over at Charlie's head, and it shone.

"I know you don't like football, Holly," he said, lying back on the bed, spreading out his arms the way you do to make snow angels. "But stay for the game today, then we'll do what you like next time."

Next time, *oh beautiful words.*

Charlie got up and turned on the biggest television she'd ever seen, getting the cheering of the crowd as the team jogged out on the field. That was one part of the game she hadn't hated. Sometimes she turned on sports events while she did housework and pretended the applause was for her.

"I could watch one game. Sure."

"Great, have a pillow." Charlie tossed her a gold velvet one shaped like a football, which she caught close to her soccer chest.

Then she lay back to watch Washington play the Dallas Cowboys with him, relaxed, since a man won't make a move on you while his game is on. Vince also jumped up on the bed with them, making the situation all the more wholesome, except for the tidal wave it caused.

"And would you explain the plays, in language I can understand?" she asked.

"Sure, if I can figure them out myself," Charlie answered, and he smiled at her. His eyes were not gray after all. They were a soft sea green.

He took her hand and kissed it. "I like you, Holly." And as she watched the football wobble up into the sky, she was beginning to see how it can lift you up, too.

And, yes, Charlie did get her home that night in time to help her son with his report on the endangered eagle.

284

Walter wanted to use the K-2000 to draw his bird, so Holly drove him over to the office, honking along the beltway with the other cars celebrating the Redskins' victory that day. They had beaten Dallas— *by one point.* Whipped those Cowboys in the last minute of the game.

And she knew now that it is the team in Washington that brings the people together.

While Walter was doing his report, she delivered a box of Snickers to Bill's desk to congratulate him on his promotion to Division Head. It came through just before Mr. Johnson went on an "extended leave of absence to spend time with his family" the memo said. Mr. Johnson had also put out a memo regarding phone calls to spouses, requiring all BelCon personnel to call home on a daily basis, "in order to enhance Company morale and facilitate familial interface."

Meanwhile, as Division Head, Bill was going for the jugular in the next new market area, bidding on a cryonics clearinghouse this time. When Leonard explained that *cryonics* means you freeze people's heads or their whole bodies, to be thawed out at a later date, Holly thought he was kidding. Leonard had changed his image by growing in sideburns. However, he hadn't gone so far as to become a funny guy. This business of freezing heads was real.

She put Bill's Snickers bars next to the *CBD* and went to check on Walter. He was fine-tuning his eagle's beak.

So she took a stroll down the hall, stopping off at Claire Whittle's vacant office, which Bill was saving for a cryonics specialist if he could find one.

Holly went around and sat in Claire's chair. This was the life, having an office with no machines in it. She should work up to editor in her next career move. She already knew the editorial markings Claire put in the margins to point out other people's mistakes.

She looked in Claire's drawers for materials about editing, but everything was pretty much cleaned out. Then in the back of the drawer she found a note pad with Claire's handwriting on it. What was this?

*Rodney swept Ramona into his arms, kissing her trembling lips, her throbbing throat, and gravitating to the delicious oasis of her cleft, lying between breasts that sat up like muskmelons to taunt his thirsting soul. "Yes, Rodney, yes," she said this time, and he squeezed her.*

Holly stopped to breath. She knew Claire was a good writer. But she didn't know she was this good. What proposal was this for, though, school lunch? The header said *Forbidden Fruit*, and they had eliminated a lot of fruit since the kids don't like it, plus the pesticide scare and all. Still—

*The blood rushed to Ramona's head.* (Maybe Claire was writing this for the cryonics clearinghouse.) *"Oh, Rodney," she moaned, "this is so good. But can it last? Can even true love last forever?"*
*Rodney stroked her scorched auburn hair, gazing out at the horizon where storm clouds brewed. "Ramona," he whispered, "as long as there are acts of God, I will gravitate to you."*

Holly was sitting still as a cactus when Walter walked in. "Mom, where have you been? Hey, I'll bet I found Rita Staples's station. You're right. It's slobby.'"
"Come and show me, son." She arose and glided along BelCon's hallway, past the supply closet with its clean smell of paper, full boxes of envelopes, and all the bright colored paper clips you could desire.

286

Rita's work area, on the other hand, was its usual mess. And she'd put more pictures on the wall, naturally without framing them. Next to the enlargement of her yappy poodle (a soiled little dog compared to magnificent German shepherds) was Rita's baby. And, look, T.D. was wearing the warm-up suit she and Fiona had given him. He did look cute bundled in his burgundy outfit, with his bright baby's eyes shining out from under his gold hood.

"Why did Rita stick a letter on the wall?" Walter asked. (Holly didn't stop him from picking at the masking tape.)

She went over to see. The letter was announcing Rita's promotion. So? Holly had one just like it.

Then she stopped and stared at something. Rita's letter said, "Promotion effective July 15." A thrilling feeling went through her. "Walter, run get my letter. It's on the wall over my desk, framed. Just take it off the nail and be careful. Hurry, and don't drop it."

He came trotting back, holding the precious document to his body, what a good kid. "Read the part where it says 'promotion effective.' Read it out loud. Take your time, son." Walter had always done well in his reading classes and was practically gifted.

He held out her framed letter. "It says 'promotion to administrative assistant, effective July 1.'"

"Oh, Walter." Holly leaped up and went over to hug him. She knew she had remembered the date right. "Isn't this great?"

"What?"

"That Rita didn't get her promotion until July 15—and I got mine on July 1. You just read it yourself."

"So, what's the big deal?" Walter wondered. Children do torment you, pretending to be innocent.

"Walter, two weeks is plenty of a big deal. It's a whole pay period, for heaven's sake, something you will under-

287

stand some day. And this shows that BelCon appreciates me after all."

"Good, mom. I'm glad. And since you got a raise, can we buy a four-wheel drive, please, please?"

"Walter, don't press me."

The thought of cruising past low police cars in a Bronco did make Holly smile as they drove home on this fine Virginia night, a place on the earth where darkness does not mean cold. There was no moon, but the car lights were golden, and the street lights were enough.

"So, how was that guy Charlie?" Walter asked.

Her car spurted ahead. "He was wonder—he was OK."

"Where'd he take you besides driving?"

"We watched the game. It was good."

"The game wasn't good, mom, it was *great*. But I don't believe you watched football." Walter flopped his head back on the seat. "So, you must be bonkers over this guy already."

"Don't be silly," Holly told him. "In a trailer house, on the first date—and with a German shepherd on the premises? But you should see Charlie's room. It's all done in burgundy and gold, with a hog hanging down in the middle of the room over this huge water . . . OK, Charlie has a water bed. And a huge TV."

"You watched the game in the bedroom of this guy's trailer?" Walter hooted. "You must have really made out there."

"Oh, Walter. I am your *mother.*"

"Yahoo," he hollered out the window to the traffic. "And she's a Skins fan, after all." Then he came back in and said more soberly, "Did he say he'd call you back?"

Holly kept on driving without saying a word. No, Charlie Valley had not said he would call.

288

Better! "He's taking me to a Redskins game next week. His friend who had a heart attack gave him his tickets."

"I don't believe this," Walter said. "You know how long people have to wait for those tickets? They put you on a list for years. You could wait until you're old. Until you're dead."

Holly sang along, "Hail . . . to the Redskins," taking her time before she dropped the next bomb. "And guess what else. Charlie has three tickets. Walter, you're invited to the game, too."

"Whoa." Walter sat up. "Really?" He looked over at her with shining eyes. And for once he didn't have a smart comeback.

"Also, it's possible to get tickets for wild card playoffs if you stand in line all night," she said excitedly. "We could do that and surprise Charlie, take our sleeping bags. It could be fun."

"Unbelievable," Walter put his head back and closed his eyes.

They had arrived in his father's neighborhood by now, and it was time to drop her son off. But Holly had forgotten to stop by the hydrant at the end of the block and driven up to Eddie's door.

OK. Here goes. She sat and watched her son get the whole way inside the lighted house before she looked away.

On her way home, Holly drove by the church in her neighborhood, where she stopped and sat in the warm, quiet night. The street was covered with yellow leaves.

"Thank you, Lord, for my life," she said softly. "For letting me have Walter." She touched the seat beside her. "And that he isn't too messed up coming from a broken home.

"For seeing Eddie and not having him hate me. He did get spit on when he came home from Vietnam. He also has that low sperm count." She looked up at the stars. "Charlie Valley is nice. He doesn't even seem to have hang-ups, not yet.

"And thank You, Lord, for my employment, especially for my promotion—*and for getting it before Rita Staples got hers*—sweet Jesus, You are too good."

# Acknowledgments

I would like to thank Joe Lee

for his generous editing and his empathy,

Aniene for her intriguing stories of the workplace,

Barbara for a mountain retreat,

Jim for sharing male fallibilities,

Jean for her mind-shaping humor,

two cats for warming the writing desk,

and my husband, Robert Redd, for warming

my whole life with his abiding cheer.

Mary Allen Redd

was born in Provo, Utah, and

received a Ph.D. from the University of Maryland.

A former technical editor for beltway bandits,

she now teaches at George Mason University

and lives in Fairfax, Virginia.

# TO ORDER A COPY of

*The World of Holly Prickle* @ $10.00

## USE THIS COUPON

Name_____

Address_____

City_____State___Zip_____

Enclose a check or money order
plus $.75 for postage and handling.

**SEND TO:** Shenandoah Books
3151 Lindenwood Lane
Fairfax, VA 22031